SHATTERING SECRETS

They'd meshed, body and soul and mind, fulfilling the promise of the spark that had flared between them the night they'd met. No other woman had ever affected him the way Lauren had, the way Lauren did. She was the other half of himself.

"How can you forgive me?" she asked.

"It's over." He didn't intend to talk about it anymore tonight. He stopped further conversation with a long lingering kiss. They stood at the top of the stairs, only a few steps away from the bedroom.

"I love you, Lauren," he whispered huskily, and with one smooth movement lifted her high into his arms. "I will always love you. There is nothing you can tell me that will change the way I feel about you."

— — —

By Kathy Lynn Emerson

Winter Tapestry
Echoes and Illusions
Firebrand
Unquiet Hearts
The Green Rose

Published by HarperPaperbacks

ECHOES AND ILLUSIONS

KATHY LYNN EMERSON

HarperPaperbacks
A Division of HarperCollins*Publishers*

This is a work of fiction. The characters, incidents, and dialogues are products of the author's imagination and are not to be construed as real. Any resemblance to actual events or persons, living or dead, is entirely coincidental.

HarperPaperbacks *A Division of* HarperCollins*Publishers*
10 East 53rd Street, New York, N.Y. 10022

Cover illustration by R. A. Maguire

First printing: March 1993
Special edition printing: February 1996

Printed in the United States of America

10 9 8 7 6 5 4 3 2 1

With gratitude for *years* of moral support, technical advice, and positive feedback,
this book is dedicated to:
Sheila Bearor, Merritt Emerson, Wendy Sirois,
Shirley Martin, and Sandra Yeaton

Acknowledgments

I would like to thank the following: John Kennedy Melling, for answering my questions about police work in England; the West Yorkshire Police for details of police procedure in Leeds; Kay Landry, for answering questions about types of therapy and therapists; and Laurie and Penny of Downtown Travel in Farmington, Maine, for helping me plan an imaginary journey. Any errors in these areas are my own and will hopefully be forgiven on grounds of poetic license.

I would also like to acknowledge the support of four very special people who have always had faith in my ability as a writer—my husband, Sanford M. Emerson; my mother, Theresa Marie Coburg Gorton; my agent, Lettie Lee; and my editor, Carolyn Marino. And, for broadening my horizons in more ways than one might suspect, I would like to thank the three talented, eccentric artists in C.A.W.—Mimi Gregoire Carpenter, Jean Ann Pollard, and Carol-Lynn Rössel Waugh.

1

It was not a mirror image.

The face in the painting was that of a much younger woman . . . a woman half her age . . . a girl, really, except that in those days girls married at thirteen and were mothers soon after.

Those are my eyes.

Lauren Ryder's steps slowed until she came to a complete stop directly in front of the portrait.

The familiar eyes stared blankly back at her—large, not as widely spaced as she'd have liked, and in hue the exact color of the first forget-me-nots of spring. The other painted features, too, were her own. Lauren thought that she might have found the same likeness in an old family photo album, if such a thing had existed, but as far as she knew there was no pictorial chronicle of her early years. Her parents had not cared enough to keep one.

Fascinated by the uncannily accurate representation,

Lauren stepped closer to the velvet cord that separated the paintings in the exhibit from the people who had paid an exorbitant fee to view them. Her outward appearance had given no hint of it when her hands suddenly went clammy. No one had seen the shudder that swept through, deep inside her, like a ghost stirring restlessly in her soul.

A security guard glanced her way but saw nothing out of the ordinary. A brunette in her mid-thirties, short in stature and as compactly built as a gymnast, Lauren Ryder wore a simple short-sleeved dress and low heels. She did not stand out in a mixture that included upscale patrons of the arts, college students, foreign tourists, and families on a weekend outing. Neither did she fit the profile the guard had been trained to recognize. There was little likelihood she'd try to vandalize the artwork.

Oblivious to all else, Lauren absorbed the impact of the vividly detailed oil painting before her. In her rented headset a disembodied voice soldiered on in a clipped British accent: "Number Twenty-nine, oil on panel, is titled *The Court of Henry VIII at Nonsuch* and was painted in the manner of Hans Holbein the Younger circa 1545. Note that the figures on either side are the images of royal servants, a groom of the stable on the right-hand side near a door that is open to reveal the gardens beyond and, in the lower left corner, a maid. It was rare to include such subjects in early sixteenth-century art and the like is found in only one other group portrait of the early Tudor period."

It was an enormous piece depicting more than a dozen people and was in such good condition that Lauren surmised it had recently been restored. She'd expected to view yet another example of the art of the German-born Holbein, or of one of his English imitators, make a close inspection of any fabrics therein, especially tapestries, then pass quickly on to the next painting. Instead she'd been brought up short by the shock of recognition. She couldn't tear her eyes away from the figure of the maidservant, this unknown girl who had been dead for well over four hundred years but who possessed not only Lauren's face but her sturdily built body as well.

Coincidence, Lauren told herself firmly, rubbing her hands over her bare upper arms as if to dispel a chill. With a quick jab at the stop button, she stopped the recorded commentary, which had moved on to Number Thirty, a painting of King Edward VI attributed to William Scrots. Absentmindedly fingering the edge of the tape player, which was clipped to the strap of her shoulder bag, Lauren studied the likeness before her.

The girl seemed richly dressed, in spite of her station in life. Lauren had never seen a costume quite like the one she wore, but she supposed royal servants must have been put into some sort of livery, in this case an orange gown, heavily appliquéd in forest green. It was lined with an ivory-colored fabric, visible because the skirt was tied back. A pleated, orange kirtle showed through the inverted **V**-shaped opening. Black shoes peeped out from beneath the skirts. Unlike the square, low-cut bodices usually shown in portraits of noblewomen of the period, the maid's outfit concealed all hint of a bosom with a black inset topped with a small standing collar. An unflattering cap, two-toned in orange and ivory, covered any hint of hair and completed the ensemble.

She had been painted in a watchful pose, regarding the antics of her betters with an expression that might have been disdain.

Several people, impatient to get a better look at King Edward's portrait, pushed past Lauren, breaking her concentration and abruptly reminding her that she was not alone. In an effort to orient herself, she inhaled deeply, taking in the myriad aromas of the crowded room, mingled essences of sweat and Old Spice, Chanel, and hair spray.

Footfalls thudded against polished hardwood floors. A door closed with a quiet *whoosh* on the line of patiently waiting spectators snaking down the corridor outside. They were being allowed inside in groups of twenty, but enough lingered each time, savoring this intimate glimpse of the distant past, that the rooms were always filled to capacity.

Remembering why she'd come—to study the needlework of the period with an eye to duplicating some of the designs in her own creations—Lauren tried to concentrate on the ornate hangings and brightly garbed courtiers in the painting in front of her, but her gaze kept returning to the girl in the corner. Unable to stop herself, Lauren bent forward, one hand snaking out toward the surface of the panel.

An order delivered in an authoritative baritone arrested her thoughtless movement. "Ma'am. Don't do that."

Lauren hastily withdrew her fingers and folded them into a fist. Guilt-ridden, she dropped her gaze, dismayed by her own behavior. She knew better. These paintings, most of them on loan and all of them invaluable, were as vulnerable to damage by overeager connoisseurs as they were to theft or vandalism. Resigned to a lecture, she turned slowly and met the disapproving glare of a green-uniformed museum guard. He didn't say another word, just indicated, with a jerk of his head, one of several prominently displayed signs in heavy black calligraphy warning patrons not to touch any of the works on display.

"Sorry." Embarrassed, Lauren fled toward the sanctuary of a group of upholstered benches at the center of the room and sat down gratefully on the only empty one.

From that safe haven she risked another look at the troubling portrait. Again, her own eyes stared back at her. But before she could ponder this oddity any further she heard a familiar voice and turned to find her sister-in-law bearing down on her.

"What on earth did you do to earn such a dirty look from the rent-a-cop?" Sandra Ryder demanded.

She landed on the bench at Lauren's side with a distinct plop. She was not a heavy woman. On the contrary, she was taller than Lauren and inclined to gauntness, but she blew into any room like a breath of fresh air—distracting, refreshing, and impossible to ignore. She never walked when she could stride, never sat when she could fling herself into a chair. Now she was exhibiting every bit of patience she possessed, for her lack of interest in this exhibit of paintings from sixteenth-century England had been evident from the moment they had arrived at the museum.

"Don't worry," Lauren assured her, "I'm not about to get arrested."

"Better not!" Sandra's eyes sparkled with amusement.

"Oh, Lord! I can just see the headlines now. 'Law Enforcement Expert Called Away From International Crime Conference to Bail Wife out of Jail.' Wouldn't that be a kicker?"

Lauren tried to return Sandra's smile but her heart wasn't in it. She was still too bewildered by her own uncharacteristic behavior, and by her peculiar reaction to Number Twenty-nine. Sandra was right to imply one thing, though. There was probably no one more law-abiding in all of New York City than Adam Ryder, Lauren's husband.

Lauren's smile no longer had to be forced. She and Adam had one of the most blissful marriages of anyone she knew. From the moment they met she'd known he was the one man for her, and Adam, too, claimed to have fallen in love at first sight. Their wedding took place before that same month was out, and neither of them had ever regretted their hasty decision to marry.

"So, how much longer do you think you'll be?" Sandra looked hopeful. "I've been all the way to the end already. Ninety paintings. I'd have gone on out but I didn't think I'd ever find you again in this maze, and they won't let anyone back inside the exhibit once they've left."

This wasn't the first time Sandra had complained long and loud about wasting the second of three days in New York at a museum. She wanted to visit Saks Fifth Avenue and F.A.O. Schwarz and the stores in the Trump Tower. She'd been somewhat appeased by the purchase of a few souvenirs in the museum gift shop, but then she was told she'd have to check her shopping bag before she could enter the exhibit. In line, where they'd stood for a good hour, she'd groused about that and the long wait and the fact that her shoes were too tight.

"Beats me why you want to spend a perfectly beautiful afternoon in here," Sandra complained as she kicked off the offending footwear and began to rub her toes.

"Business," Lauren reminded her. Personally, she couldn't understand the appeal of using a lovely autumn day for shopping.

"I'd think you'd be disappointed in these pictures," Sandra remarked. "They don't look anything like the covers on those historical novels you're always reading. And as for your craft business, you've already designed more needlework patterns than you know what to do with."

"I'm always on the lookout for inspiration." Lauren hesitated, reluctant to risk making herself feel more foolish than she already did, but in the end she yielded to her need to know. "Do me a favor, Sandra? Go look at that painting, the one that fat woman in the purple jumpsuit is staring at, and tell me if you can spot anyone in it who looks, well, sort of familiar."

"If you've seen one picture of Henry VIII you've seen them all," Sandra grumbled, fishing under the bench for her discarded shoes.

"Humor me."

Wincing in an exaggerated bid for sympathy, Sandra forced her feet back into her shoes, stood with a grimace, and then, as if resigned to her fate, strode purposefully toward Number Twenty-nine. After a moment, Lauren got up and followed.

"So, anyone look familiar?"

"Sure."

Lauren slanted a nervous glance in her sister-in-law's direction, enough to tell her that Sandra was amused again but also perfectly serious. "Who?"

"Exactly."

"What?"

"Not what. Who."

"Sandra, you aren't making any sense."

"I'd be making perfect sense if you were into cult classics. See that guy, second from the right, sour expression, the one with the staff and the fancy gold necklace?"

Lauren nodded, more confused than ever.

Sandra's grin widened. "He's the image of Patrick Troughton. You know. The actor. He played the second Doctor Who."

As a muffled snort of laughter sounded directly behind them, Lauren belatedly caught on. Her sister-in-law was addicted to the British-made television series that was shown in endless reruns on their local PBS station.

"You're quite right, you know." Lauren glanced over her shoulder to discover a small, elderly man who was still chuckling at Sandra's remark.

"Looks just like him, doesn't it?" Sandra asked.

"Indeed. There's a reason, too. Allow me to introduce myself. I'm Professor Steven Markam. Before my retirement I specialized in Tudor history. You may recall that a number of years ago there were two television series, one on Henry VIII and his wives and one on Elizabeth I. The casting people deliberately sought out actors who physically resembled the characters they were to play, and based costumes and makeup on extant portraits of those historical figures. You see before you Thomas Howard, 3rd Duke of Norfolk. Patrick Troughton was hired for that role because of his uncanny duplication of the Duke's features."

"Told you," Sandra said, nudging Lauren in the ribs with her elbow.

Lauren didn't answer. She was staring at the painted maidservant again.

Was that all it was? A chance resemblance?

Well, of course that was the answer.

A small smile lifted the corners of her mouth as she looked one last time at her own likeness and then turned away. If the BBC's casting department had been able to find twentieth-century look-alikes for kings and queens and noblemen, then obviously present-day doubles existed for the common folk as well. While Sandra continued to chat amiably with their new acquaintance, Lauren gave a soft sigh of relief and moved on to the next portrait.

Two pin-on name badges were removed in unison and stuffed in jacket pockets as their wearers claimed a table in the hotel's lobby bar. One bore the name Daniel Ryder, *chief of police, Lumberton, Maine.* The other identified its wearer as Adam Ryder, *consultant,* and a blue dot denoted his status as a speaker at the conference.

"What's your pleasure, gentlemen?"

The young woman who had come to take their drink orders habitually smiled at everyone she served, but in this case it was no hardship. Both men had the sort of rugged good looks that appealed to her.

"What have you got on tap?" Dan asked, returning her approving look.

She ran down the list of domestic and imported beers from memory, which gave her the chance to make a closer inspection of the two men. She didn't need nametags to tell what conference they belonged to.

"Coors Light," Dan said with a rueful gesture. She tracked the movement and saw that a hand wearing a wedding ring hovered over the beginnings of a decided paunch. Without missing a beat she shifted her attention to the second man.

Adam Ryder was six years younger and weighed twenty-five pounds less than his brother. Just sitting there he was an imposing presence. He gave her his drink order in a voice that could melt a woman's bones. It was deep, dark, and nearly as sexy as the lock of dark blond hair, highlighted by random streaks of silver, that fell rakishly over his forehead. Tilted up at her was a face dominated by a strong, square jaw and a thick mustache which, like his hair, had the beginnings of a dashing salt-and-pepper look.

"My wife and sister-in-law will be joining us soon," Adam Ryder said. "I'd appreciate it if you'd keep an eye out for them. When they arrive, I'd like you to bring us a bottle of champagne." His smile was slow, sensual, and so full of private pleasure that the waitress felt a sharp stab of envy.

"That's one lucky wife," she managed to say.

"It's our wedding anniversary."

"Lauren deserves champagne for putting up with you for five long years," Dan joked when the waitress left them.

"She's the best thing that ever happened to me."

Dan grinned. "Could be. Could be. Of course, if you hadn't been filling in for one of my sick officers, you'd never have gone out on that call in the first place."

Adam knew his brother well. He said nothing, just waited.

"So, I was thinking, how about you splurge on an extra bottle of the bubbly for Sandra and me?"

"Why not? But, then, by rights, I should have champagne sent to Thomaston, too, as a thank-you gift for Greg Wilks, the man who really brought us together."

Dan chuckled. "Wouldn't go over too well with the warden."

A scowl darkened Adam's features as he remembered that Wilks would be out in another year. Six years in Thomaston, the state's maximum security prison, and six years on probation wasn't nearly long enough for the scum who'd broken into Lauren's house and assaulted her. "He's lucky I didn't shoot him," Adam muttered.

"I've always wondered just how close you came that night."

"Too close. I was burned out. Badly." He shook his head. "It still amazes me that I let you talk me into being sworn in again to help you out. It hadn't been a month since—"

He fell abruptly silent as the waitress returned with their drinks. Dan took a long swallow of the beer, but Adam, instead of drinking, ran one blunt fingertip around the rim of his glass. That incident was better forgotten. He'd rather think about the life he'd built since, with Lauren at his side.

He glanced at his watch, suddenly anxious. "What's keeping them? I expected they'd be back by now."

"Need you ask? Sandra can't pass a store without going in."

From what he'd heard, dangers lurked in the streets of New York even in broad daylight. Adam couldn't help but worry about Lauren, on her own in that jungle. She was a unique combination, intelligent and self-sufficient, but at the same time sweetly old-fashioned in her outlook. She could hold her own marketing the line of textiles she'd developed, but she had a deplorable tendency to take what people told her too literally, missing the nuances, oblivious to the possibility of other interpretations. At times this produced amusing results, and then she was the first to laugh at herself, but once in a while there were more serious consequences. Adam didn't like to contemplate Lauren interacting with the street hustlers of Manhattan.

"They'll turn up soon," Dan said with a confidence his brother envied. "While we're waiting I could use your advice on something."

"What's the problem?"

"The town's approved putting video cameras in the patrol cars."

"That's good."

"It might be, but you tell me, Adam, how I can risk putting a camera in Clubber's cruiser."

In spite of a brave effort to quell his automatic reaction, the beginnings of a grin showed on Adam's face. The situation wasn't funny. He knew he shouldn't allow himself to be amused by it, but he was.

John "Clubber" Doucette was, most of the time, everything Dan could ask for in a member of his police department. Clubber was diligent in the performance of his duties, well versed in the current laws and, to the relief of his fellow officers, not only great at making presentations in the local schools but willing to volunteer to do them, thus letting the rest of the force off the hook. Clubber had, however, one glaring flaw. He couldn't resist the blandishments of women who found a man in a uniform the ultimate turn-on. The origin of his nickname had long been the subject of much speculation.

Dan was fighting a smile of his own. They'd both heard the story going around at the conference of an officer who had forgotten that his video camera was set to track his movements and was aimed at a homing device pinned to his jacket. The jacket had ended up in the backseat of the cruiser. So had the officer. As a result, he inadvertently starred in an X-rated movie and lost his job.

"I mean it, Adam. What am I going to do about Clubber? He's getting worse."

"Have you considered turning a fire hose on him?"

Sandra's exuberant greeting brought an abrupt end to their discussion. "Sorry we're late," she called out from the far side of the lounge. "I've never seen so many toys in one place in my entire life. The kids would have loved it." Apparently Sandra had loved it, too, for she was loaded down with shopping bags and carrying a large, brightly wrapped box under one arm.

Adam's gaze shifted quickly to Lauren. He was on his feet an instant later. "Are you all right?"

"Fine. Just a little worn out from trying to keep up with Sandra."

He pulled out a chair for her, more concerned

than he let on at the sight of her pallor. She seemed nervous and distracted, too. They'd agreed the previous night, after their first day in New York, that the hectic pace of the city was not for them, that they much preferred the quiet life they led at home. Even so, Lauren's apparent exhaustion worried Adam. She was usually full of energy. He'd never considered that she might come back from this afternoon's excursion too tired to enjoy the romantic evening he had planned for them.

Dan winced as most of Sandra's parcels landed in his lap. "Did you leave anything in the store?"

She dropped the remaining bags on the floor between his chair and the empty one she now claimed for herself. "Be nice," she admonished him, "or I won't give you your present."

"Why can't you be more like Lauren," Dan grumbled, indicating the one small parcel Adam's wife carried. "She doesn't spend all her husband's hard-earned cash."

Adam barely listened to the good-natured bantering. All his attention was focused on Lauren. Was it just that she'd spent an entire day with Sandra? Adam liked his brother's wife, but a little went a long way.

At that moment the waitress arrived with the champagne, and Lauren brightened visibly. A smile of pure pleasure transformed her. "What a lovely way to begin the evening!"

Several hours later, when Adam and Lauren returned to the hotel, he was feeling pleased with the success of his elaborate plans to celebrate their anniversary. He'd whisked Lauren into one of the carriages that went through Central Park, and after the standard ride the driver dropped them off at a restaurant Adam had been assured would not only provide a quiet and intimate setting for two lovers but would serve good food as well. Everything had been perfect, right down to the delivery of a spray of five red rosebuds when they reached their table.

"Sorry it has to be such an early night," he murmured as they stepped into the elevator together. He didn't know how it was possible, but he loved Lauren more with each passing day. He couldn't remember being happier or more content than he was at this moment.

"No problem. I know the conference starts up again at the crack of dawn." An erotic invitation sparkled in her eyes as she held out both hands to him, a message so blatant that it made his head spin and tightened his body with desire. "I think staying out till the wee hours in the city that never sleeps is probably vastly overrated. I've been quite certain, ever since we finished dinner, that what I'd really like to do most is come back here and celebrate our anniversary properly, in that nice comfortable bed in our room."

"I don't know if I can wait that long," Adam admitted gruffly. He was glad they were the only ones in the elevator.

With exquisite tenderness he slowly slid his hands up Lauren's arms until they reached her shoulders and the edge of a low-cut neckline. A warm glow suffused her skin, more evidence that even after five years their desire for each other had not diminished. If anything, it had grown stronger. When Lauren moved closer, easing her arms around his waist and snuggling against him, it was all Adam could do not to plunge his hands beneath the soft fabric of her dress to the softer flesh it concealed.

"We're alone," she whispered, tempting him further. Her fingers left a trail of fire as they inched toward the top button on his shirt.

He caught her hand. "Patience, my love."

Oblivious to the floor number that lit up when they stopped, Lauren continued to cuddle. Arms wrapped around each other, they moved down the corridor. Only when they reached the door did she finally notice that something was different. "Adam? This isn't our room."

"It is for tonight." He managed to manipulate the key card while she was still gazing up at him with a puzzled expression on her face. As he'd instructed, the interior had been left dimly lit. Before Lauren could turn her head and see inside, he scooped her up and carried her over the threshold.

Lauren gasped, her expression reflecting both surprise and delight as she got her first good look at their new accommodations. "Oh, Adam," she whispered, "you booked the honeymoon suite."

Lauren's horrified scream echoed in the night.

For a moment she didn't know where she was.

"Lauren? Sweetheart? What is it?"

Strong, masculine arms cradled her. The voice was as soothing as the gentle embrace.

Adam's voice.

Slowly the desire to run from some amorphous terror was replaced by a primal need to be held and protected. She was shaking, and to her amazement she discovered that her cheeks were wet. She'd been crying in her sleep.

"That must have been some nightmare," Adam murmured close to her ear. His arms were around her, wrapping her in warmth and security.

Intuitively certain that Adam could keep her safe, Lauren clung to him tightly. Remnants of an appallingly realistic dream lingered, as vivid as her memories of their perfect evening together. They'd ended it in this bed, wrapped together, exhausted, replete. There was no earthly reason for her to have had a nightmare after such beautiful love-making.

"Sweetheart? Do you want to talk about it? Sometimes it helps."

"I'm not sure."

"You don't have to try to remember if it's already fading. I just thought—"

"It won't go away." There was an edge of panic in her voice. She didn't know how she could be so certain, but she was sure that the details of this dream were not going to fade, not ever.

"Then tell me. What did you dream about that upset you so much?"

She drew strength from his solid warmth, courage from the way his arms circled her, keeping danger on the outside. Maybe he was right. Maybe if she described what she'd experienced in her sleep it would diminish the nightmare's continuing effect on her. She could stop trembling, stop being afraid.

"I was in a cart, dressed in a dirty, yellowed shift," she whispered. "I don't know when it was, or where this was happening, except that it must have been hundreds of years ago."

Adam's lips brushed against her forehead. "You went to that exhibit today. It's not so odd you'd come away from it immersed in pictures from another century."

"But this was so vivid. I could actually feel the splinters in the wood of the cart, and the bruising way it jounced over a rough, unpaved street. There were smells, too." Her nose wrinkled, and she realized she could enumerate them, from horse dung to offal to the pungent stench of human fear.

"You were having a historical nightmare. Offensive aromas go with that territory." His words soothed her. He was right. High-born ladies in the novels she read were always pressing pomander balls to their noses to ward off an assortment of unpleasant odors.

Emboldened, Lauren let subconscious memories of her dream drift closer to the surface. "My surroundings were kind of vague," she told him, "but I know there was a crowd. They were jeering and throwing things at me. The sounds and sights kept fading in and out, so that I felt as if I'd really tied one on. I wasn't exactly frightened, not until the cart jolted to a stop. Then I couldn't seem to breathe. I was suddenly terrified and hands were grabbing at me, trying to force me to step down from the cart." She drew in a shuddering breath. "That's when I woke up."

"It's okay, Lauren. It's over now. The paintings you saw today must have made an impression on you, and we did eat all that rich food tonight." Adam bent his head and began to kiss her with rapidly rekindling passion, but for the first time in their five years of marriage Lauren did not immediately respond to his ardor.

"It seemed so real." The panic had returned to her voice. The sky above had been a cloudless cerulean canopy. To die on such a day seemed cruel.

"It was just a dream, sweetheart." His caresses were undemanding, but Lauren squirmed until he released her. She no longer wanted to be touched.

"You don't understand," she cried, and came up onto her knees on the rumpled bed, clutching the sheets protectively in front of her breasts.

"Tell me, then. I want to."

"That's when the dream ended, but I know what happened next." Her eyes were wide, dark, and unfocused, an effect that was startling in her too pale face.

"Lauren?"

Pulled back to herself by Adam's alarmed voice, Lauren shuddered. She had to tell him the rest quickly, before she lost her nerve. "They were going to burn me at the stake," she blurted. "For murder."

"It was a dream, Lauren. You didn't kill anyone." He still sounded concerned but his words were tinged with the first hint of annoyance. When he reached for her again Lauren let him tug her back into a gentle embrace. As before, it was comforting to be held, but she could not quite rid herself of the feeling of revulsion that had swept through her when she realized the truth.

"It's all right now, Lauren," Adam insisted. "It's over. It was all a dream."

"You don't understand, Adam," she repeated.

Her voice trembled and was so soft, muffled against his chest, that he had to strain to catch the rest of her words.

"I *did* kill him."

She closed her eyes tightly in a futile attempt to block out the horror of what she was confessing.

"I murdered mine own husband."

2

Loud knocking woke Lauren. She sat straight up in bed, as her hands shot up to her mouth to prevent a startled cry from escaping. Her head was pounding, and for a moment confusion reigned. She wasn't certain where she was, and wondered why she wasn't wearing a nightgown. Then her frantic, searching gaze fell on the spray of roses Adam had given her at dinner the night before. Exhaling slowly, Lauren relaxed. She was in the honeymoon suite. Adam had placed those flowers on the nightstand earlier, on his way to the first conference session of the morning. He'd kissed her sweetly in farewell, worried because she'd slept so poorly after that nightmare. He'd told her not to get up, to laze as long as she liked, and to her own surprise she had dozed off again.

"Lauren? You can't still be sleeping!"

Sandra's impatient call penetrated the thickness of the suite's outer door, propelling Lauren into action.

At home she got up early, a morning person by temperament. Adam was the one who needed that first cup of coffee to render him fully alert. She fought an unaccustomed grogginess as she looked for something to cover her nakedness. Her eyes felt gritty and she became aware of the dull throb of an impending headache.

"Lauren?"

"Coming!"

Fumbling her way into the lightweight flowered caftan she'd brought to use as a bathrobe, Lauren stumbled out of the bedroom and into the suite's outer room. Adam had already opened the drapes, and bright sunlight was pouring in, making Lauren blink from the glare. Then she winced, getting her first clear view of the decor. The previous evening, dimly lit, the surroundings had seemed romantic, but in the full glory of the day, wallpaper, carpet, and upholstery, all in various shades of pastel pink, made her think of cotton candy, frothy and much too sweet. Had Adam seen the color scheme before he booked the room? Somehow she doubted it, but she had to admit that its cloying colors had mattered little with the lights turned down and the promise of exquisite lovemaking in the air. Lauren was wearing a smug little smile when she finally opened the door to her sister-in-law.

Sandra, too, made Lauren blink, for she was attired in a loose jade top over linen slacks so white they hurt the eyes. "Oh, Lord! Don't tell me Adam's still here?"

Lauren's smile widened. "If he'd still been here, I doubt we'd have heard you knock."

Sandra entered the suite, a refreshing addition to

the pastel landscape, as soon as Lauren waved her in. "Well this proves it!" she declared. She stood in the middle of the room, hands on hips, tote bag dangling from one shoulder, and turned slowly in a circle, giving the place a thorough once-over.

"What proves what?" Lauren rubbed at her eyes and yawned hugely.

Sandra adopted a prim expression, one she occasionally put on in her job as Lumberton's town librarian. The effect was spoiled by the twinkle in her dark brown eyes. "I always assumed, based on my own marriage to a Ryder male, that Adam would be a man who knew how to keep his wife happy."

She began to prowl, inquisitive but unself-conscious about it. Her chuckle was deliberately salacious as she stopped beside the comfortable, if garishly upholstered, sofa and bent to scoop up the lacy slip Lauren had been wearing the night before. "It's nearly eleven, you know. With Adam's presentation scheduled right after lunch, I figured it was late enough to risk interrupting you two lovebirds."

Disconcerted by Sandra's mention of the time, Lauren glanced toward the bedroom. "I need to dress. Pack, too." They'd planned to check out, leave their suitcases in the hotel's baggage room during the afternoon session, and head for the airport as soon as it was over. Their flight back to Maine would leave LaGuardia early in the evening.

"Don't forget this." Sandra tossed the slip her way.

Lauren deftly caught it. "Believe me, I won't forget a thing."

For a moment she was warmed by heated recollections of the way she and Adam had celebrated their first five years of wedded bliss, but as she closed the door behind her, shutting Sandra out, other memories intruded, vivid images from the nightmare. Standing in the middle of the romantically decorated bedroom of the honeymoon suite, clutching her slip in a convulsive grip, Lauren fought against the onslaught. She tried to tell herself that bad dreams vanished in the morning light, but this one persisted. It haunted her. Worse, she could remember more details now than she had in the middle of the night.

She'd been given a posset to ease the pain.

Lauren blinked but the vision would not vanish. She felt rough hands on her bare arms as she was dragged forth from her foul-smelling cell and forced to climb into the waiting cart. Then her hands were bound behind her, and she could feel the rough rope biting into the tender flesh at her wrists.

Suddenly, he was there, the man who loved her, lifting a cup toward her parched lips. "Drink it all," he insisted in a tormented voice.

In that moment she could see him clearly, his solid build, his clean russet-colored doublet, the agonized look on his dear face. His features were large, roughly hewn, but his pale blue eyes were the gentlest she'd ever encountered. One of his big, blunt-fingered hands held the cup close to her mouth while the other came to rest at the nape of her neck, stroking and at the same time forcing her to swallow. A shudder went though her.

"'Tis bitter," she objected after the first sip. An aftertaste fouled the flavor of the local ale.

"Aye." A wealth of meaning surrounded his assent. Their love for each other had been bittersweet from the first, and she knew then that the cup contained some powerful potion, an herb that would render her senseless ere the first flames reached her naked foot. Helpless to save her life, it was the only thing he could do for her now. Her eyes fixed on his, she drank it all down.

"Lauren? Do you want me to order coffee from room service?"

Dragging herself back to reality was an effort, but after a moment Lauren managed to answer Sandra, though she had no idea exactly what she said. Resolutely, she set about washing and dressing and then repacked the few items they'd removed from their suitcases the previous night. The aftereffects of the dream still lingered. Lauren felt strangely out of sync with her surroundings and was glad that the hotel staff had already done most of the work when they moved the luggage from one room to the other.

Lauren checked the bedroom and adjoining bath one last time to be sure she hadn't overlooked anything, then folded the bulging garment bag and snapped the locks closed. The final tiny click seemed to restore her accustomed self-confidence.

Home.

Relief swept over her in a palpable wave. Late tonight they'd be home. Lauren was certain she'd be able to put the disconcerting dream behind her once she was out of the city and back in Maine. She'd always been safe there. Home was a place where one could forget any unpleasantness, real or imagined.

Reluctant to dwell on the reason for her certainty, since that, too, was best forgotten, Lauren picked up all three of their bags and rejoined Sandra in the outer room.

"All this luxury," her sister-in-law commented, "and your view is just as lousy as ours is."

"I hadn't noticed," Lauren said. Obligingly, she put the bags down and pirouetted so that Sandra could admire the linen suit she'd made for the occasion. One of her trademark tapestry-design scarves added a splash of color to the ensemble.

"You had other things to distract you," Sandra acknowledged, "but trust me, you didn't miss a thing." She nodded toward the window. "We have here a pigeon's-eye view of a Sizzler restaurant, a glimpse of one corner of a theater marquee, and, at an angle that would be a Peeping Tom's delight, a look into a shop that sells cels."

"Sells what?"

"Cartoon cels. You know, from animated cartoons. Cost the earth, too. I used to think your stuff was overpriced. Now I suspect you may be selling it too cheap."

"Thanks, I think."

"I hate these sealed windows."

Sandra was off on another tangent, telling Lauren how she and Dan had managed to open one in their room and then had to wedge an ashtray into the space to keep it from slamming shut again. Lauren paid little attention, distracted by her discovery that Adam had left the notes for his speech on the end table. She picked up the first page, skimming the neatly typed text, her heart swelling with pride and love as she read over the well-thought-out phrases. The second page had doodles in the margin. Adam had the endearing habit of drawing pictures, usually of animals, when he was deep in thought. The rough drafts of the manuscript of his textbook on policies and procedures for small correctional facilities had been littered with them, and with the occasional clever caricature of officers of his acquaintance.

Lauren wasn't surprised to find a pencil sketch of herself on the bottom of the third page, but though she'd seen such efforts before, this one gave her an odd sense of déjà vu, reminding her in an uncomfortable way of her experience at the exhibit of sixteenth-century portraits. She was sure it was her exposure to all those detailed paintings from another era that had prompted the nightmare. Adam had suggested the same thing, and she hadn't even told him what a turn it had given her to see her own likeness in one of them.

"Oh, good! Here's our breakfast." Sandra bounded toward the door.

"I don't think changes in routine agree with me," Lauren murmured as she gathered the pages together and placed them next to her purse. She'd take them along and save Adam the trouble of coming back to the room for them.

"Would you have come on this trip if it hadn't been your anniversary?" Sandra supervised the room service delivery and took charge of the coffee pot.

"Not likely. This is the first time I've been farther from Maine than Boston in years."

"Good heavens, Lauren, I hadn't realized. I mean, lately anyway, Adam travels all the time."

"I'm happiest staying home. I miss him when he's gone, but usually he's only away a few days at a time and the reunions are lovely." The caffeine was having an immediate and welcome effect. Her head cleared; tense muscles began to relax.

"How about a quick trip up Madison Avenue?"

"Please! No more walking. My feet aren't speaking to me as it is. I'm not even up to any more museums."

Sandra brightened at once. "I nearly forgot." She left off eating the muffins she'd ordered to go with their coffee and began to dig in the oversized canvas tote bag she always carried. After a moment, beaming triumphantly, she came up with a postcard. "I was writing a note this morning, to my aunt who lives in Florida, and I didn't even look at the picture on the front first, but then I flipped it over and you could have knocked me over with a feather I was so startled."

Guessing what she would see, Lauren maintained a stoic calm as she took the postcard from Sandra's outstretched hand. As she'd expected, she found a color reproduction of *The Court of Henry VIII at Nonsuch.* It was difficult to make out details of the much reduced painting, yet there was still a certain familiarity about the maidservant in the corner. "A memento of your friend, the Doctor," she murmured, returning the card to Sandra.

Her sister-in-law wrinkled her nose as she stuffed the card into an outside pocket of the tote to mail later. "That, too, but boy did I feel dumb when I realized what it was you expected me to spot yesterday."

Lauren quickly set her cup down, hoping Sandra wouldn't notice the sudden trembling in her hand. The hot liquid slopped over, spilling beyond the saucer onto a white napkin. Lauren stared at the spreading stain in dismay.

"You meant the girl off to one side." Sandra was still bent over her bag, intent on searching through an inner compartment. "I should have seen it at once. It's the way she holds herself. Just like you do when you spot something you don't quite approve of. Like that awful display in the jewelry store window last Fourth of July."

Lauren hedged. "There couldn't have been all that much resemblance."

Upright again, triumphantly flourishing a slip of paper with an address on it and another postcard, this one with a picture of the Statue of Liberty, Sandra qualified her statement. "True. She was just a *young* thing, wasn't she? It was more like if you and Adam had a daughter, *she'd* look like that."

Lauren's silence went unnoticed. Sandra was busy addressing the postcard and scrawling a quick note on the message side, oblivious to the fact that her carelessly uttered words had pained her younger sister-in-law. Lauren retrieved her rapidly cooling coffee and concentrated on draining the cup. Sandra didn't realize. How could she when no one knew the truth but Lauren and Adam and Lauren's gynecologist? They'd shared the knowledge for nearly four years now, the hard fact that no matter how much she might want to, Lauren could not bear children. Adam insisted her barrenness didn't matter, pointing out that Dan had already taken care of passing on the Ryder genes, but it left Lauren feeling both sad and a little guilty because she would never be able to give the man she loved a son.

Adam Ryder stepped up to the podium, the pages Lauren had brought him at lunch held lightly in one hand. He didn't really need the notes. His memory was excellent and he liked to vary his talk to suit the reactions of his audience, but it warmed him, as it always did, that she took pains to look out for his well-being. Even better was her presence in the end seat of the fifth row.

He checked the microphone for squeals and began. "When three inmates succeed in committing suicide in a jail with a capacity of thirty in a period of just over a month, a large part of the fault lies in that facility's policies and procedures. . . ."

Adam was well launched into his topic, giving examples and citing statistics when he noticed he'd lost Lauren's attention. At first he didn't think much about it. After all, even though she had never come with him to one of these conferences, she had heard variations of this particular address many times. Not until he reached the heart of his thesis did Adam realize that Lauren was more than inattentive. She looked distant and troubled. Deep frown lines creased her forehead and she was nibbling delicately on her lower lip.

As Adam's talk wound down, his concern grew, for it had crossed his mind that she might be ill. He brought the lecture to a close, made short work of the questions from his audience, and went to Lauren's side.

"Are you all right?" Adam kept his voice low and pasted a smile on his face for the departing officers. He slid one arm protectively around Lauren's waist and managed to steer her out of earshot. She looked dazed, though she went with him willingly enough. It seemed to take hours to shake off well-wishers and move far enough from the exit to ensure privacy. They ended up in the corner where pitchers of ice water and glasses had been set up. Adam quietly shifted his hand from her waist to her forearm and tightened his grip, as if he feared she was about to bolt. "Are you all right?" he repeated.

Wide, puzzled, blue eyes turned in his direction. "I'm fine, Adam. Is there some reason I shouldn't be?"

"You tell me. Where were you for most of the hour?"

Her voice conveyed mild reproach. "You must have noticed me in the audience, right next to Sandra. You couldn't miss her, not in that fluorescent green. We were there all through your talk."

"I was aware of the location of your body. The whereabouts of your mind was the thing that concerned me."

"I don't understand what you mean."

"Sweetheart, you're a lousy liar." He'd have smiled if he hadn't been so worried, but his voice did soften. "I don't care whether you paid attention to my spiel or not. I didn't expect you to hang on every word, not when you've heard it all a dozen times before. I'm not annoyed. My feelings aren't hurt. I just want an honest answer. You're not acting like yourself, Lauren."

"I wanted to hear you speak, Adam. Truly, I did. It's different when you're just practicing. You're more intense before a crowd. One moment I was involved in what you were saying, and so proud of you, and the next . . ." As her voice trailed off she shrugged, as helpless to explain to him as she herself was to understand what had happened to her.

"Lauren, there's nothing you can't share with me. I need to know what's bothering you so I can help."

She placed her hand over his on her arm. The lecture hall had cleared now and they were alone. Even Dan and Sandra hadn't lingered, but there was a workshop scheduled for the next hour. Adam estimated they had no more than ten minutes in which to talk without interruption.

"I'm not some suspect you're questioning, Adam. I'm your wife." She tried to make a joke of it. "Unhand me, sir. I think you're leaving dents in my arm."

He loosened his grip but did not release her. "I've got a right to worry about you when you've been behaving so oddly. Now, tell me what distracted you. Tell me, Lauren."

"It's just that foolish nightmare. I guess I was thinking about it again."

He wanted to pursue the matter, to pressure her into telling him what was really troubling her, but for the moment he contented himself with tugging her into his arms. "Forget about it," he murmured against her hair. "You didn't murder your husband. I'm alive and well, and if we weren't in a public place I'd prove it to you."

"It was so strange." Her face was flushed, her expression sheepish as she lifted her head. "I was listening to your speech. I really was. I was thinking how charismatic you are."

"Yeah, right."

"You are." One finger came up to caress the side of his face, tracing the line of his jaw. "You look quite dashing and your voice is wonderful. I was thinking how lucky I am, and then, out of nowhere, this memory surfaced." She hesitated, frowning slightly. "Well, it wasn't exactly a *memory.* I mean, I was hardly remembering something that actually happened to me. It was just in my imagination that I saw myself in the leading role. I suppose I must have been recalling a scene from a movie I've seen or one in a book I've read."

"Tell me."

"The picture in my mind was very real," she said, and moved deeper into the haven of his embrace. "I was looking down on a great hall. You know the sort, with a dais for the family at one end and a musicians' gallery at the other. I was up in the gallery. I could see the rest with incredible clarity, as if I'd really been there."

"Maybe you have been." Adam pitched his voice low, to soothe, and let his hands begin a slow massage of her back and shoulders. Her explanation relieved his mind. Now all he had to do was get her to relax. "You were in England years ago, weren't you? At school? Isn't it likely you once visited such a place?"

"Maybe." Lauren sounded doubtful. "I can't remember it if I did."

An odd expression flickered across her face and was gone before Adam could identify it. He didn't pursue that angle, satisfied that he had hit upon the correct explanation. Lauren didn't like to talk about her youth, but he knew enough to realize that her family life had been unpleasant. Once she'd remarked that all the years before her arrival in Maine were best forgotten. She'd only begun to be happy, she'd said, after moving into the house they now shared.

The tension beneath his fingers eased a fraction. She rubbed against the front of his suit coat like a sleek little cat. He didn't want to ask, but he felt compelled to. "Was there more to the daydream? Something disturbing?"

He felt her nod, and after a moment she attempted

to explain. "I was in this musicians' gallery and I saw a man come into the hall below. I didn't know his name, but this was the second time I'd caught a glimpse of him and I felt inexplicably . . . drawn to him."

"Drawn? You mean attracted sexually?" It was absurd for him to feel envious of a figment of Lauren's imagination, but he did.

Lauren's nervous laugh sounded high and unnatural in the deserted lecture hall. "I wanted him. Just like that. Husbands have beaten their wives for less."

It was an effort to keep his tone light, but Adam managed. "You must have read that sign in Dan's office, the one that says, 'the beatings will continue until morale improves.' " He felt her smile against his chest. "I promise not to beat you, and I'll try my damnedest never to bore you into fantasizing again."

"Whatever triggered my daydream, it was not boredom. You are by far the most exciting man I've ever met." An impish grin appeared as she once more lifted her head. Her fingers began to climb his tie. "In fact, I'm beginning to wish we hadn't already given up our room."

"Behave yourself, woman."

Two policewomen appeared in the doorway, followed by a steady trickle of conference-goers. "Let's get coffee, or a drink, before the closing session," Adam suggested, yielding the room to the invaders.

"I thought you wanted to hear Jake Lawson speak." The world-renowned criminologist was scheduled next, in the last hour before the crime conference formally ended with the presentation of the last award.

"I'd rather be with you."

To Lauren's relief he dropped the subject of her wandering attention. She tried to forget all about it, too, but a short time later, when one of Adam's colleagues distracted his attention in the lobby bar, she realized that she needed to assimilate what had happened to her. It had been impossible to explain, even to Adam, just how much she'd become a part of that disturbing daydream. Perhaps if she considered logically and unemotionally what had happened to her she could make some kind of sense out of the experience.

Lauren prided herself on her pragmatic nature. She was determined not to give in again to such foolishness. Bad enough that an irrational trepidation, a vague sort of fear, had been stalking her ever since she woke from that nightmare trembling and in tears.

She willed herself to focus on what she had seen while sitting in that lecture hall. Her body had been in the twentieth-century conference hall, but in her mind she had seen . . . no, had *been* a girl kneeling on the wooden floor of a musicians' gallery, a long, narrow, dimly lit room built over the entry to the hall and open all along that side. She'd had a bird's-eye view, looking out from between the balusters to see clearly all the way to the dais. Through the archway behind the high table she'd glimpsed a set of broad stone steps curving up out of sight.

There was a brightly colored canopy suspended over the seats on the dais, Lauren recalled, those few real chairs upon which the family sat while everyone else, even the most important guests, had to make do with benches or stools. There was an oak ceiling above that and along the side walls were traceried windows and a richly carved wall chimney. The tapestry opposite it depicted a hunting scene.

At one end of the dais a bay window provided light, allowing her to admire the workmanship in the damask tablecloth. It was wrought with a curious variety of blue and yellow flowers and completely covered the board. Over it was a diaper tablecloth sewn with a pattern of crossed diamonds.

Slowly Lauren began to relax. Her interest in fabrics and design was of long standing, and since she made her living with them perhaps it was not so odd that she'd daydream about tapestries and tablecloths. It was probably significant that she'd pictured one of her own original designs, the pattern on the damask, in the scene.

The other tables had also been covered with cloths, she remembered, but not such fancy ones, and at each place a trencher, napkin, and spoon had stood waiting. Wine, ale, and drinking vessels were lined up on a buffet. Gleaming gilt and silver plate was set out in a plate cupboard to make a bright, impressive display.

Why had it seemed so dangerous to be there?

The answer came at once. She'd been hiding, praying that no one would find her, hoping that since there were no musicians playing that day no one would come into their gallery. She'd watched the first wave of blue-liveried servants as they entered, bringing basins, ewers, and damask towels for ablutions. A maidservant set platters overflowing with apples and cherries in place, one on each table, and all was in readiness. Watching, her anticipation grew as guests began to drift into the great hall and take their places. There was much noise, both conversation and the scraping of stools and benches as people sat according to rank. The line of demarcation was a massive salt, a handsome thing, double gilt, with elaborate images carved into the cover and sides.

Lauren took a sip of the white wine Adam had ordered for her, momentarily disconcerted when his troubled gaze met her eyes over the rim of the glass. He knew. He knew she was thinking about her lover again.

Lover? She hadn't even met the man yet. Abruptly, new images filled her mind, blocking out thoughts of Adam.

Everyone was settled. The steward rose from his stool and tapped his long, white wand on the top of the table where he presided over the most prominent of the secondary guests. Voices obediently rose in prayer, and when all the company chanted "Amen" the noise level increased tenfold. The first course, which had been collected through a servery hatch from the kitchen and carried along the corridor connecting it to the great hall, was brought in through the arch beneath the musicians' gallery. She could smell the richly spiced chewits and heard her own stomach growl. It had been a long time since she'd last eaten.

Then he was there, just entering the great hall, and she experienced a different sort of hunger. He—

Adam leaned across the small, round table in the lobby bar. Lauren blinked in surprise as she was catapulted back to reality. Adam's friend was gone and she hadn't even noticed him leaving.

"Come here, love." Adam's voice was low and sexy. His eyes glittered with an emotion she could not quite read, but Lauren obligingly bent toward him, her pulse racing, anticipation in her heart.

"I love you, Adam Ryder," she whispered just before their lips met in a searing kiss.

"I've discovered something about myself on this trip," he confessed before he settled back into his chair.

"What's that?"

"I'm possessive when it comes to my wife. I don't much like other men, even murdered husbands, cropping up in your subconscious."

3

"*You really are* nervous about flying, aren't you?"

Lauren acknowledged her sister-in-law's observation with a wry smile and a nod. It wasn't so much being in the plane as the dizzying view from the window that threw her. If she didn't have to look out, she could almost convince herself she was riding in a rather luxurious bus. Adam squeezed the hand clutching his arm as they entered the boarding tunnel, offering silent reassurance.

"I'm a much better flyer than I used to be," Lauren said aloud. "I picked up a lot of good tips from a book. If I avoid coffee, carbonated beverages, and restrictive clothing, and all newspapers and television news, why I hardly even think about dying in a fiery plane crash."

The flight attendant's smile looked a little strained as she overheard Lauren's facetious statement.

Just as they reached the gaping aircraft cabin door, a second uniformed woman emerged, ignoring both her colleague and the boarding passengers to reach for a phone set into the wall of the walkway. "This is Corinne on Flight 546 to Portland, Maine," she said into the mouthpiece. "Our coffeemaker isn't working."

"You'll all have to have wine, too," Lauren joked, trying to ease the sudden increase in her level of tension. She always ordered one glass as soon as she was airborne, even when she was just on the short hop to Boston, a trip she made periodically for business reasons. "Plain white wine is a well-known tonic for the uneasy traveler."

She found 14-C, her aisle seat, and thrust her carry-on luggage into the overhead compartment. Adam was next to her, in the middle, with a stranger at the window. The section on the other side of the narrow passageway had only two seats, and they were occupied by Sandra and Dan. They'd just settled in and fastened their safety belts when every light in the airplane abruptly blinked out.

Lauren sucked in a harsh breath, losing whatever sense of security had been instilled by the presence of her family. She clutched the armrests with a white-knuckled grip as a terrible suspicion sprang, fully formed, into her mind. *Coffeemaker* had to be some kind of code word. Was the entire electrical system on this plane defective? Her worst fears seemed confirmed when a man in a mechanic's coveralls and oversized ear protectors boarded to engage the flight attendants in a whispered consultation. No one had any word of explanation for the passengers.

"Coffeemaker, my eye," she muttered darkly.

"Lighten up, Lauren." Sandra was laughing, as if this was just another great adventure. She appeared supremely unconcerned. "You can dine out for months on a story like this."

Dan evidenced greater sympathy for her ever-increasing nervousness, but little real understanding. "Come on, Lauren. You've seen those commercials on television, haven't you? They turn an entire ocean liner around to go back for the coffee beans. Stands to reason the airlines would sanction a little delay to fix the pot, just to be competitive, you see."

"Sure. They always rearrange the flight schedule at one of the busiest airports in the country just so the passengers will be able to order fresh coffee."

"Makes perfect sense to me," Dan teased.

Adam said nothing. He'd never flown with her before this trip, but he'd known for years that she considered planes a necessary evil. When time permitted she made a five-hour drive from their home in the mountains of western Maine to Boston rather than go by air.

As the minutes ticked slowly by, Lauren's nervousness grew. Was the electrical system kaput? Was a fire in the wiring likely? Or maybe there was a bomb on the plane. No, her common sense objected. Not a bomb. They'd have evacuated everyone if that were the case.

Lauren tugged on Adam's sleeve. "Doesn't this faze you at all?"

"There's some sort of electrical problem. They're fixing it."

"We're sitting here in the dark."

"Think of it as romantic."

"Adam, this thing depends on computers and

readouts and"—words failed her "—electrical stuff to fly! What if they *don't* fix it."

At least Adam didn't laugh, nor did he try to humor her out of her concern. He relied on the same techniques he used in doing his job, citing proven facts, employing logic, reasoning with her, one intelligent adult to another. "Think of it this way, Lauren. If they catch the problem on the ground, then they repair it before we take off. That means we have a very safe flight because everything has just been checked and double-checked. This delay is reason to be relieved, not worried."

"If we die in a plane crash, I'll kill you," she was able to joke. His explanation did make sense. She could already feel herself beginning to relax.

She calmed further when Adam started to talk about the deck the two of them were planning to build at the back of their house before the snow flew.

Twenty minutes passed. Then the interior lights came back on as suddenly as they'd been extinguished, together with a reviving blast of cool air. Lauren would have felt better if she hadn't known that at any minute their plane was actually going to do the thing she dreaded most. It was going to take off.

As the aircraft taxied out onto the runway, Lauren readied herself. She unwrapped a stick of gum and put it into her mouth. Then she closed her eyes tight and began to chew steadily. Without the gum, her ears would pop. That was a miserable feeling. Even worse was the sensation of rising rapidly. Lauren didn't like high-speed elevators, either. She refused to set foot in the glass ones.

The sounds of flight made her uneasy as well.

There were those odd bumps and thumps as the plane changed altitude or speeded up. The clunk as they raised the wheels always seemed ominous to her, for even though she knew what it was she had a difficult time containing her imagination. Surely such a loud thumping must herald certain disaster.

Lauren coped with her irrational fears by concentrating all her attention on a silent chant, a prayer, really. It was the only thing that could keep her mind off the fact that the ground was being pulled out from under her at a ridiculously high speed.

The refrain was a simple and direct plea for divine protection, repeated over and over until the plane leveled off and she dared open her eyes again.

If she concentrated, Lauren knew she could almost put herself into a trance.

"Lauren!"

Adam had one hand on each of her shoulders and was shaking her with surprising roughness. Her eyes flew open to discover that his face was only inches away from hers, his expression reflecting both exasperation and, inexplicably, embarrassment.

"Is something wrong, Adam?"

"You were getting a little . . . loud, honey."

Carefully she unclenched fingers that were still clinging to the armrests. She'd never chanted aloud before, not that she knew of. Surely someone would have told her.

The stranger in the window seat, an elderly lady with fluffy white hair and a face full of laugh lines, leaned over to smile and nod at her. "Went to Catholic school, eh?"

"I beg your pardon?" Confused, Lauren simply stared at the older woman.

"All that Latin you were spouting." The woman persisted, a trace of Nova Scotia in her voice. "That was right out of the old liturgy, eh? It's been a long time since I heard Mass in Latin, but when I was a young girl everybody knew enough to mumble along." She shook her head, lamenting changes that had taken place decades earlier. "It's a dead language these days."

Lauren felt the color drain from her face. "I was speaking in Latin?" Adam's nod confirmed it. "I don't know any Latin. I . . . I'm sure I don't."

A panicky sense of unreality threatened to overwhelm her. It was hard to think clearly and even more difficult to breathe properly. When the lighted signs flicked off, indicating they'd already reached cruising altitude, she fumbled with her seat belt, her fingers frantic and clumsy.

"Oh, God," she whispered as the vividly detailed images began to assault her. "It's happening again."

Lauren's only thought was to escape, to get away from the stares, the questions. She heard the concern in Adam's voice, but his words did not register as, on shaky legs that would barely support her, she started down the aisle toward the rest rooms, thankful the narrow space wasn't yet blocked by a serving cart.

Off balance, Lauren bumped from side to side, hitting first one seat-back and then another. There were one or two grumbles of complaint but she didn't stop to apologize.

She passed through the tiny kitchen area, where flight attendants were too busy setting up the drinks cart to notice her agitation, then finally reached the refuge she sought. Inside the lavatory with the door securely latched, she turned to stare at her own image in the mirror above the small sink. Who was that woman? She wasn't sure she knew any longer. Defeated, Lauren leaned forward until her forehead rested against the cool surface of the glass. Her eyes drifted closed.

She was coming out of an old stone church. Its doors had been flung wide open to accommodate the revelers spewing forth. Lads in leather tunics chanted and capered, showing off the bride laces they'd stolen. The priest stood apart, lest he seem to sanction any tradition handed down from pagan times.

Some boys had pipes and drums to add to the noise. Older, sober, and more somber than their sons were the yeomen-farmers in the crowd. In plain buffin doublets and kersey stockings and heavy hobnail shoes, they stood cheek by jowl with artisans in leather jerkins and red Monmouth caps. Their wives were present, too, in Sunday best, starched white caps discreetly covering their hair. These were people she knew, had known all her life, but though she felt their familiarity she had no names to attach to their faces.

She felt excitement coupled with dread, a fear that grew when the man at her side laid rough hands on her. She saw herself start and heard her own yelp of protest. Her bridegroom was small and wiry, but very strong, and he smelt of sweat and spilled ale. No one else objected and he did not desist. Instead his hard hands moved up her body, squeezing her breasts possessively, then cupping her face. One jagged fingernail scratched her cheek. She had a brief impression of bright, cruel eyes and a nose marred by deep pockmarks before he kissed her, thrusting a distasteful tongue into her mouth and leaving both her lips and her chin wet when he withdrew it. The essence of rotted teeth and spiced wine from the bride cup lingered.

When the lord of the manor emerged from the church to stand beside the priest, the crude fondlings blessedly ceased. The lord was of medium height for a man and sturdily built and, as befitted a member of the local gentry, was decked out in Mechlin lace and Cordovan leather boots. Thinning gray hair showed beneath a scarlet bonnet with white plumes. His facial features were sharply defined and unmarred by scars. Some village girls thought him handsome and went willingly to his bed . . . the first time. He was a powerful man in the village, the honored guest at every wedding, wielding absolute control over those who worked his land, and provided services to the manor. His tenants were dependent upon his goodwill, but they could not like him.

The short, plump woman who had been his wife for many years came up on his other side, wearing a bone grace of the newest fashion on her head. She stood no higher than her husband's broad, velvet-clad shoulder, and while the wedding guests watched he took her elbow, ostensibly to guide her descent from the porch of the church. She could not quite hide her wince of pain. He did not trouble to conceal the pleasure he took in causing it.

"A blessing," the black-robed priest insisted, and began to speak in Latin.

Adam's voice, soft and urgent, broke her concentration. "Lauren? Are you okay in there?"

She came back to the present in a rush, just as the

plane hit an air pocket and threw her against the sink, causing her to gasp aloud.

At the small, pained sound, Adam began to pound on the door. "Damn it, Lauren, open up."

"Sir?" The flight attendant's voice was quiet, pitched low to calm the harried passenger.

"My wife's in there. I think she may be ill."

"Would you like me to—"

Before she could suggest letting him in, Lauren voluntarily released the lock on the inside of the door. "I'm all right, Adam," she whispered, but she had to sink down onto the only available surface. She felt too drained to contemplate the long trip back to their seats.

A moment later he was crowding into the small space with her. "Lauren?"

"Do you need assistance, sir?"

"No. No, she's just not a good flyer. We'll be out as soon as I get her calmed down." It was an exercise in contortion to reach behind him and lock the door again, but Adam managed it. "What the hell is going on, Lauren?" he demanded in a harsh whisper. "I know you don't like being on planes, but this is something more than that."

"I'm fine."

"Then look at me."

She couldn't make herself lift her eyes to meet his. Too many images still danced in her head, pictures that made little sense and seemed to have no rational explanation.

There was scant room for maneuvering in the aircraft rest room, and the ride was getting rougher. An announcement came over the public address system asking all passengers to return to their seats and fasten their safety belts because of turbulence. As if to lend credence to the flight attendant's words, the plane was buffeted by a gust of wind and Adam nearly tumbled into her lap. Only the fact that he'd already braced his hands against the wall behind her head kept him from crushing her.

"This is ridiculous," he grumbled as he attempted, unsuccessfully, to right himself.

Lauren tried to help, but froze when her arm accidentally struck his fly. The intimate contact jarred them both. Her head snapped up. He lifted his eyes to the low ceiling and clenched his jaw.

Whatever strange connections had allowed Lauren to tap into an elaborate costume drama were severed as completely as if she'd seized the remote control and hit the button to stop a playback. The fog she'd been in lifted, and in that first second of clear thinking Lauren vowed she would never allow this kind of thing to happen to her again. She did not want to experience any more glimpses of another century, another Lauren.

"How on earth do they do it?" Adam's voice sounded strangled.

"Who? And do what?"

"Those people you hear about who make love in airplane rest rooms."

"The mile-high club." The corners of her mouth twitched, and though she felt uneasy rather than excited by the idea of making love in such cramped quarters, she was suddenly much more herself again. He wasn't serious anyway. "You're not saying you think we ought to join?"

His hazel eyes met hers and Lauren noticed that

the pupils were dilated. He really was turned on by the idea and their proximity.

"It does have an interesting initiation rite," he whispered, apparently unaware that she didn't share his enthusiasm. "I think I'd be tempted if I could only figure out the logistics."

He bent down, twisting painfully to bring their lips together. His were gentle against her mouth. It was a loving, soothing kiss, but she wasn't aroused by it and she was relieved when Adam awkwardly levered himself upright again.

"I wouldn't know where to put what, and even if I could figure it out, Mrs. Ryder, I am too old and set in my ways to care to try it. Come back to our seats with me, and, I promise, in just a few short hours, we'll be in our own bed, with plenty of room to do whatever we like." He waggled his eyebrows at her, a playful expression that promised pleasant adventures to come.

Lauren managed a credible smile and followed him out of the cubicle.

That Latin business bothered him.

Hell, so did the way she was acting now, as if nothing out of the ordinary had happened while they were away. They'd ridden with Dan and Sandra as far as their old Victorian farmhouse in Lumberton Falls. There Adam retrieved his own car for the remainder of the journey. His covert survey, made while they were stopped at Lumberton's only traffic light, told him that Lauren looked tired but serene. Her hands rested, relaxed, in her lap. Her eyes were focused on the road ahead.

"I'm glad we're almost home," she said, as if she sensed his intense scrutiny. Their house, still several miles distant, was the simple Cape with dormers Lauren had moved into when she came to Maine to live.

Adam mumbled agreement. He'd been approaching with his gun drawn the first time he saw it. His expression darkened as he remembered that night.

Near midnight on the Saturday of Labor Day weekend, Lumberton's police dispatcher had received a phone call from an agitated female claiming someone was breaking into her house. She'd barely had time to give her name and location before the line went dead.

Adam had lost no time responding, arriving within ten minutes at a house well shielded from the two-lane highway by surrounding trees. He radioed for backup from the county sheriff's department but went in alone, afraid to delay. With extreme caution he moved toward the house on foot. The caller's name had been Kendall. Lauren Kendall. He'd never met her, but he had heard that there was a woman living alone out here near the town line, operating some kind of craft business out of her home.

His hands sweaty, in spite of the crisp night air, Adam had fought a battle for self-control as he moved like a silent shadow from tree to tree. He wanted to rush to the rescue but his instincts, honed by more than a decade in police work, had urged continued stealth.

The Kendall house was fronted by a wide porch. There were lights on both upstairs and down, but heavy draperies had kept Adam from seeing inside. He holstered his weapon and followed the burglar's route through a basement window. It swung inward, and as

Adam's fingers closed on the sill he felt the stickiness of fresh blood. A grim smile overspread his taut features. Good. The slime had cut himself when he broke the glass. That meant he was hurt, which was no more than he deserved. Better still, it meant he'd left evidence. Blood was as identifiable as a fingerprint.

Adam slid through the opening feet first. It was a tight squeeze for a broad-shouldered man encumbered by a bulky uniform jacket and a belt loaded down with police accessories, but he made it, dropping soundlessly to the cellar floor. There he waited, scarcely breathing, while he got his bearings. The moon had provided enough light to find his way around outside, but now he was obliged to use his flashlight to reconnoiter.

The cellar stairs were close at hand, just to the left of the spot where he'd landed. The door at the top was closed, but a narrow band of light showed beneath it. Adam began to ascend, his gun once again drawn and ready.

There was no one on the first floor, but as soon as he opened the cellar door, Adam heard the altercation above. A guttural male voice was cursing fluently. There was a crash, the sound of a booted foot striking a door. Wood splintered and a woman's high-pitched scream echoed through the house. Adam began to run, searching for the stairs that would lead him to the second floor.

"She'll pay for the extra trouble," the man said; then he yelled, "Come here, you bitch!"

Adam took the steps two at a time. For a second both attacker and victim were framed in the open door at the top of the stairwell. Lauren Kendall was a small woman, plainly terrified, but she stood her ground, defending herself with a pair of scissors.

Her assailant knocked them aside with one vicious blow. Then he grabbed for her. Lauren Kendall evaded, ducking and dodging, but her long, white nightgown tripped her up. Her feet tangled in the lacy hem, and she fell heavily backward just as Adam crested the stairwell.

If he'd been able to get a shot off without risking her life he would have fired, but the man had flung himself on top of his victim, catching hold of a band of lace at her throat. He tore at the fabric, slapping her hard across the face at the same time, completely unaware that a third person had come into the room until he felt the cold barrel of Adam's gun against his temple.

"Let her go and move real slow and easy." Adam's voice and hands were steady, but he knew how close he was to losing control. What had happened during the last arrest he'd made before leaving the sheriff's department had been declared an accident, but he meant to take no chance that history would repeat itself while he was doing a favor for his brother.

As soon as Lauren Kendall scooted away, Adam instructed his prisoner to lie facedown on the floor. He could hear her moving about behind them while he went through the routine of handcuffing, patting down, and giving the Miranda warning. He was determined that this woman's attacker would not get off on any technicalities.

"Thank you for coming so quickly," she said as he hauled the manacled man to his feet. She'd donned a floor-length, burgundy-colored velvet robe, and although her face was very pale it did not seem likely that hysterics were imminent. Relief was evident in her soft voice, but a puzzled expression flitted across her features as she glanced from his face to the name badge above one pocket, then met his eyes once more.

"Are you okay, Ms. Kendall?"

"Lauren, please."

"Are you okay, Lauren?" He liked the name, and he liked the way she was quickly recovering her aplomb. She was obviously the kind of woman who could be counted on in an emergency.

"For a moment I felt as if I already knew you, Officer Ryder." She shook her head, trying to clear away any lingering confusion, then essayed a shy smile. "I'm fine now, and I owe you more than I can ever repay."

"A cup of coffee would probably do both of us good," he told her, more to give her something to do than because he needed additional caffeine in his system.

"I think I could use a nice hot drink," she agreed. "If you'll excuse me, I'll just go start a fresh pot perking."

With his free hand, Adam unhooked the portable radio from his belt and brought the police dispatcher up-to-date on the situation. "There should be another officer arriving shortly," he called to Lauren as she started down the stairs.

"I'll unlock the door."

She became practical in the aftermath of a crisis, another trait he valued, but he could not let her disappear just yet. "Are you sure you're not hurt?"

With a rueful grimace she touched her cheek as

she looked back over her shoulder. A handprint was still visible on her pale skin. "A few bruises, I think. Nothing that won't soon fade."

Adam tightened his grip on the prisoner's arm. The man had subsided into sullen silence, giving him no excuse for rough handling. Adam didn't recognize him, which surprised him a little. Most burglaries were committed by local talent.

Below, Lauren called out a greeting. She'd turned on her dooryard lights just in time to catch Adam's backup getting out of his patrol car.

The deputy left ten minutes later to transport the prisoner to the county jail. Adam stayed behind to collect the evidence, take Lauren's statement, and drink her coffee.

"Of course I'll testify, Officer Ryder," Lauren said.

"Adam."

"Adam," she repeated, and offered to pour more coffee into his mug.

He nodded, in no rush to leave her. "Are you as calm about this as you seem?"

"I watch television. I know the show is over once the police come and take away the crook."

The naive self-confidence of her statement brought a frown to his face. "In fact, it's just beginning. That scum will probably be out on bail until his trial."

She asked intelligent questions and he answered, hoping to calm the very fears he'd deliberately evoked. Soon he discovered that her conversation exerted a calming influence over him as well.

Somehow he ended up talking about himself, telling her how he'd started in the business fourteen years earlier as a corrections officer. He'd worked his way up to a patrol job, later spent two years as an investigator, and then took over as chief deputy when the previous second-in-command keeled over of a heart attack. Everyone had expected him to run for sheriff when the incumbent retired. Instead, just a few weeks earlier, Adam had made the decision to resign his commission and start a consulting firm. He'd been working that night for the town police, on a part-time basis, only because his brother was the chief.

He might have stayed there longer, sitting at that dinette table, talking about his plans for the future, and drinking coffee, but a static-laced voice calling him to a traffic accident on the other side of town brought the interlude to an abrupt end.

He returned the portable radio to his belt after a brief exchange, in code, with the dispatcher. "I have to go."

"Thank you, for everything." She held out her hand and he took it, intending to engage in a businesslike farewell, but something happened the moment their fingers touched that neither had anticipated.

Adam's head jerked up, his intent, questioning look colliding with her startled gaze. In the blue depths of her widening eyes he saw, to his relief, that he was not alone. She felt it, too. The same electricity that was making his fingers tingle, his body come alive, was only part of the circuit—it completed itself in her.

Lauren shook her head, her lips curving into a smile. "And you think *my* mind wanders."

Adam seemed to have driven most of the way home from Lumberton Falls on autopilot, remaining distracted even as he activated the garage-door opener and backed inside. He'd been parked for a solid minute before he came to, realizing that he'd already shut the engine off only when he started to do so again.

"It's late," he said, "nearly midnight."

Lauren got out to flick switches that turned on lights in the dooryard, on the porch, and in the vestibule just inside their front door. While Adam unloaded their bags from the trunk, she headed for the house. By the time she unlocked it a monstrous gray cat had materialized just inside the door, glaring malevolently.

"You had plenty of food and water," Lauren told her, skirting around the roadblock to put her purse on a table, "and a clean litter box."

"But she hasn't had the personal attention she considers her due." Adam came inside with the luggage, and as soon as he set it down he scratched the hefty little animal behind the ears. Whatever intense thoughts had preoccupied him during the drive from Dan's, he'd put them behind him now.

"She's just miffed at being left to her own devices for so long." It had been three whole days and then some.

Lauren's sense of relief and well-being increased as she joined Adam in coaxing a nuzzle from their offended feline. She'd grown more and more confident with each mile that brought them closer to home. Now that she was actually here, she felt absolutely certain that her life had returned to normal. A soft, delighted laugh burst forth as she scooped their beloved pet into her arms. She nuzzled a furry neck, murmuring the cat's name and appropriate endearments and promises never to desert her again.

"What did you call her?"

Startled by the harshness in Adam's voice, Lauren slanted a questioning glance in his direction. He was staring at her with the oddest look on his face. "I called her Pounce."

"Lauren . . . I don't understand."

"What's so hard to understand? Her name *is* Pounce."

Then it hit her. She was standing there in the kitchen, holding the cat they'd owned for most of their married life, insisting her name was Pounce when she knew perfectly well that they'd named her Hassle, for all the trouble she'd caused them when she was still a kitten.

"I must be more tired than I thought." Lauren tried to laugh the incident off, but she didn't quite succeed.

Adam's curiosity had been aroused. "Who is Pounce?"

"A cat I had as a girl."

"You never mentioned her before."

"I had forgotten all about her till now." Frowning, Lauren put Hassle down, picked up her flight bag and purse, and moved toward the back of their small house and the stairs that led to the second floor. That had been the literal truth, and it was as disturbing as anything else that had occurred in the last couple of days. She *had* forgotten, completely, that she'd ever owned another cat before she and Adam got Hassle.

Too many unexpected things were popping into her head, some of them irrational, all of them vaguely troubling. If this sort of thing kept happening, Adam was going to think she was crazy.

She was beginning to wonder about that herself.

4

Lauren never heard Adam open the door to her workshop, which took up half of a converted stable, sharing space with a two-car garage. He wasn't surprised. He frequently worked with the same single-minded concentration himself. What he'd never been able to understand, though, was how she could manage to do it with the television set blaring away in the background. Lauren always had it turned on when she worked, claiming it helped occupy her mind when only her fingers had to be busy.

He had watched her in silence for a few moments, reluctant to interrupt, before he noticed that she was not alone. Hassle was curled up on top of the needlepoint canvas stretched on the standing floor-frame. Its attached bench was vacant, for Lauren was using a lap frame to stitch a small piece of crewelwork. She was seated on a padded stool between her worktable and the rack where she sorted various colors and thicknesses of yarn. That ladderlike contraption scaled an entire wall, each dowel laden with strands of wool, except for the one that held the black sewing silk Lauren used for Spanish work.

Adam frowned as the cat opened one green eye and promptly closed it again. Lauren had been avoiding any references to the previous weekend since their return, and when he'd asked about that earlier cat, Pounce, she'd all but snapped his head off. As far as he knew she'd had no more of those odd fantasies. Neither had she made any more peculiar slips of the tongue, which gave him hope that whatever had been bothering her in New York was now a thing of the past; still, it puzzled him that she'd be so sensitive about the subject of a childhood pet.

There had always been cats and dogs in the household when he and Dan were growing up. He'd missed having pets when he lived in an apartment that didn't allow them, and had thought it strange when he was first getting to know Lauren that such a loving, giving person had chosen to live alone for nine years. She hadn't acquired a single stray. She hadn't even put up a bird feeder.

He supposed that her wretched family life accounted for the lonely life-style Lauren had chosen. Her mother had died of cancer when Lauren was barely twelve. Adam wasn't sure when Mr. Kendall had died, but he did know that by the time Lauren had moved to Maine permanently she was on her own.

Hassle yawned, stood, stretched, turned in a circle, and settled down again, all without acknowledging her master's presence. Adam was standing right next to Lauren before she looked up and noticed him.

"Hi, gorgeous."

"Hi, good lookin'." She detached the small piece of embroidery from her frame and held it out for his inspection. "What do you think? This idea just came to me out of the blue. It has a sort of Renaissance flavor, don't you think? Can you make a sketch of it for me?"

"Sure. Later." He dutifully glanced at the design, but set it aside without really seeing it so that he could bend down and kiss Lauren hello.

"You hardly even looked at it," she complained when she emerged, a trifle breathless, from his embrace.

"I was desperate. I haven't held you for hours." He kissed her again to prove it, savoring the softness of her lips beneath his.

"Flatterer. Now flatter this." She thrust the embroidered linen square at him again.

Adam dropped one last kiss onto the end of her nose and straightened up, taking the crewelwork with him. "You don't need me to tell you your ideas are good."

"Sure I do." She stood, too, and began to fold the lap frame.

"Nope. You just keep me around because I can copy to scale." Lauren could put her ideas directly onto any fabric with her clever needlework and colored yarn, but she had difficulty transferring the designs to paper. Soon after their marriage Adam had taken over the task of sketching new patterns so that they could be silk-screened onto scarves or made up into needlepoint kits.

"I keep you around for your hot body," she assured him with mock seriousness, then looked anxious as he finally turned his full attention to her newest creation. "What do you think? Do you like it? If you hate it, tell me. They can't all be gems. This—"

"Is . . . different," he interrupted. Adam moved closer to the light, but he had not been mistaken about the carefully stitched details. Blunt words slipped out before he could soften them. "Do you really want to show deer guts trailing down a scarf?"

Lauren blinked at him in surprise, then quickly snatched the sample away. "It was just an experiment."

"It blew up. Better turn off the Bunsen burner."

Too late to temper his words he realized how much this had meant to her. Tears shimmered in her expressive blue eyes as she turned from him and began to tidy the shop. A heavy silence fell between them, broken only by the steady stream of annoying babble from the television.

Adam's eyes narrowed as he watched Lauren return the lap frame to storage and run the needle she'd been using through an emery strawberry to clean and sharpen it. Then she returned it to its special case. Each needle was kept in its own case. He knew she had hundreds, in all imaginable sizes, and she treated each one as if it were irreplaceable.

All the time she was closing up shop, Lauren avoided Adam's gaze. She wasn't angry, just hurt, but making her feel bad had not been the way he'd intended to start their weekend. It was their first at home together since mid-August and he wanted it to be special. Guilt nagged at him as he tried to think of some way to erase the effect of his hasty words. He could have been more subtle and let her decide for herself that this design was all wrong for her.

He would have done well, he realized, to emulate Lauren's own technique when she'd encouraged him to write about what he did for a living. That book's success still astonished him. It was now being used as a textbook in college criminal-justice programs all over the country, producing steady royalties and increasing the demand for his appearance as a paid speaker.

Lauren's support had made all the difference in the world. She'd never been less than honest in giving her opinion, but somehow she'd managed to criticize without sounding critical. Her positive suggestions had spurred him on, helping him over the rough spots. Could he do any less for her?

Lauren fussed around the workshop, returning her scissors to their protective sheath, straightening supplies that were already in order, and finally removing Hassle from her chosen nest. Protesting loudly, the fluffy, gray cat was escorted outside. All the while Lauren tried to pretend she wasn't in the least upset by Adam's criticism, but he knew her too well to be deceived. Catching her hand as she reached for the television remote-control, he lifted her fingers to his lips.

"Sorry, hon. I could have phrased that better. Your subject matter just caught me by surprise." To his knowledge she'd never before depicted a hunting scene, and certainly not one that featured such gruesome attention to detail.

"Hunting does produce dead animals." She looked a little like a wounded doe herself as she retrieved her well-kissed hand.

"I know that. So do your customers. But that doesn't mean they want to be reminded of it quite so graphically. It's quite a departure for you, Lauren. I mean, you get queasy at the sight of a road-kill."

"Maybe the people who buy my needlepoint kits are getting tired of flowers and birds. Did you ever consider that?"

Her sudden hostility surprised him, making Adam wonder why she was so sensitive about this particular design. "Are you tired of them?"

She nibbled delicately on her lower lip until he wanted to take her into his arms and kiss away her distress. It was far too late to call back his critical words, even if he wanted to reconsider his opinion. He didn't, he admitted to himself, but it pained him to see Lauren this upset.

"I thought I was satisfied with the things I've been doing," she said in a small voice. Her fingers toyed with a thimble, rolling it over and over on the top of the worktable. "I should be happy with them. I mean, I have plenty of variety in what I do. There are the kits, and the tapestry designs for the folks in Boston to silk-screen onto scarves, and I'm exclusive provider of cutwork lace to a top dress-designer, and I still do the odd tapestry panel and a bit of blackwork."

Listing her own accomplishments did not seem to

be cheering Lauren up. Anxious to erase the bleak expression on her face, Adam scanned her workshop in search of inspiration. In spite of his natural ability as a copyist and his tendency to doodle when his mind was elsewhere, he did not consider himself an artistic person. His writing was largely an exercise in organization and logic. He didn't think of it as an expression of a creative side. Now the only idea he came up with seemed sadly lacking in originality. He made the suggestion anyway. "If you need to try new things, why not exploit your secret vice?"

"Television?"

"Why not? Design something that reflects whatever it is that attracts you to . . . that." With bewildered distaste he nodded toward the set, which was broadcasting a close-up of a particularly obnoxious game-show host.

The preposterous proposal provoked a strangled chuckle, as he'd hoped it would. "You *are* kidding?"

"Depends. Do you like the idea?"

"I think it's absurd."

He pantomimed wiping sweat from his brow. "Whew! A close call."

"You, Adam, have a singularly cynical opinion of daytime programming."

"Yup." He reached for the remote control, but she caught his hand.

"Don't you dare. I freely admit this is not as intellectually stimulating as, say, listening to public radio, but it has been invaluable to me over the years."

"Uh-huh." Her tongue, he hoped, was firmly

lodged in her cheek, but even if it wasn't, at least he'd succeeded in cheering her up.

"How do you think I keep up on fashion trends?" she asked, her eyes twinkling in anticipation of his response.

"I'm not sure I want to know."

"By watching the soaps, of course. They're an important part of the research I do for my business." Lauren's impish grin abruptly faded as she glanced toward the screen. "I've learned a lot from game shows, too."

"You'd do better to watch the news."

"No thanks." Her odd tone of voice made him uneasy. Now that he thought about it, Adam realized that Lauren avoided watching the nightly news. She did the dishes instead, and although she was a voracious reader, preferring books to television when she wasn't working, she hardly ever looked at magazines or newspapers. She complained that they were depressing, too graphic, too inclined to dwell on unpleasantness and report only bad news.

Lauren turned off the television and, linking her arm through his, tugged him along out of her workshop. Hassle was waiting for them at the end of the curving flagstone walk edged with lilac and forsythia bushes that led to the house. Her yowls of protest could be heard clear across the dooryard.

"There's your answer," Adam said. "Do a design with cats."

"This was not one of our better game plans!" Adam nursed the thumb he'd just battered for the third time. He'd been on his knees on the pressure-treated planks. Now he tossed the hammer down and shifted his weight, settling back on his haunches to glower at the offending tool.

Lauren ignored him, certain he didn't mean it. They'd been planning to replace their temporary porch, a small stoop, with a real deck ever since the previous summer when they'd had sliding glass doors installed at the back of the house. Before that the only rear entrance had been through the cellar.

All the necessary materials had been on hand since July, but the days they'd meant to work on it had all turned out to be too hot, or too wet, or their plans were preempted by more compelling commitments. Far too often Adam had been out of town on days made for deck building. His job frequently required that he observe the department he'd been hired to advise during its busiest period—the weekend.

Efficiently dealing with her next nail, using swift, accurate strokes, Lauren scooted sideways to the spot where she intended to pound in the next one. They'd started early that morning, while the hoarfrost still dotted green grass and multicolored fallen leaves with white. They'd put supports in place, constructed a base, erected the posts for the railing, and begun to put down the flooring. As the early October day wore on, it had become warmer, turning into one of those flawless Indian summer days found nowhere but New England. They'd discarded sweaters well before noon and worked steadily, taking only a brief break for lunch. Another hour, Lauren decided, two at most, and they'd be finished, even to the addition of the cross and top pieces of the railing.

The job hadn't proceeded entirely without setbacks. Adam had an unfortunate habit of striking his thumb rather than the head of the nail, and she occasionally missed, too, bending her target instead of driving it in. As if she'd jinxed the stroke by thinking about it, Lauren did just that on the next nail. With a resigned sigh she came up on hands and knees and used the claw at the back of her hammer to extract this latest miscalculation, then laid it on the decking and proceeded to pound it straight again.

"We can afford to toss them away, you know," Adam teased. "You don't need to salvage everything."

"Waste not, want not. Shame on you, Adam. Think of it as recycling."

"I can't think at all with this view."

She assumed he meant the brilliant display of leaves in their backyard. A plot of open land roughly the size of a baseball diamond was enclosed by a variety of trees, from white birches to evergreens to apples and mountain ash. The hues defied description. The old sugar maple alone was decked out in at least four distinctly different shades of orange and red. "Mother nature's patchwork quilt?"

Then she saw that he had not resumed work but sat, tailor fashion, elbows on knees, chin resting on fists. He was leering appreciatively not at the profusion of vivid colors but at her bottom. Her recent movements, Lauren realized, had produced a bounce of the backside for every stroke.

She made a face at him over her shoulder. Instead

of driving in the straightened nail she turned and threatened him with her hammer. "I'll pound something nearer and dearer to you than that thumb if you don't get back to work."

"Slave driver."

"Yup. Besides, we're almost finished. Just think how much use we're going to get out of this deck once it's done."

"I can think of a pretty good use for it right about now." Without further warning he dove at her, disarming her easily. They rolled together on the hard wooden surface, the carefree sound of their laughter bubbling over into the balmy air.

"Watch it, mister," Lauren gasped out between giggles. "A law-enforcement expert trained me in self-defense."

He'd insisted on that soon after they were married, astonished that she'd been living alone for so long, so far from the nearest neighbor, without a thought about protection for herself. Until the night they met she'd never imagined she would need it.

She rolled on top of him, landing so that she straddled his hips, but she lost her sense of control when he manacled a wrist with each hand. "Which dirty trick are you going to use?" he inquired politely.

Lauren met the wide, masculine grin with a mischievous smile and tossed her head in a futile attempt to dislodge the lock of hair that had fallen in front of her eyes. "I'd have to be crazy to warn you."

"Guess I'll just have to immobilize you, then. To be on the safe side." One swift movement tucked her beneath him, trapping her body under his own.

Her wrists ended up pinned on either side of her head.

"Beast!"

"You love it! Besides, we've got a tradition to uphold here."

When he bent to capture her lips, Lauren surrendered willingly. Against the cradle of her thighs she felt the full extent of his desire for her and it aroused her as nothing else could. No one had ever made her feel the way Adam did, especially when he was in a mood that was playful as well as amorous. It was as if they'd been born knowing how best to pleasure each other.

He stripped away her short-sleeved sweatshirt, baring her unconfined breasts for his kisses. She attacked the buttons on his well-worn flannel workshirt, all but ripping them loose in her frantic haste to touch the skin beneath. Hands collided reaching for zippers, hindered then helped each other remove the remaining barriers. Adam's mustache tickled as he rained kisses down her legs and back up again.

"I love it when you do that," she murmured.

Then, her attention concentrated on their swiftly mounting mutual passion, she lost her ability to speak and all coherent thought as well to the maelstrom of their loving. Electricity gave way to fireworks, pyrotechnics that soon exploded into ecstasy.

Lauren came slowly back to the reality of a late afternoon in early fall. The sun warmed her bare flesh, dispelling the slight chill of a gentle breeze. Another week and it would have been too cold for this, she thought.

The smell of sawdust surrounded them, so strong

that it nearly blotted out all other scents. Lauren inhaled deeply and discovered that she could detect a hint of spruce and the distinctive fragrance of pine. She sniffed again and was rewarded with the faint aroma peculiar to dry, fallen leaves. The sweet decay of crabapples lying beneath the trees came to her next and she sighed, replete. They'd picked the perfect day. This was the perfect place. He was the perfect man.

"Good thing we're screened from the road by trees," Adam murmured.

Belatedly Lauren realized that she had ended up on top, protected from contact with the hard, chemically treated surface; Adam had borne the brunt of the abuse.

"So considerate," she murmured. "Shall I kiss all your bruises and abrasions and make them better?"

Adam's response was involuntary and very gratifying, but his rueful grin contradicted the wicked gleam in his eyes. "Later," he promised, and landed a sharp swat on her backside. "Up and at 'em, sweetheart. That was our coffee break. Now it's time to get back on the job."

She dressed slowly, appreciating her view of Adam resuming his clothing. The oaks and birches, poplars and alders, even the brightly hued maples were only a backdrop for him, incapable of distracting her attention, and as she watched Lauren was sorely tempted to try to change his mind. She was certain she could. Adam always insisted she was his one weakness.

* * *

One entire wall of the cottage was faced in brick, containing a hearth and a bake oven with a wooden stop. She set aside the quilted sarcenet cap she'd been embroidering with friars' knots, to symbolize love, and bent to stir the pot simmering above the fire, hoping the savory cullis within would help appease him. He would be in a vile temper when he returned. That much was certain. Even if he was not cup-shotten from too much ale, he was ever choleric.

The cottage was on the far side of the stream from the manor house, with a view of its rooftops and chimneys. It had first been claimed by his father when their present monarch's sire defeated good King Richard at Bosworth. She peered out with anxious eyes and spotted him fast approaching their small timber-framed house. As the man who was her husband hurried across the small wooden bridge, she backed away from the door.

Out of habit she cast her gaze upward to the low rafters in a futile plea for heavenly protection. Then his arrival blocked all other thoughts from her head. He loomed threateningly in the entrance, although he was not a large man. The very sound of his booted feet on the stone-flagged floor seemed ominous to her.

He stopped inches away from her and spat, sending the foul stream directly into her face.

"Harlot! Cockatrice!"

Each harsh word was accompanied by a slap, one from each hard hand. The blows stung her cheeks and brought tears of pain to her eyes, and yet she knew he was not putting much force behind them. He'd beaten her before, beaten her senseless on more than one occasion. She knew he was saving his strength for the punishment he would mete out to her later.

"You are no better than a Winchester goose," he shouted as she backed away. Her hands came up to stave off the next hit. He knew. He knew she had cuckolded him.

"You dare defy me?" he bellowed, incensed by her futile effort to protect her face. "Lower your arms, trull. You deserve a sound thrashing for your sluttish ways, and as your husband I've every right to give it to you. You are my property, my chattel. Under the law I can beat you to death if I choose to. None will stop me. You have much offended me, wife. You do not deserve to live."

Silent defiance flashed briefly in her eyes even as she ducked her head and sidled out of his reach. She had survived earlier heats, but never had she seen him so far gone into rage. He was livid with anger, beyond reasoning even if there could be any argument. He did have the right to use her as he would, would have it even if she had not dishonored him by taking a lover.

She knew it was useless to plead with him to spare her and that resistance would only further inflame him. Escape could but delay the inevitable, and yet she found herself poised for flight as he advanced toward her once more.

An animal snarl issued from his bloodless lips, increasing her terror. She clung to the memory of the happiness she had found in those few precious, stolen hours. Love could not save her, but it did sustain her.

"Will you run and hide, quail?" His pockmarked face twisted into a horrifying sneer, revealing the blackened stubs of his teeth. "Bawd. Strumpet. There is no refuge for a stale as foul as you. A murrain on you, wanton jade."

Pushed at last to attempt to defend herself, she whispered, "I am no whore, husband."

"You have no honesty, either, inconstant drab. A bitch in heat hath more discretion." The words were spoken in almost conversational tones.

She had to bite hard on her lower lip to keep from pleading with him for mercy. There was no forgiveness in him. This return to apparent calm was a sign she knew too well. It was but the lull before a new spate of violence erupted.

He chuckled. His voice went very low as he made her a promise. "I will deal with him, too. Never doubt it."

The whimpered protest was ripped from her against her will. "No!" she cried. She could not bear the thought that he would be harmed, the one man who had shown her kindness, the man who had taught her that she had the capacity to love.

Her husband's rheumy eyes narrowed dangerously, and spittle appeared at one corner of his thin, merciless mouth. His whisper sent an icy chill into her veins, making the very blood run cold. "You will lie together for all eternity, you damned whore! At Court, they say, a man needs must wear his horns and pretend all be well, but here he hath another choice."

"Will, no!" She gave a long, keening cry, and of their own volition her hands extended themselves toward him, beseeching his mercy even though she knew full well that all her pleas were uttered in vain.

His breath began to come in short spurts, as if her terror excited him.

Knowing it was futile to try sweet reason, still she

made the effort. "You have the right to kill me, husband, but if you take away another's life they will make you pay for it with your own."

He laughed again and took another threatening step toward her. "You forget that I am bailiff here. I am the one collects the rents, my rancid sweeting. Think you Sir Randall will be deprived of such a loyal servant? Not for the sake of an unfaithful wife. Nay, nor not for the sake of that lewd creature, her base lover, neither. The fellow is not even a true-born Englishman."

Indignation at the idea that his wife had preferred a foreigner to himself turned Will's expression even uglier. His voice dripped venom as his fists clenched convulsively. "I will kill him slowly. None will trouble to stay my hand nor will any seek to avenge him when the worms have their turn at him."

With a sinking heart she knew he spoke the truth. Her lover had friends and family but they would be powerless against men of Sir Randall's ilk. Will had long been that ill-tempered knight's most valuable retainer, and Sir Randall, who owned all the land hereabout, was also the local justice of the peace. He could try a case or dismiss it on a whim, choose to mete out punishment or ignore wrongdoing as if it had never been. It would not trouble him that she had given his wife years of good service, or that her lover was a member of the household, too.

Will backed her away from the door, cutting off that avenue of escape, but she was desperate enough now to try another way. Spinning on her heels she began to run, sprinting up the narrow flight of stairs that led to two small rooms above. The ceilings were low and uneven, timber-framed like the walls, and the front chamber, which boasted a small fireplace, was almost entirely filled with their bedstead. She seized the only other piece of furniture, a heavy wardrobe trunk, and attempted to pull it in front of the door.

He was too swift for her. With brutal strength he shoved both door and trunk aside and pushed into the room.

She did not have time to think about what she was doing. She scrambled backward, realizing too late that she'd cut herself off from the window that had been her goal. Trapped between the bed and the hearth she flattened her back and palms against the wall. Her fingers closed around the handle of a heavy iron rod they used to stir the fire.

"Whore!" he cried, clambering across the dagswain blanket that covered their lumpy straw mattress. His hands were outstretched, grabbing for her throat, and she saw her own death in his mad eyes.

She swung the poker awkwardly, striking him on the temple with a blow that stunned him but did no permanent damage. She had a fleeting thought for her lover's comforting embrace, an instant's desire to find him, to convince him to run away with her; but in her heart she knew that any flight was doomed. They might gain a few more blissful hours together, but as long as Will Malte lived he would seek revenge. He would come after them, track them down to the ends of the earth if need be, and then he would make good his promise to kill them both.

There could be no escape for her, but she had in her hands the means to save her lover's life. With all the force she could muster she brought the poker down, striking Will with it again and again until blood and brains flowed freely and she was quite certain that he would never hurt anyone ever again.

Lauren woke abruptly, bathed in sweat, tremors shaking her as she levered herself upright. Beside her in their big Victorian bed Adam slept on, blissfully unaware that his wife had just murdered her husband.

5

Dan held his hand over the mouthpiece of the telephone and waved Adam into his private office. "Close the door behind you," he said; then, into the phone, "Yes, Karen." He winced at a reply Adam couldn't hear before continuing his attempt to placate the woman on the other end. "No, Karen. You're absolutely right, but—"

It was a conversation that seemed likely to go on for some time. Adam prowled restlessly in his brother's domain which, unlike his own place of business, bordered on the sloppy. Dan knew where everything was, but no one else had a clue.

"Come on, Karen, you know I can't do that, not without a court order." Dan rolled his eyes toward the ceiling, then closed them and tipped back in his chair. "Karen, I—" His feet hit the floor with a thud and the look of surprise on his face would have been comical if Adam hadn't already guessed what lay behind Karen Doucette's phone call. "She hung up on me!"

"She's got a right to be upset."

"Not with me." His eyes narrowed. "How much have you already heard? I've been trying to keep things quiet."

"Give it up. Lumberton's not that big a town."

Dan's sigh was heartfelt. "I suppose it's too much to hope that the rumors are accurate."

Adam shrugged. "I haven't heard that Clubber was on duty."

"Thank God for small favors. No, he was on his day off. Karen thought he'd gone bird hunting." A faint smile flickered across Dan's face, acknowledging the unintentional pun. "Damn fool left two garage-door openers in his car. Karen found them, naturally got curious, and spent the next couple of hours driving all over town trying to discover whose door the second one opened."

"Anya Carson's?"

"Yeah."

"The way I hear it, Karen walked right in on them."

Dan simply shook his head. "Guess they figured there was no point in locking the door between the garage and the house."

The two brothers exchanged a telling glance. Sympathy for Clubber warred with their shared belief that a man shouldn't cheat on his wife in the first place. "Karen wanted me to turn his paycheck over to her. Said I owed it to her."

"You're Clubber's boss, not his keeper."

"I could have sent him to the week-long training session on AIDS awareness."

"Come on, Dan. Do you think he'd have believed it might apply to him?"

Dan noticed that his brother was roaming from window to bookcase, file cabinet to desk. "What's got your tail in a twist? Damn sure it's not concern over the future of Clubber's marriage."

Adam didn't meet his eyes, fixing his gaze on the depressing view of the dreary parking lot beyond the window instead. The weather since Saturday hadn't helped his mood any, or done much for Lauren's. Typically perverse, the peak fall foliage days had been overcast, with frequent rain showers like the one in progress this morning.

"I'm worried about Lauren, Dan."

"What's the matter with her? Sandra said she saw her yesterday at the supermarket and she looked like she hadn't slept for a week."

"That's about the size of it. Not a week, but more than three days now."

Dan gave a low whistle.

"She may be getting in a few catnaps, but my best estimate is that she's gone close to ninety hours with little more than that." It was a circumstance that had left her testy and hadn't done much for his attitude, either.

"That's a hell of a case of insomnia. Any idea what's causing it?"

How did he describe the mounting tension of the past few days? Adam struggled for words. He had a wife who insisted she'd been unfaithful, though not to this husband, and that she'd murdered her husband, again not the one she had now.

"It started with a nightmare Lauren had while we were in New York," he told Dan. "After we got back home everything seemed fine at first. Then, just a week after the first dream, she had another one that really spooked her."

"Sit down," Dan ordered. "I'm getting a crick in my neck from watching you pace." He waited until Adam complied, then steepled his fingers under his chin, leaned back in his chair, and demanded details.

"I feel like a rookie making a report," Adam complained. "It's a case where I've misplaced all the evidence, too."

Dan grinned.

"Don't laugh."

"I wouldn't dare, Adam. I wouldn't dare. Why don't you just go ahead and tell me what Lauren dreamed about?"

"Don't laugh," he warned again. The details of Lauren's first nightmare sounded even more preposterous when repeated to Dan than when she'd told him. His brother wisely made no comment.

Adam drew in a deep breath and pushed forward with his story. "She didn't tell me as much about the second nightmare. Didn't even wake me up when it woke her. I'm not sure she would have said anything at all if I hadn't noticed how jumpy she was afterward. When I insisted on knowing what was wrong she confessed that she'd had a nightmare about the actual murder."

"She dreamed she killed her husband?"

Adam frowned, remembering how he'd felt when she told him that. "It was like pulling teeth to get much out of her, but Lauren eventually admitted that this . . . husband . . . was about to strangle her when she hit him in the head with a fireplace poker."

"Self-defense, then. That sounds more reasonable."

Adam cocked an eyebrow at him, incredulous. "Right."

"You know what I mean. So, did Lauren say why he was trying to kill her?"

"She told me that he knew she'd been unfaithful to him." Dan frowned and opened his mouth to comment, but Adam glared his brother into silence. "Don't even suggest it. Whatever made her dream about infidelity and murder, it wasn't anything to do with *our* lives."

"No need to get defensive, little brother. I'm puzzled, though. Sure, those dreams sound unpleasant, but Lauren's a sensible woman. Why is she letting them keep her awake nights?"

"Damned if I know." Unable to sit still any longer, Adam bolted out of the chair and resumed his restless pacing.

"Are you sure there were only two nightmares?"

Dan's suggestion stopped Adam in mid-stride. There had been that daydream in New York. In clipped sentences Adam related what little Lauren had told him about her vision of a great hall and a musicians' gallery and a lover.

"So, there's that vague historical setting. Again."

"Yeah. Medieval, I guess. You know I'm not much on history."

"Did the last nightmare take place in a castle, too?"

"I never said it was a castle. I don't know what kind of building it was. Lauren didn't tell me anything on Sunday about where she was when she killed him. If a fireplace poker was the weapon I guess it could have been in the same place, though. Weren't those big old dining halls heated with fireplaces?"

"Could be. Could be. Then again, I know about as much about history as you do."

"What difference does it make, anyway? None of it was real."

Dan didn't answer. He swiveled slowly in his chair, setting Adam's already strained nerves on edge with each strident squeak. Adam was about to clamp a hand on the chair-back to stop the noise, when his brother came to a halt of his own accord and offered a new slant on the situation. "There might be a connection between Lauren's nightmares and that painting she and Sandra saw in New York."

"What painting?"

"You remember the exhibit they went to?"

"Sure. I already suggested to Lauren that all that historical stuff might have been the source of her first nightmare." He stared unseeing at the parking lot, so intent on Dan's explanation that he didn't even notice when Clubber Doucette's cruiser pulled in.

"Sandra was telling me about one particular painting. According to her, Lauren had a real peculiar reaction to it. Sandra says it took her a while to catch on, though she did notice right away that Lauren was shook. She finally figured it out the next day. There was this girl, see, in the picture, and she looked a lot like Lauren must have when she was a teenager. Sandra was asking me just this morning if I thought Lauren would have any interest in genealogy, since it was probably some ancestor of Lauren's in that painting. Sandra thought it might be fun to see if they could trace her family tree back that far."

"Lauren doesn't even like to talk about her parents. I can't imagine she'd be interested in previous generations."

"Just a thought. Just a thought. Anyway, there's your answer. The visit to the museum did prompt that nightmare. Made Lauren imagine herself in that setting."

"Why? The picture didn't show an execution, did it?"

"From what Sandra said I think it was a scene at Court. Lords and ladies and all that."

"Doesn't explain why there was a second dream, anyway," Adam grumbled. His elbows rested on the window frame while all ten fingers worked to destroy any semblance of order left in his hair.

"Did Lauren give you any other details? I don't know much about interpreting dreams, but aren't nightmares supposed to be a reflection, heavily disguised, of what a person's really worried about?"

"I've repeated everything she told me, and as far as I'm concerned it's more than enough. I've got to tell you, Dan, that I don't much like this business of my wife dreaming about other men."

Adam caught himself just as he was about to rake his hands across his scalp again.

"The whole thing is just crazy." One hand came down on top of Dan's file cabinet with a resounding thump. The dirty metal felt gritty against his skin as a cloud of dust rose. "Don't you ever clean in here?"

"No. Destroys my filing system."

Clubber Doucette opened the door without knocking and stuck his head in. "You got a minute, Chief?"

Dan glanced his way in annoyance. "Come back in ten minutes. I want to talk to you."

"You got it. Morning, Adam."

"Clubber." Turning, Adam acknowledged the other man with a curt nod and a cold stare.

"Hey, I like the hair." Whistling cheerfully, Clubber exited Dan's office and headed for the coffee machine, leaving it for Adam to cross the room and close the door behind him.

"I'm worried about her, Dan."

"Come on, Adam, don't you think you may be making too much of this? The bottom line is that Lauren hasn't been sleeping well. Maybe all she needs is a good over-the-counter sleeping pill."

"She doesn't want to sleep, Dan. That's the real bottom line. I think she's afraid to relax that much, afraid she'll have another nightmare. The last two nights she didn't come to bed at all. She sat up drinking coffee. Damn it, she's going to make herself sick if she keeps this up."

"Could be . . . if she's not already ill."

Adam went very still. "Meaning?"

"Meaning that if she's been this long without sleep she's already in bad shape. I went seventy-two hours without sleep once when I was in the service. We were trying to get a plane airborne before the carrier docked. I was hallucinating by the time the chief ordered me to go to bed. Could have sworn I was heading for an open door. Walked right into a bulkhead."

"She's due to crash, then."

"I'd say so. I slept round the clock when I finally hit the sack."

"Maybe there won't be any more nightmares after she catches up on her sleep."

"If there are it won't be the end of the world. Even the worst-case scenario is that she's having some kind of breakdown. If she is, you can get professional help for her."

"She's not crazy, Dan."

His brother's pensive silence spoke volumes.

"I was just about to try to nap a while on the sofa," Lauren told her sister-in-law in an irritated voice, hoping she'd take the hint. It was an outright lie, but Sandra, on the other end of the phone wires, had no way of knowing that.

Lauren scarcely listened to Sandra's long list of sure-fire cures for insomnia. Her powers of concentration were deteriorating rapidly, along with everything else. Her stomach was tied in knots, and so laced with acid from all the coffee she'd drunk that the lining had probably started to resemble Swiss cheese. Heartburn exacerbated the discomfort, and ragged nerves left her twitchy. Her eyes were scratchy, she'd lost all interest in food, and as the total number of hours without sleep accumulated she was getting increasingly more clumsy, dropping things as periodic waves of dizziness washed over her.

Lauren stared at the phone for a long moment after she heard the disconnecting click, trying to think what to do with it. Finally she left it off the hook, ending any possibility of further interruption.

She was too tired to feel betrayed that Adam had talked to Dan about her problem, or angry that Dan had promptly repeated everything to his wife.

Sighing, Lauren turned back to the array of embroidery she'd taken out of storage just before Sandra's call. They were the prototypes for her tapestry designs. She spread them out in the order of their creation, displaying her earliest professional work on the small table in the dining nook.

She'd settled into this house, which at the time had been little more than a summer home, had it winterized and rewired, and applied herself with total dedication to producing saleable creations in crewel and needlepoint. She hadn't needed to supplement the income from her trust fund, but she had wanted to feel useful, to have a career. The first efforts, square panels for handbags, had a distinctly medieval origin and featured unicorns, ladies with lutes, and knights carrying shields.

"Phase Two," Lauren mumbled, laying out a row of colorful geometric patterns along the carpet that flowed unbroken from dining area into living room. She'd kept the same familiar stitches but given the designs a more modern flavor.

The third period coincided with the beginning of her married life. These were Victorian designs, influenced by the period of the historical romances and mysteries she liked to read.

With one hand to her aching temples, Lauren tried to think why she had even wanted to look at these samples in the first place. She couldn't remember. Frustrated by her inability to think clearly, she gathered everything up and thrust the pieces helter-skelter back into the cedar-lined storage closet that divided the dining nook from the entryway and kitchen.

She should eat something, she supposed, and plucked a fresh-picked apple from the bag Adam had brought home from a roadside stand. Taking it with her she wandered back toward the living room, pausing to stare through the sliding doors at the rain-soaked deck.

The room behind her was reflected in the glass. The sofa sorely tempted her, but Lauren knew she didn't dare give in. Every time she let her guard down, day or night, the dreams attacked.

Not all of the scenes that popped into her head were violent or terrifying. Some of them revealed mundane or inconsequential things, a hauntingly familiar face to which she could not attach a name, or a place she knew she'd been to before. They were moments of no particular importance, and yet she visualized them in infinite detail.

With a final, wistful look at the soft sofa cushions, Lauren began an orgy of housework, hoping that would keep her awake. She dusted everything in the den, a small room at the back of the house on the other side of the stairs from the living room. Then she started to clean the bathroom, which was tucked in between the kitchen and the door that led to the cellar, but she had difficulty aiming the scouring powder. After the third try she gave up. She tried taking the throw rugs to the front porch to shake them out, but quit when she lost her balance and nearly fell over the railing.

"Walking disaster area," she muttered as she dug out the vacuum cleaner and started on the carpets. The drone of the small engine had a soothing effect, lulling her into another time, another place. A sunny meadow supplanted the living room.

She was running through the tall grass toward a gnarled apple tree. She climbed high into the branches and began to munch apples, but they were green and before long they unsettled her stomach. She was going to be sick, and fall out of the tree, and no one was nearby to help her.

"No!"

The vacuum protested as Lauren shoved it viciously away from her, then hummed steadily again as she glared at it.

Lauren took deep breaths, willing her heart to stop thudding so loudly. After a moment she was calm enough to shut off the vacuum cleaner and return it to the utility closet.

It had happened again.

She didn't understand why she was suddenly plagued with such a vivid imagination. She didn't want it. She wanted to go back to living a normal life.

Adam was sympathetic, but he didn't really understand.

"Put it behind you," he'd advised after she gave him the essentials of her second nightmare.

That was easier said than done.

She'd tried to forget.

Despondent, Lauren made her way to the second floor. She was so tired. She'd slept very little. She couldn't seem to get more than an hour or two at a time before the dreams woke her.

Adam didn't know the half of it, she thought. She had not told him when, belatedly, she came to the chilling realization that the square she'd embroidered portrayed the same hunting scene she'd first seen on a tapestry in the great hall. She'd never filled him in on the additional details of that room, the ones that had come to her in the lecture hall and the lobby bar. Neither had she mentioned the vision she'd had on the plane, of the wedding.

If only she could sleep and not dream.

She stood in the middle of the boudoir they'd created, resentful of the fact that it no longer held only good memories. Early in their marriage, she and Adam had taken out a wall and joined the small room Lauren had slept in before they were wed with another the same size. Professionals had installed the bright red plush carpet, but Lauren had chosen and hung the red and white flocked wallpaper with its pairs of lovebirds in heart-shaped swings. She'd designed the bedspread and curtains and upholstered the furniture in velvet to match the decor.

"Is this the playroom?" one of Adam's nephews had asked the first time he'd clapped eyes on the spacious new bedchamber.

Adam had told him it was. Then he'd teased Lauren mercilessly, claiming the room reminded him of an Old West bordello. The beginnings of a smile played across Lauren's lips. Adam hadn't been put off by that. In fact, if the nights they'd shared in their ornately carved mahogany bed were any indication, they'd both been inspired by their surroundings. She ought to be dreaming of gunslingers and saloon girls, or of Indians who kidnapped white women and fell in love with them.

Lauren frowned, noticing one corner of the small mid-nineteenth-century settee they had found at an auction. Hassle had been using it as a scratching post. Lauren found she didn't have energy enough to be annoyed. Wearily, she sank down onto the damaged piece of furniture and promptly forgot all about her cat's destructive tendencies.

You have to think, Lauren told herself, but she was too tired to be rational. Her mind wandered and she couldn't seem to catch it for more than a few moments at a time.

Should she be relieved or frightened by the fact that there seemed to be a story developing, though not in any particular order? Those very ordinary glimpses of village and manor made her more uneasy than the violent episodes. They seemed so real. Faces recurred, faces of people she knew, even if she did not have names for them. They were connected, to her and to the household of Sir Randall.

"Sleaford," she said aloud. "Sir Randall Sleaford."

She had no idea where the name had come from, but she was certain it was the right one. Sir Randall Sleaford was Will Malte's employer. Sleaford was the man who'd stood on the church steps at their wedding, the man who was cruel to his own wife and even more brutal in his dealings with others.

The chill damp of the October afternoon outside her windows seemed to seep into the bedroom with her. Lauren rubbed her hands together, trying to warm them. Slowly she lifted them, palms up, in front of her. There might not be any blood upon them now, but those hands had killed a man.

Adam was late getting home, delayed by a last-minute phone call canceling an assignment in early December. Another county budget had just gone into the red, and his services were expendable.

It surprised him to find no lights burning in either the house or the workshop. Even more unusual was the phone; the kitchen extension was off the hook. After replacing it he hurried upstairs. Lauren was in their bedroom, sound asleep, curled into a ball on the settee. At first he was relieved, but then he came close enough to hear the harsh, labored sound of her breathing.

"Lauren?" He tossed his jacket and tie in the general direction of the closet and leaned over her to brush his lips against her forehead. The skin was so cold to his touch that Adam glanced quickly at the thermostat, though he could feel for himself that the room was comfortably warm. "Lauren?"

She moaned in her sleep but did not open her eyes. He hesitated. He hated to wake her when she needed rest so badly, but he didn't like the way her hands were clasped tightly together, nor the tortured sounds she was making as she dreamed. As he reached for her again she sat up and opened her eyes, but she didn't seem to see him. There was a dazed look on her face.

"Lauren?"

At the sound of his voice she blinked, then shook her head in denial. "No. My name is Jane Malte."

"Damn it! That's enough!"

Her sharply indrawn breath reminded him that fear had accompanied the nightmares. With considerable effort he managed not to shout, but he had to fight hard against the nearly overpowering urge to demand that she stop all this nonsense at once.

"I was dreaming," she said in apologetic tones.

"I know. Do you want to talk about it?"

Silence hung heavily between them, until Adam made her slide over. He sat down beside her on the settee, his arm settling across her shoulders. As soon as he tried to tug her close against his side she shied away.

"Don't shut me out, Lauren." The sudden loss of

her trust left him feeling painfully empty inside. He wanted to force her to turn to him for help, to demand his right to cherish and protect her. Instead he used gentle strength to draw her closer and in an unnaturally husky voice admitted his own fear. "I don't like this . . . space between us. The longer we go without talking about it, the wider the gap will become."

"I know."

"I hope I'm making too much of this, but I'm worried about what's happening, Lauren. I don't know what you're thinking. I hate this feeling that you may be afraid to share what's troubling you with me. We've always tackled things together before. Why not this?"

"I don't know what *this* is." The words were accompanied by an agonized sob. "I don't know why I pulled away. I love you, Adam." She turned her face into his shoulder and began to cry.

Adam's arms tightened around her. "Go on. Get it out." He held her close, one hand moving in soothing circles over her back, until she subsided into mere sniffles. It was hard to let go when she started to sit up, but he did, reaching for the tissue box and keeping his voice low and level as he handed it to her. "Better?"

"Yes. No. I don't know." She gave up trying to answer and noisily blew her nose. "I can't think straight anymore."

"Sleep deprivation."

"Adam? I . . . I'm afraid to sleep."

"You'll have to sleep eventually."

"I know." Her shoulders heaved in a shuddering sigh. "Staying awake didn't help, anyway. The most extraordinary things have been popping into my head."

He wondered if she was referring to hallucinations or daydreams. Adam settled her against his chest again, tucking her head in under his chin and wrapping his arm around her shoulders. "Talk to me, Lauren. Give us a fighting chance to figure out what caused this problem in the first place."

"According to Sandra you already know why the nightmares started."

Adam cursed silently, damning his brother's inability to keep anything from his wife. "She called you?"

"I may have been rude to her. I can't remember exactly what I said."

He thought about the phone he'd found off the hook. "She probably deserved everything you dished out. She's got a bad habit of meddling." She also had, he grudgingly admitted to himself, an uncanny ability, about half the time, to suggest viable alternatives to thorny problems. "Did she tell you her theory that the girl in the painting might be an ancestor of yours?"

"Is that what she meant?" Lauren stirred restlessly. She sounded done in.

"Are you too sleepy to talk about this now?"

"Tired, not sleepy. My mind's still in overdrive. Not coherent, just . . . spinning. I feel like a mouse in one of those wheels. I'm getting nowhere fast. Other times it's more like a maze, and I'm one of the dumber lab animals. I can't find a way out on my own."

"I'll help you. Together we'll find a door."

"What if it's locked?"

"We'll find a key, or I'll use my trusty lockpick."

There was a short silence. Lauren's hand rested on his wrist, her fingers toying with the edge of his cuff. "I'd never be unfaithful to you, Adam," she said in a small voice.

"Hell, I know that." His free hand covered hers, stilling the fitful movements. "I know you're not about to murder me, either. Whatever is causing these dreams, it's not some subconscious urge to do away with your spouse. I've got sense enough to see that."

When she shifted her head to look up at him he realized she was fighting to keep her eyes open. "We'll talk later," he said. More to himself than to Lauren he added, "We'll get you some help. I promise."

Her reaction was instantaneous. She went stiff in his arms, then levered herself away from him. Her expression reflected confusion but it was laced with a new wariness. "What do you mean . . . help?"

"I mean that if these dreams are symptoms of some real problem, not anything homicidal, just a . . . problem, then we should consider seeking professional help to get rid of them." The idea had taken him all day to get used to. He couldn't blame Lauren for being resistant to it, but he hadn't anticipated the vehemence of her reaction.

"A shrink."

It wasn't a question but he nodded anyway.

"You think I'm crazy, don't you?"

"I think you're going to make yourself crazy if you don't get some rest." She tried to jerk away from him and stand, but he caught her arm. "No, Lauren, I do not think you're crazy, but it's obvious something's wrong. These aren't normal dreams. The sensible thing to do is ask for help."

"From a shrink?" Revulsion colored her voice, making the word sound like the worst kind of epithet.

Pulling free of his grip she rose too quickly and nearly lost her balance. Adam steadied her as he, too, stood upright. Then he turned her around to face him and held her firmly by the shoulders. "Lauren, look at me. Why are you so opposed to this idea?"

"I don't want some stranger messing with my mind. It's difficult enough talking to you about my dreams." Her eyes were wide and frightened, but more telling still were the dark circles surrounding them and the redness within.

"That's the point, I think. An outsider has some perspective and the training to figure out what's going on in your head."

Incipient hysteria tinged her words of protest. "I don't want to know! I just want the dreams to stop."

"We'll talk about it after you get some rest."

"I can't sleep. I may never sleep again."

"If things are that bad, then you'd better consider seeing a medical doctor. Damn it, Lauren, you're standing here trembling with fatigue. You can't go on like this. Maybe a sedative—"

"No pills. You know I don't like pills. People get addicted to pills."

"I don't like the idea of depending on prescription drugs myself, but we're not going to accomplish anything when you're so spaced out from lack of sleep that you can't carry on a rational conversation."

She promptly burst into renewed tears. "I'm so scared, Adam. Maybe I *am* losing my mind!"

"It's okay, sweetheart. Don't worry. No matter what's happening to you, we'll get through it. We'll find out what's causing the problem and get treatment and make you well." He sat down, shifting her in his arms until she was cuddled on his lap.

Lauren wiped at the tears in her eyes with the backs of her hands and swallowed convulsively. The edge of panic had not left her voice, but she had regained a modicum of control over her emotions. "If I go to a shrink will I have to talk about my childhood? My parents?"

"Would that be so awful?" Adam had no clear idea what treatment did involve. All the cases of mental illness he'd come across in police work had been in crisis by the time he encountered them.

"There's something I'd better tell you."

He braced himself for some unpleasant revelation about her early years. He thought he was prepared to hear anything, inured by years in law enforcement to all kinds of depravity.

Lauren lifted her head and met his sympathetic gaze. "I won't be able to tell a shrink much," she whispered. "The truth is, I can't remember a single thing about the first eighteen years of my life."

6

There was a brief pause as Adam attempted to absorb what she'd just said. "Let me get this straight." His voice held a skeptical note no amount of love for her could hide. "We've been married five years and you're only now getting around to telling me you have amnesia?"

"It didn't seem that important."

"Good God, Lauren. That's half your life you're talking about. What did the doctors say?"

She blinked at him, momentarily unsure of his meaning. It was becoming increasingly difficult for her to hang on to the thread of conversation. "What doctors?"

"Whoever you consulted when it happened. Was there some accident? A blow to the head?" When she hesitated too long over her answer he gave her a little shake. "Look at me. That's better. Now, tell me what caused your memory loss."

"I don't know."

"Couldn't the doctors—"

"Will you stop going on about doctors. I didn't see a doctor."

"How could you *not* consult someone?"

There was utter disbelief in Adam's voice. Lauren didn't know why she should be surprised by his reaction. Doubts were natural, especially from someone with Adam's background and training. To a man who'd spent most of his life in one branch of law enforcement or another her claims must sound not only outrageous but downright suspicious.

"You needn't sound so exasperated with me."

"I don't understand any of this. I won't pretend to be an expert on memory loss, but I do know it occurs much more frequently in fiction than it ever does in real life. Damn, Lauren. Why didn't you go to a doctor? Didn't you want to get your memory back?"

"Don't yell at me!"

He gaped at her. "I wasn't yelling."

He'd sounded unbearably loud to her, but maybe he hadn't even raised his voice. Her mind was probably playing tricks on her again.

She flexed her fingers against his shoulders, surprised to discover that she'd already sunk her nails so deeply into the fabric that tiny depressions remained in the soft cotton.

After a deep, slow, steadying breath she tried to force her scattered thoughts to regroup. The long nap she'd had that afternoon had reduced some of her confusion, but she was still lamentably short of sleep. It took incredible effort to think clearly. There was that pounding in her head to get through for one thing, and her stomach felt queasy, too. Even worse, she was horribly afraid she was going to start crying all over again. She'd done more blubbering in one day than she usually did in a year.

"Please don't yell at me," she murmured distractedly. "I can't think at all if you yell."

"Lauren, I promise I won't raise my voice above a whisper, but I'd like an explanation. Why didn't you go to a doctor when you lost your memory?"

She slid off his lap, surprised that he let her go. It was even more remarkable that he stayed put. Only his intent stare followed her as she cautiously moved away.

"It never occurred to me that a doctor could help."

A small voice, far in the back of her mind, wondered why it hadn't. Fear, she supposed. They'd been wary in those days of any authority figure, just as they'd been unwilling to trust anyone over thirty. A rueful smile contorted her features. Somehow she didn't think Adam would understand that rationale.

Aloud she said, "There was someone with me when it happened, someone who was able to tell me who I was, to fill in the missing details of my life. Medical advice didn't seem necessary."

Adam didn't try to hide his astonishment as he came to his feet in a rush. Across the width of the room his eyes bored into her and she could sense the intensity of his agitation. "Let me get this straight. You never told anyone about this memory loss?"

"Not until just now."

Continued silence on the subject would have been wise. She saw that now. Rob had warned her to guard their secret well. He'd told her time and time again to trust no one but him, and shrinks, he'd always insisted, were the very worst people to confide in.

"Lauren, you—"

"Why *should* I have told anyone? I was able to find out who I was, and once I'd relearned all the essentials of my background there was no need to make a big deal out of having forgotten them."

Adam's face still reflected his disbelief. "This is a little hard to swallow."

"Harder than the dreams I've been having?"

"Yes. No. Hell, Lauren, I don't know." Predictably, one hand furrowed through his hair, but for once Lauren failed to find the habit endearing.

"You don't believe me."

She flung herself across their bed, burying her face in the brocaded spread. The raised pattern pressed into her right cheek, leaving swirling indentations in the soft skin, but her senses were more attuned to Adam's movements than her own. She felt the vibration of each step as he came toward her across the room. The hairs on the back of her neck prickled when he hesitated, standing beside the bed, staring down at her prostrate form. Then one of his knees depressed the mattress near her left foot. Slowly, as if loath to startle her, he eased himself down beside her.

Lauren opened her eyes.

He lay sprawled on his back, his hands behind his head, his expression stoic as he gazed at the ceiling. He made no attempt to touch her, but when he spoke his voice was soft and urgent, pleading for her cooperation. "Start from the beginning," he requested. "You lost every scrap of memory? All knowledge of who you were?"

"Yes. Eighteen years—gone in a flash." She tried to snap her fingers for emphasis but couldn't even manage that feat.

"None of it has ever come back to you?" He still didn't look at her, which, perversely, made Lauren wish he would reach out and tug her close to him. She felt cold without his arms around her, bereft of the security she knew she'd find within his embrace.

"Nothing," she confirmed. Instinctively seeking his warmth, she inched closer, until she could nestle against his side. Her head came to rest in the crook of his left arm.

As if he'd been waiting for the signal, Adam moved, resettling them both so that Lauren's ear was directly over his heart.

"At first I couldn't even remember how to read or write. I had to be taught to sign my own name." She managed a weak smile. "The only thing I could manage without any instruction was needlework. It took years to pick up everything else."

"This is an incredible story, Lauren."

"Do you believe me?"

"Of course I believe you. That's not the point. What's giving me trouble is the fact that you waited until now to mention something so earthshaking to me."

"It's not a subject I like thinking about." She hesitated, wondering how much more to reveal. Her instincts told her it would be best if she told him as little as possible. "By the time we met, twelve years had passed. I was fully functional."

The steady rise and fall of Adam's chest relaxed Lauren even as she struggled to decide how to deflect new questions. His breath stirred tendrils of her hair with comforting warmth, but he didn't speak. After a moment she realized he'd accepted her explanation and was willing to let her proceed with the story at her own speed.

"I couldn't remember a single thing I'd learned in school," she said after a moment, fighting the lethargy that now stole over her limbs, "or any of the everyday knowledge people pick up just living. I had to be taught the value of coins and how to use a fork. I didn't know the names of rock groups or remember how to drive a car, though I had a valid driver's license."

It was so comfortable lying next to Adam, she thought. She didn't want to move, didn't want to think, certainly didn't want to remember that she hadn't even been sure what a car was the first time she'd seen one after her memory loss. The first airplane had terrified her. Even a ride in an elevator had been a frightening new experience.

"I always thought skills stayed," Adam murmured against her temple. "Things like driving."

A bleak, dispirited tone crept into her voice at the thought that Adam might not believe her after all. "They didn't for me."

How impossible would it have been to cope, she wondered, if Rob hadn't been there for her? She knew she ought to tell Adam about Rob, but something held her back. She was excruciatingly tired and it was terribly hard to recall the reasons secrecy had seemed so important.

"You managed to relearn a great deal," Adam ventured.

She mumbled sleepily, "Praise the Lord and turn on the television set."

"So that's what you meant when you said you'd learned a lot from game shows."

Did that sound like the kind of thing he'd say if he believed her? Maybe Adam was even starting to understand why she'd kept quiet about her amnesia all these years. "The first months were hard," she whispered. "Scary. But I've put that whole period of my life behind me now. When I moved to Maine I started fresh."

"You kept to yourself a lot then."

"Mmmmm. A veritable recluse."

Images of the nine years of near solitude in this house flickered through her tired brain. She'd stayed close to home with her embroidery and her television and her books, hundreds of them on every subject imaginable. There had been so much to catch up on once she'd honed her reading skills sufficiently. "Time to finish adjusting," she said. No one had bothered her. Maine had been the ideal place for her recovery, for it was a state where eccentrics were so commonplace that no one thought twice about it when a person chose to keep to herself.

Lauren fought a yawn. She didn't dare sleep, but neither did she want to face the inevitable interrogation. Adam was silent now, but she knew him well. He was turning questions over in his mind. Sooner or later he'd ask them all, and she didn't dare attempt answers when her thoughts were this jumbled. The risk of another nightmare suddenly seemed the lesser of two evils. Sleep appeared to be an escape route. Resolutely, Lauren closed her eyes.

Adam's voice intruded, soft but insistent. "What's the very first thing you remember?"

Lauren tensed in his arms. There it was: the question she most dreaded, the question she could not answer without triggering a dozen more. He'd only be upset by the truth, she told herself.

"Do we have to talk more now, Adam?" she said evasively. "I'm so tired."

"Lauren—"

"I need sleep. You were right. I do need sleep."

What began as feigned exhaustion quickly became reality. Lauren was completely spent, emotionally and physically, and discovered that it felt so deliciously wonderful to lean against Adam, so safe, that she at long last relaxed in his arms.

"Need sleep," she repeated, and drifted off without another thought.

This time, Adam decided, Lauren was so soundly asleep that nothing he could do would disturb her.

She'd be uncomfortable sleeping in her clothes, especially if she was down for the count. Round the clock, Dan had said. It was going to drive him crazy waiting that long for answers. Working quickly and efficiently, Adam stripped off Lauren's jeans and sweatshirt and replaced them with a soft, flannel nightgown. He tucked her into bed and stood frowning down at her, plagued by indecision. It was an unusual state for him to find himself in, but then he'd never before been faced with a situation that even remotely resembled this one.

His strongest impulse was to shake Lauren awake again and demand more details. He sensed there was a great deal she hadn't told him. It was almost as if she wanted to hide something from him. She'd never been able to lie. Her face was too open. Adam suspected she was holding back crucial facts about the onset of her amnesia. In particular she hadn't wanted to tell him about her earliest memory, which made him think it must have been an extremely unpleasant one.

Amnesia. The mind boggled. If anyone else had spun him such a yarn he wouldn't have bought it for a minute, but Lauren could not lie to him.

No wonder she'd always been reticent about her early years.

Procrastinating, Adam retrieved his jacket and tie from the floor and hung them neatly in the closet, then finally, reluctantly, he left the bedroom, closing the door behind him to keep Hassle out.

He crossed the narrow upstairs hallway to the room he'd turned into a home-office.

His official place of business, dating from before his marriage, was located on the third floor of a building in downtown Lumberton. This room was the place where he worked on articles for professional journals and revisions for the second edition of his textbook. It was a more comfortable environment, more conducive to writing.

Hassle was curled up in the top basket of a four-tier stack of letter trays that sat on the work station next to Adam's personal computer. When he reached past her for the phone, she opened slitted green eyes and glared at him, apparently offended by the interruption. Adam ignored the cat, and the stack of notes for the next consulting job and the student papers he'd collected the previous night in the police ethics class he taught at the University of

Maine's Lumberton campus. He dialed Doctor Warren Brinkwood's home number from memory.

An answering machine took the call. Adam hung up without leaving a message. This was Wednesday, he realized, which meant he should have known Doc would be out. Since his retirement the previous year, the Ryder brothers' lifelong family doctor had become a creature of habit. Every Wednesday he went to his daughter's house for the evening.

Adam debated the wisdom of leaving Lauren alone when she was so deeply asleep that she'd never hear a smoke alarm, but he didn't intend to be gone long and there was no reason to suppose disaster would strike during the next couple of hours. He no longer questioned her need for professional help. She wouldn't like it when she found out that he'd gone behind her back, but it was for her own good. Filled with a sense of the rightness of his mission, Adam drove to his brother's house.

The dog guarding Dan Ryder's back door had been named Not-a-cat, but in truth he was more pussycat than sentinel. Even if he hadn't recognized Adam he wouldn't have barked. Adam let himself in through a mud room that connected to the old-fashioned kitchen and paused to drop a light kiss on the cheek of the woman he found there.

"Is your father here?" he asked.

Sandra was concentrating on getting a meal on the table and barely glanced at him. "He and Dan are in the living room," she said. "Are you eating with us? If you are, set another place on your way through the dining room."

It was easier to comply than explain why he had no appetite.

"You look like hell," Dan greeted him. He didn't bother to get up. He was too comfortably ensconced in the recliner Sandra had given him on his last birthday. A beer can in one hand, a plate of cheese and crackers near the other, and a calico cat curled up asleep on his lap, he was the very model of a modern couch potato. The television was tuned to a local news program for the latest chapter in an ongoing battle between a feisty D.A. and the state's undercover drug-enforcement unit.

"You wouldn't look much better if you'd been trying to talk sense to someone who's hallucinating, having bouts of uncontrolled weeping, and is downright paranoid about going to sleep for fear of nightmares."

"Huh!"

The snort of interest from the other side of the snack tray came from Doc Brinkwood, a tall, spare man in his seventies who was still both straight of limb and sharp of mind. He'd given up active participation in the medical profession the last time the rates for malpractice insurance went up, but he rarely hesitated to offer free advice. It came full of personal opinions and since those in medicine shared with law enforcement professionals a certain dark, irreverent attitude toward life, Adam was not surprised by the older man's cavalier use of pejorative terminology.

"Used to be we'd institutionalize all those weird wackos," he grumbled. "Just incarcerate the worst nut cases till they calmed down some."

An image of Lauren, locked away, abruptly became very real for Adam. The possibility appalled him, giving his voice a strangled quality, even to his own ears. "That's what you'd recommend?"

"Probably couldn't these days. They've laid off so many people at the state hospital with their damned cost-cutting that the inmates are running the asylum. Who're you talking about, anyway? Didn't think you still arrested folks."

"He's talking about his wife, Doc."

Looking askance at Dan, the older man sputtered for a moment, then turned his full attention back to Adam. "Get in here, boy, and fill me in. Can't diagnose properly without all the facts."

Frozen in the archway between dining and living room, still trying to deal with the possibility that Doc's dire prediction might come to pass, Adam hesitated. Was he doing the right thing? Would Lauren understand why he'd gone ahead with his plans while she slept?

"Sit," Doc ordered irritably. "Dump Zip out of that chair and talk to me. You say she's seeing things?"

Reluctantly Adam took the chair Doc indicated, moving aside the white and gray coon cat already occupying it. "Maybe this wasn't such a good idea." Doc was a judgmental old man. His views on mental illness were probably hopelessly out-of-date.

"Spit it out," Doc commanded.

A lifelong habit of following doctor's orders was hard to break.

"Lauren has been having rather vivid dreams, day and night," he said carefully, "and just tonight she told me that she has amnesia."

"Details, boy."

He was aware of a certain sense of irony as he began to outline what little he knew. Only that afternoon he'd been trying to convince himself that there was no longer any stigma attached to what he'd euphemistically called Lauren's nervous disorder. A breakdown was just another illness, he'd reasoned after leaving Dan's office. He'd even told himself that mental problems were less traumatic to deal with than physical ailments, deciding that talking about one's fears had to be less painful than suffering through surgery. He was no longer sure that was true.

Sandra stuck her head into the room early in his account, listened from the doorway long enough to grasp the situation, then disappeared to feed her two young sons. She put the rest of the food on warming trays for the adults to eat later and returned to the living room in time to hear Adam recap his most recent conversation with Lauren.

"I left her sleeping. I suspect she'll be out for hours, but I want to be home when she wakes up. Trouble is, I don't know what to say to her."

"Huh," Doc said. His white brows beetled in thought and he drummed his fingers on the arm of his chair.

"Before you threw in the amnesia angle I was going to suggest you talk to the stress-management guy at the college," Dan said. "Memory loss puts things in an entirely different light."

"Does it? Why?" Sandra perched on the edge of the sofa, her expression an echo of her father's. "Seems to me these dreams could be an attempt to remember whatever it was she forgot."

"There's the little matter of their historical setting," Adam reminded her.

Sandra waved a dismissive hand. The jangle of her silver bracelets added a jarring note to an atmosphere already charged with tension. "Haven't you ever read any books on dream interpretation? Things are never what they seem."

"My daughter, the expert on everything." Neither Doc's sarcasm nor the sour expression on his face daunted Sandra.

"Let's hear your suggestion, then." Her voice issued a challenge and she leaned across the end table to reinforce the impression, inclining her whole body forward.

Doc ignored her and turned so that he was facing Adam. "Got to tell you right from the get-go that this case is beyond me. I was never more than a simple, old, country G.P., so—"

"Oh, Lord, Dad. Give us a break." A testy glare didn't deter Sandra one bit. "You aren't old and you were never simple. Humility doesn't suit you."

"I'm not being humble. I just know my own capabilities. When I had my practice I was always smart enough to turn problems like this one over to an expert. First off, you need someone trained in dealing with sleep disorders. That's the ticket."

"I'm a little leery of head doctors, Doc," Adam said.

Brinkwood looked amused. "And why's that?"

"I suspect it's because I've seen too many mishandled court cases. I haven't much respect for most insanity defenses." In Adam's experience, both the D.A. and the defense attorney always seemed able to find experts willing to swear to diametrically opposed views of the defendant's mental state.

Doc chuckled, understanding. "Doesn't inspire much confidence in the profession, does it? Still, these psychiatric folks aren't all quacks, and I'm going to tell you which ones to avoid. Don't go near Dr. Liam Greeley, whatever you do. He's an M.D., a practicing psychiatrist, which means he's allowed to dole out medication. Loves to do it, too, whether the patient really needs drugs or not. Prozac for everybody! Why, with a former patient of mine—"

"Dad," Sandra interrupted. "You're off on a tangent. You know perfectly well Lauren doesn't need a psychiatrist. It's a psychologist she should think about consulting, or a psychotherapist."

This time his glare contained both pride and affection. "Huh. Kids don't know their place these days. She's right, though. I can recommend several good men."

"Are we talking about analysis?" Adam asked.

"Nobody does that Freudian crap around here. Takes too long. Costs too much. This is Maine, not California."

"The generic term is therapy," Sandra said under her breath. "Very nonthreatening."

Adam still wasn't convinced, but he had to admit that therapy did have a less formidable sound to it than analysis.

"Now listen up, boy. Some of these therapists have Ph.D.'s, and some have less impressive sounding degrees but are just as savvy. What you have to do is decide whether you want to go to a licensed clinical psychologist or to a licensed clinical social worker. A clinical social worker uses a psychologist as a preceptor to oversee the counseling work."

Compared to keeping Lauren medicated or locked up, having her talk to some sort of counselor seemed reasonably painless. Adam managed a curt nod of agreement. "I guess it won't hurt to try. Who do you recommend?"

"Get the boy a notepad, Sandra."

"Only if all three of you will go sit at the table and eat. I'll dish up the food while you dish out advice." She shooed them into the dining room to serve the long-delayed meal.

Adam tasted none of it, though he forced himself to eat. The notepad sat next to his plate, and within ten minutes he had jotted down capsule descriptions of every therapist in a sixty-mile radius. He was frankly astonished, both by their sheer numbers and by the variety of techniques they used.

Sandra, who had been quietly consulting the Yellow Pages, cleared her throat. "You didn't mention Dr. Camilla Andrews, Dad."

"One more to stay away from." Doc's lips twisted derisively. "She's got a Ph.D., though God knows in what, but she uses crystals and tarot cards to help her patients get in touch with past lives."

"The ad says she offers holistic treatment," Sandra objected.

"I think I can safely cross her off the list." Adam felt his features relax into the first real smile of the evening.

Sandra gave a snort that sounded remarkably like one of her father's. "Don't you think you're being a little shortsighted? After all, Lauren's dreams are taking place in the past. How can you simply rule out reincarnation?"

"As my grandsons say, Sandra, get real."

"I love you, too, Dad." She turned to Adam, her expression uncharacteristically serious. "Why don't you let Lauren decide who she'll see? After all, it's her mind that's disturbed."

"I think I can speak for my own wife. She'll opt for middle ground. No drugs. No seances." He glanced across the table at Doc, who was just polishing off his second slice of apple pie. "You think this Dr. Beaumont is our best bet, don't you."

"He fits your middle-ground criteria. Regards problems with dreams as a dissociative disorder."

"Beaumont," Adam repeated, glancing at his hastily scribbled notes. Dr. Jarvis Beaumont, Ph.D. His office was in Twin Cities, about a forty-five-minute drive. That wouldn't be a problem until winter set in, but Adam was hoping that by then Lauren would be completely cured. How long could it take to zero in on a problem like this? It wasn't as if they were going to ask him to restore her memory.

"I'll give Beaumont a call in the morning," Doc offered. "See what I can set up for you."

Sandra's barely disguised sarcasm and the clatter of cutlery on china put an end to Adam's complacent mood. "I'll bet Lauren would be more comfortable talking to another woman. Even if you won't consider Dr. Andrews, there are lots of female therapists on Dad's list."

"Butt out, Sandra," Dan warned as he rose from the table to return to recliner, beer, and television set. "Adam knows what he's doing."

Lauren woke slowly, dimly aware that she felt more rested than she had in days and that she had a desperate need to use the bathroom.

She'd no sooner finished than Adam appeared in

the door of their bedroom. She blinked at him in confusion. What was he doing home when bright sunlight was still pouring in through the break in the curtains? He should be at work.

Slowly comprehension dawned. He'd stayed home to take care of her. She recalled most of their last conversation and remembered, too, that she'd avoided answering Adam's question by falling asleep.

"What time is it?" she asked. "For that matter, what day is it?"

"Thursday afternoon. You've been zonked out just short of twenty hours."

"No wonder I had to pee!"

Adam's smile seemed forced, and as she watched he rubbed his eyes and rotated his shoulders, stretching the cramped muscles. He'd never learn not to hunch over when he worked at his word processor, she thought fondly. Then she wondered if he'd slept at all since yesterday.

"Are you hungry?" he asked.

"Now that you mention it, I'm starved."

"Get back into bed and I'll bring you a tray."

"You don't need to fuss over me."

"I want to," he insisted.

"I'm interrupting your work."

"It'll keep. That's the advantage of being my own boss. Not only can I work at home on occasion, I can even knock off early if I want to."

"Goofing off in the middle of the afternoon is the first step on the road to ruin," she said, teasing, but she obediently crawled back under the covers. She did feel rather weak.

"To hell with the Puritan work ethic."

He left the doorway and approached the bed, his gaze sweeping over her as if he wanted to reassure himself that she really was all right. He rearranged the sheet and blanket, tucking her in with exquisite care. Then he brushed his lips lightly across her mouth.

"No Puritans in this house," she whispered, "just a practical old Yankee."

"Right. So you stay put. I need to make a backup disk. Then I'll head downstairs and I'll be up again before you know it with something for you to eat. It shouldn't take me more than half an hour to do everything. Okay?"

"Okay."

The idea of being pampered appealed to her, and the realization that she'd slept all those hours without dreaming lifted her spirits enormously. She sent a cheerful smile in Adam's direction as he left the room.

Maybe things had returned to normal. If she could talk Adam out of asking questions . . .

Fat chance.

With a sigh Lauren plumped and rearranged the pillows and settled herself against them to await her husband's return. She wasn't alarmed when her thoughts started to drift backward. This time she recognized the direction in which they were headed. This recollection was of something that had really happened to her, rather than the beginning of another fantasy involving that mysterious sixteenth-century servant girl, Jane Malte.

Remembering what she'd experienced seventeen years earlier might make her feel a little guilty, Lauren supposed, but it couldn't possibly be as unnerving as one of her daydreams. She relaxed and allowed that first clear memory to surface, that moment Adam had been so curious about.

Initially there had been a sense of disorientation, caused by the fact that she didn't know who she was or where she was or whom she was with. Then, in the next instant, she hadn't cared about any of those things. She'd been too caught up in the throes of a sensational orgasm.

7

The beautifully formed young man grunted with masculine satisfaction as he pulled away from the girl he'd just made love to. Unconcerned about his total nudity he rose from her side, then turned back to stare down at her, a vague, bewildered look on his face.

She stared back, taking in the youth's slender physique, lean but not hard. It had not yet begun to show visible evidence of his dissipated life-style. His eyes would have given him away, had she known then what it was she was seeing in them. He was stoned, too far gone to be certain what it was he was seeing, either.

She blinked dazedly at him, uncertain of his identity but fascinated by the halo of white blond curls that framed his face. The countenance itself was pleasant to look at, dominated by a thin blade of a nose.

His sensual lips moved, mumbling a whole string of words, all of them quite meaningless to her. He waited, as if for a reply, but when he received no answer he quietly melted away.

Only after he'd left her lying alone did she became aware of her own nakedness. The distinctive scents and sensations of recent sexual activity still lingered. A final tingle reverberated deep in her womb, a potent reminder of just how wonderful this man had made her feel. Subtle aches at the juncture of her thighs seemed proof they had both labored enthusiastically to achieve that pleasure.

Gradually a less welcome sensation impinged on her consciousness, a throbbing pain in the sole of her right foot. She started to sit up, but a wave of dizziness sent her reeling back onto the mattress. She felt nausea rise in her and fought it down, closing her eyes tightly against encroaching vertigo.

After a time she risked examining her surroundings once more. The foot still radiated pain, but the room had stopped spinning. With extreme caution she directed her gaze down the length of her prone body.

The valley between her breasts was glistening with sweat, but that was more than just an aftereffect of her carnality. She was burning with fever. One hand strayed to her forehead and found it dangerously hot, but in the very next moment she began to shake uncontrollably. Chills racked her undernourished body, and the skin that had been damp and overheated suddenly went cold and clammy.

Lauren, safe in her own bed in her own house, shuddered at the memory of how ill she had been. As she contemplated that part of her past from the safe distance of many years, she found she understood everything much more clearly than she had at the time.

At first she'd even had difficulty communicating. It seemed that her memory of the English language had been lost along with everything else.

The haze that still obscured many of the details of those early days was partly the result of the fever, but equally at fault was the thick, sickly sweet cloud of marijuana smoke that constantly pervaded the atmosphere of their flat.

She'd slept a great deal, Lauren remembered, with that same beautifully built young man at her side. In spite of his drug use he'd had a strong sexual appetite. Neither one of them had bothered with clothes, since it was then high summer.

Sultry heat penetrated the walls. Open windows let in only humid air as he nursed her, after a fashion, and used her for his pleasure. He'd been a selfish lover, only interested in his own satisfaction, but she hadn't know that then, or that it had been more by accident than design that she'd so often achieved her own.

Still, he'd not been unkind. On the day the last of the fever had finally left her, he put her into the old, cracked, clawfoot bathtub and filled it up. She could still remember sitting at the tap end while he washed her, gently, all over, even cleansing her hair, which had been very long and very tangled. Then he'd made slow, delicious love to her right there in the soapy water.

She never thought to object to anything he did, for he was all she knew, her only protection in a world she could not begin to comprehend. During the few times he left her alone she was tormented by the fear that he would not return. The glimpses she got of the outside world, through the windows of the flat, terrified her. She was convinced she would die without him to look after her.

She tried repeatedly to talk to him, to ask questions, but although it seemed to her that her words were clear, he only shook his head and looked puzzled. His speech was equally incomprehensible to her at first, but eventually she began to understand a little. Her feeling of confusion and disorientation persisted, but ever so slowly she began to adjust to her situation.

She watched him all day long. They shared a tiny three-room apartment, and he went out only to get supplies. By imitating his actions she learned how to flush a toilet, boil a kettle of water, make instant coffee, and smoke a joint. When she discovered an assortment of clothing in a closet, he helped her figure out how to put on various pieces of it. Then he amused himself by taking them off her again.

She never thought of their living quarters as squalid, even though they were filthy and bug-infested. She had no memory of living in any better place. She accepted as normal that a mattress on the floor served as their bed. The other furnishings were limited—a rickety wooden table, two caned chairs, an overstuffed sofa whose innards hung out in great tufts, and a set of expensive leather suitcases which did triple duty as end tables, footrests, and drawer space.

Morning light was filtering through filthy windows when she woke for the first time without a pounding headache or any other pain. Silhouetted in the glow, surrounded by dust motes, looking more like a fallen angel than ever, her lover had been watching her sleep.

"Lauren?"

She frowned at him, puzzled, and tried to reproduce the word, but apparently her pronunciation was off. He made her repeat it after him, again and again like an echo, until she got it just right.

"You're Lauren Kendall," he said.

Already accustomed to his voice, his accent, and his speech patterns, she soon comprehended his meaning. He was trying to tell her that her own name was Lauren Kendall.

His was Rob Seton.

"Do you remember anything about yourself?" he asked.

She shook her head and waited, watching his face. His grave expression gave nothing away, but for once his narrow blue eyes were clear, the pupils their normal size. He'd caught his long, usually unkempt hair back from his pale face, fastening it into a ponytail with a rubber band.

"Okay," he said. "Here's the story. You are Lauren Kendall. You're eighteen years old and you don't have any family. There's only me, and I'm going to tell you everything you need to know about yourself. Got that?"

"Got that," she parroted back at him.

"You did too many designer drugs. Burned that memory right out. It's okay. I know all kinds of personal stuff about your life. I'll fill you in on what's important."

He began that day, supplying detail after detail, making her repeat everything, correcting her speech as she did so. He stressed that they were both

Americans, although they were at that particular moment in a place called England.

She understood that these were two separate places, but little more, and she had no idea what Rob meant when he laughed and said he was Henry Higgins in the flesh.

She did know, when next he attempted to leave her behind, that she was curious about the world beyond their three rooms. "I want to go out," she said.

"No, you don't," he told her. "It's too dangerous. Besides, if you heard the accent it would just confuse you."

She hadn't considered insisting. She'd accepted his complete domination over her smallest action.

When Rob realized that she had no memory of how to read, he began to teach her to sound out words on the printed page. She loved the magazines he brought her, especially the ones with lots of colored pictures. They showed her how people dressed for various social occasions and revealed a number of activities she'd never dreamed existed. Rob had to explain what soccer was, and golf, and opera.

Slowly she gained knowledge of everyday life in the 1970s and with it a little more self-confidence. She still felt fearful when he left her alone, but she began to follow her own instincts without waiting for his commands. She cleaned, and learned to cook, and when she discovered a small sewing kit tucked away in the pocket of one suitcase, she set herself to the task of repairing clothing. She cried when Rob lost his temper. How could she have known that he preferred the knees in his jeans torn?

He was furious when he found the rips had all been neatly darned.

"Big day, Lauren," he announced one afternoon. She had no idea how much time had passed since she'd lost her memory. Interpreting calendars had not yet been added to her curriculum. Thinking back she supposed it had still been summer, or perhaps early fall, for the weather had been pleasantly warm.

"Why?"

"I'm going to teach you to write. This is your passport," he said, producing it from the one small suitcase he always kept locked. He flipped the dark green folder open to reveal a square black-and-white photograph. "That's you, believe it or not. For some reason passport photos always look like hell."

She stared at the image, intrigued. She couldn't remember ever having been shown a picture of herself before. After a moment she carried the passport to the small cracked mirror over the sink in the bathroom and studied the side-by-side reflection of her face and the one in the photograph.

Rob had been right. The picture was not a flattering one. In fact, if he hadn't told her it was a likeness of herself she doubted she'd have recognized that fact. In the small square her hair was wildly styled, obscuring much of her face. The head-on pose made it difficult to ascertain the length of her nose. To make matters worse, the camera had caught her scowling fiercely at the photographer. Lauren's eyes narrowed. It seemed to her that even her teeth looked odd in the picture, though she couldn't put a finger on exactly why.

"Lauren, come out of there," Rob ordered.

Naturally, she obeyed at once, dismissing her sense

of unease. If Rob said that was her picture, then it was.

"There's your name, and date of birth," Rob pointed out as soon as she returned to the living room and sat down beside him on the worn couch, "and your birthplace."

"Darien, Connecticut," she said, remembering what he'd already told her. Connecticut was a state in America.

"It gives the state and country here." His finger indicated the place. "Here's your height, hair color, and eye color."

She knew those, which meant she could read them. "Five feet, three inches. Brown. Blue."

"Right. And this is your signature here." He jabbed at it for emphasis and slanted a sharp look in her direction. "That's what I want you to learn to copy."

He supplied paper and a pen and supervised her efforts until she could duplicate all the swirls and straight lines perfectly. Then he put another piece of paper in front of her, one which already had several paragraphs typed on it. "Now, sign this."

"What did all that writing say?" she asked when she'd complied with his wishes.

"That was a letter to the executor of your trust fund, Lauren. On your eighteenth birthday the income became yours with no strings attached. We were planning to claim it before things got dicey."

"Why?"

"So we could go home. Just as soon as we get the money you just asked for, we're heading back to the States. No more hiding out. No more living in dumps like this one."

* * *

Lauren seemed lost in thought when Adam returned with her tray. For a moment he wondered if she was seeing things again, but then she looked up and noticed him and smiled, and he was temporarily reassured.

Her appetite had clearly been restored by her long rest, for she devoured every scrap of the grilled cheese sandwiches and tomato soup he'd brought. With a contented sigh she dropped her spoon into the empty bowl and leaned back against the pillows.

"Replete," she murmured.

"Good."

She regarded him with stoic resignation. "I suppose you have some questions?"

"A few, but there's something else we need to talk about first."

A brittle smile surfaced, the companion to a decidedly defensive note in her husky voice. "I really did lose my memory."

"I believe you, Lauren." He took the tray away from her and retreated a few steps to place it on the marble top of the nearby vanity.

"Will you bring me my brush while you're right there? I must look a sight."

He glanced up sharply as he reached for it. His own image in the triple mirror stared hollowly back at him. The last few days hadn't been easy on either of them.

With the same fluid movement that brought him back to sit at the foot of their bed, angled so that he could monitor her reactions, Adam presented her with the brush. It was part of a handsome nineteenth-century tortoiseshell set she always left displayed on the top of the antique vanity, and he thought, not for the first time, how perfectly she fit into these surroundings. There had always been something a trifle old-fashioned about Lauren. That had been, he supposed, part of her appeal to a man like himself.

She took the brush from him and began at once to work the snarls out of her hair. Her movements were stiff and awkward, betraying her unease. She was suspicious of him, and no wonder. She knew it wasn't like him to beat around the bush. He usually came right to the point even though, more often than he liked to admit, he cursed himself afterward for having been too blunt.

A moment's self-doubt assailed Adam but he brushed it impatiently aside. He'd done what he had to do. Lauren would understand that, once he'd had a chance to explain his reasons.

"While you were sleeping I talked to Doc Brinkwood about what you told me. We had two conversations, in fact. He tells me there's a kind of amnesia that leaves its victims bereft not only of their identities but also of the most ordinary skills. In severe cases the victims even have to learn how to talk all over again."

"Temporary global amnesia," Lauren said. She was brushing with industrious strokes, hiding behind a brown waterfall of her own creation.

"I thought you said you didn't go to a doctor."

"I read up on the subject. It was one in which I had a personal interest. Anyway, the key word is temporary. It doesn't usually last more than a few weeks."

"There are apparently exceptions."

"Apparently."

"Doc seemed to think we should be more concerned about your hallucinations than about your memory loss."

"Daydreams," she corrected. "From lack of sleep."

"Are you sure?"

"I'm hoping. I haven't had any new ones since you found me sleeping on the settee."

He shifted uncomfortably. She didn't seem upset that he'd talked to Doc Brinkwood. That was a good sign. He started to tell her what Brinkwood had set up, then hesitated.

Adam was disgusted with himself for being so indecisive, but he weighed the choices one more time and once again altered his plans. He'd been reluctant to put her through an interrogation, and yet now her words had reminded him of the sense he'd had, the previous afternoon, that she was holding back something vital. He couldn't let that go.

"I hope one good sleep has cured you, too, but I've got a feeling things aren't going to be that simple. I want to know everything, Lauren."

Her already pale face went whiter than before, and the brush stilled. "Everything?"

Set on an unalterable course, he persevered. "I want you to start with that picture in the museum and take me though every nightmare, every daydream. All the details. Then we'll decide what to do."

"A confession?"

He was puzzled by the hint of relief he detected in her voice. "A report," he said, correcting her.

Like the one he'd made to Dan the previous day, only this one would be complete.

She still looked doubtful. Adam racked his brain

for a way to lighten the heavy atmosphere between them.

"Just the facts, ma'am," he finally said, using his best Jack Webb imitation. The effort earned him a fleeting smile.

"You have to understand one thing, Adam. None of this makes much sense to me." Lauren hesitated, nibbling delicately on her lower lip. "Will you promise not to interrupt?"

He nodded.

She took a deep, steadying breath, but her voice was still shaky as she began to speak. "You're right," she admitted. "It probably did start with that picture in the museum. Seeing what could have been my own face like that was eerie."

Lauren stared off into space, her fingers unconsciously toying with the brush that now lay on top of the covers. "I sent for a catalog of the exhibit. There should be a reproduction of it in there. You'll be able to see for yourself."

Adam wondered if he would see a likeness. As Lauren began to recount the nightmare she'd had in New York, his eyes were drawn to the framed nineteenth-century fashion prints with which she had decorated their bedroom walls. Each showed two well-dressed women engaged in conversation. Their clothes, ornamented with bustles, ruffles, and fichus, were the focus of the illustrators' efforts, detailed and unique. The faces, on the other hand, were all of a kind.

He'd seen a few old portraits over the years, primitive renderings of Maine's founding fathers and the like. They'd always seemed to him to bear a strong resemblance to one another, a sameness that undoubtedly reflected the artists' lack of skill. Would this painting in New York fall into the same category? It was possible it showed a face so generic that a hundred different women could claim to find their own features in it.

"Adam?"

"Sorry. My mind wandered."

"I know I asked you not to comment, but I did think you intended to listen." Gentle amusement laced her words.

Cautiously he began to relax. She needed to talk. He'd been right to insist on it. He arranged himself more comfortably at the end of the bed, leaning back against the footboard, and said, "I'm all ears now."

He could hardly be otherwise, he realized, as she proceeded to fill in the details she'd been able to remember later. There were far too many images of that lover, the one who'd handed her a drugged cup of ale.

Adam soon discovered it was harder than he'd expected to remain silent. He fought valiantly against a recurring impulse to ask questions. It was obvious to him that Lauren had gone over all this information many times in her own mind, seeking in vain for some rational explanation for the onslaught of images and dreams.

That she was already telling him all she knew was in itself alarming. He'd had no idea that she'd experienced so many of these strange visions. They went on and on, all the way up to yesterday's dreams.

"I suppose I saw the child Jane eating apples because I'd just been munching one myself," she mused. "Then, just before you came home and woke me, I had the last glimpse of her, at her trial. Sir Randall

Sleaford was presiding. A clerk was there to take notes. There was no jury, just the two of them, the justice of the peace, and his minion. The clerk called out, 'Jane Malte, come into the court,' and I saw myself enter the room. A constable came with me, to be sure I didn't escape, but I knew already that there was nowhere to run. The proceedings were very quick. I was accused, then sentenced. No defense lawyer. No appeal. No mercy." She paused, looking thoughtful. "I know why, now."

Her gaze was fixed, unseeing, on the brush she still held in her hands. The fingers wrapped around the handle were white-knuckled with the force of her grip.

"Why was he so determined to punish you?" Adam asked, bending closer so that he could see his wife's eyes. "You acted in self-defense." With a grimace, he hastily corrected himself. "*She* acted in self-defense."

Lauren's lips twisted into a sardonic smile as she looked up and met his searching gaze. "Jane Malte was an unfaithful wife, and Sir Randall's wife had been unfaithful to him, too, many years earlier, when they were both at the Court of Henry VIII. I suppose Lady Sleaford's lover was someone influential, maybe even the king himself. That would have prevented Sir Randall from doing anything about it at the time. Later, though, he made her pay. He took another opportunity to punish her when he condemned me to death. She liked me, you see."

For a long moment Adam said nothing. Lauren spoke with such absolute conviction that if he hadn't known better he'd have sworn she was describing a real event and real people from her own past.

He cleared his throat and once more leaned

back against the high curve of the mahogany footboard. Lauren frowned, her wariness returning with an almost tangible force. She was nervous about his reaction to all she'd told him, in desperate need of his reassurance. Adam offered what he could, aware even as he spoke that it was going to fall short of her expectations.

"Doc recommended that you talk to a Dr. Jarvis Beaumont, Lauren. He's managed to make an appointment for you for tomorrow."

Lauren's eyes narrowed before she turned her face into the pillow. "You talk to him," she muttered against the slipcover. "I don't want to."

"Lauren—"

She wouldn't look at him, but he was certain that out of his sight her sharp, white teeth were worrying that much-abused lower lip. After a long moment she murmured, "I'm certain that was the last dream, Adam. I don't need treatment."

"It wouldn't hurt to keep the appointment," he coaxed. "Think of it as preventive medicine."

In an effort to convince her, Adam launched into a glowing account of Jarvis Beaumont, then threw in Doc's biased descriptions of the methods used by Dr. Greeley and Dr. Andrews for contrast.

Lauren shifted restlessly but did not turn over to face him. "I understand why you picked him, Adam. Dr. Beaumont sounds very reasonable in his approach, but his philosophy isn't the problem." Lauren had abandoned the hairbrush, but her fingers now clutched spasmodically at the covers.

"What is, then?"

"I don't want to talk to anyone else about this." She

began to fold and refold the edge of the sheet. "It was bad enough telling you."

"If you won't consult Beaumont about the dreams, will you let him treat you for the amnesia?"

At last she rolled over and met his eyes, letting him see that her own were full of resentment. Her chin tilted to a stubborn angle and she sat up. The way she was holding herself, erect and very still, conveyed her determination.

"I refuse to discuss either one with some stranger. I coped with losing my memory on my own. I can certainly deal with the occasional bad dream."

"Lauren—"

"I mean it, Adam. Go ahead and keep that appointment if it will make you feel better, but don't expect me to show up."

His frustration had been held in check too long. Adam surged violently to his feet and in two steps had reached the head of the bed. He glowered at his wife. She glared defiantly back.

"Last night," he reminded her, biting off each word, "you agreed you needed help."

"I may have agreed to consider asking for it. I am quite certain I did not commit myself to anything more."

"You implied you'd talk to a shrink."

"Will you stop hovering over me! If you're trying to browbeat me, it won't work. I'll make my own decisions about my own life."

He sat down abruptly, bringing his hip tight against her thigh. His face was intimidatingly close to hers. Adam seized both her hands, and with a sense of shock felt how cold they were.

"I thought we had a partnership, Lauren."

"I married you. I didn't give you the right to make decisions for me."

"You made the decision, of your own free will. Last night you knew that you needed help and you were willing to ask for it."

Anger brought two bright spots of color to her cheeks as she tried to tug her hands free and failed. "I didn't know which end was up last night and you know it, Adam Ryder. I can't be held accountable for *anything* I said when I was that confused."

With sudden, devastating clarity, Adam realized that the woman to whom he had been married for five years, the woman he'd believed he knew, had never intended to tell him about her amnesia at all. She'd deliberately kept that part of her life secret from him.

"If you hadn't been so out of it you'd never have mentioned losing your memory, would you?"

"Of course not."

"Damn it, Lauren!"

He freed her, thrusting himself away from her. He was too agitated to sit next to her any longer without giving in to the temptation to shake her until her teeth rattled. With long angry strides he circled the room, keeping his hands stuffed into his pockets to prevent himself from inflicting irreparable damage on the bric-a-brac. His eyes never left her face.

"You weren't going to say a word, and now you claim you aren't prepared to talk about it anymore at all. How do you think that makes me feel?"

She was watching, cautious and tense, as he paced. "You never seemed to have any great desire to know the details of my past," she said carefully.

"My mistake, obviously. Then again, you might have offered to tell me about yourself."

She reacted to the grumbled complaint with continued defensiveness. "You never asked me much. I didn't think what happened before we met mattered to you."

He couldn't trust himself to respond. The double-stitched denim edge of the pockets of his jeans bit into the backs of his hands as he clenched them into fists. He glared at Lauren from the opposite side of the bedroom.

A tiny smile tried to surface on her pale face. "You seemed satisfied that you knew everything that mattered after you made sure I wasn't already married."

Adam glowered at his wife as jealousy joined the other unsettling emotions churning inside him. The combination made his voice gritty, his words vicious. "I should have. By God, I should have. I was obviously so blinded by desire that I abandoned common sense."

The chemistry between them had been right from the beginning, overshadowing every other concern. By the end of the first week they'd made love.

Adam hadn't expected a thirty-year-old woman to be a virgin and he hadn't asked about old lovers. He'd assumed, basing his conclusion on Lauren's reclusive life-style and the physical indications that it had been some time since she'd been with a man, that there had not been many. He'd guessed only one.

"How do you know you weren't married?" he demanded. "How do you know for certain that you aren't still married? Amnesia! Who knows what—"

"Adam!"

"What?"

She winced at the harshness in his voice, but then drew herself up again, posing regally against a backdrop of lace-trimmed pillows, and sent him a look that would have done Queen Victoria proud. "I may not remember things first-hand, but I certainly was told enough details of my own life to be able to assure you that I wasn't married. I was in very proper boarding schools most of my first eighteen years."

His eyes narrowed. "The fact remains you don't remember and you can't have been told every detail. No one person, no matter how good a friend, could know everything about you." An unpleasant suspicion assailed him. "Just who was this friend, anyway?"

"That's not important."

"The hell it's not!"

But she was adamant. No amount of argument would change her mind. She would not say another word about the past.

There seemed no way out of her quandary. Either of the two solutions she'd thought of would produce tensions in her marriage that Lauren simply did not want to deal with. Sighing unhappily, she sat down at her standing floor-frame and took up her needle.

It still astonished her that last night, after that terrible quarrel with Adam, she'd been able to fall asleep. For the first time in days she'd slept a normal eight hours. There had been no dreams, no nightmares.

This morning she and Adam had barely spoken. The rift between them had seemed like a living presence as they went through the normal routine of breakfast and kiss goodbye. He'd left for his office, but Lauren knew that he'd be keeping that appointment later, and she was terribly afraid that he would not stop asking questions.

How could she ever tell him about Rob? Or about the kind of life she'd led with him? Adam wouldn't like it, not one bit. He'd be annoyed by the revelation that she'd lived with another man for the better part of three years, but he'd be livid when he discovered that his wife had experimented with illegal substances on a regular basis and never thought anything of it.

Adam hadn't even been tempted to smoke pot when he was in college. He'd always been outspoken, too, about his belief that there was a clear distinction between right and wrong. How would he react to the news that she hadn't always understood the difference? That she'd broken the law repeatedly and with the full knowledge that she was doing so?

The only alternative was to continue to refuse to talk about her past, but that solution carried a high price. Honesty and loyalty mattered to Adam as much as did obedience to the law.

The embroidery in front of Lauren occupied her hands, but her thoughts strayed again to Rob. She had to sort out how she really felt about those years, search for the reasons she'd stayed with him after she realized that his only interest in her was the steady income from her trust fund.

Was there a way to make Adam see that there were shades of gray? She wasn't proud of that period in her life, but there was no way she could change what had happened.

She continued to work on the canvas, directing her mind back to events of the 1970s. Those memories had just begun to come into focus when, without any warning, they were abruptly supplanted, replaced by a vivid image of a gentlewoman's solar.

Embroidery tents were in place, left up at all times so that servants, even the men, could use their free moments productively. The girl Jane was there, younger than in the painting but older than she'd been when perched in that apple tree, and she was very nervous.

Her large, blue eyes widened even more as she gazed, awestruck, at the room around her. Never had she been invited into such a splendid chamber. Arras-work hung over every inch of the inner wall. Real glass windows ran in a row along the outer one, allowing the occupants a view of field and orchard. Even the rushes on the floor were grander than any Jane had ever walked upon, releasing the sweet smell of rosemary with every step.

"Your name is Jane?"

The girl's head snapped around. For a long moment she simply stared at the richly garbed woman addressing her, drinking in the wonderful sight of her rich red branched-velvet gown, her silver sussapine kirtle, her brocaded stomacher and sleeves. They'd said in the village that Sir Randall liked his wife to wear fine clothes, but this was past all of Jane's imaginings. In comparison her own drab woolens seemed even poorer. She hastily lowered her gaze.

"Answer me, girl. Is Jane your name?"

"Yes, ma'am."

"Well, then, Jane, bestir yourself. You are here to show me how well you can work."

"Yes, ma'am." She was anxious to please. She'd be beaten if she went home a failure.

With more patience than Jane had expected from so grand a personage, Lady Sleaford showed her the stitches she must use to duplicate the design of a tapestry in embroidery. "A true tapestry is woven," the lady of the manor explained, "but we may more easily produce hangings with this needle painting."

Too shy to reply, the child applied herself to the task set for her, filling in a leaf with close herringbone stitches.

Anne Sleaford inspected the work closely. Then she surveyed the child. After a long, nerve-wracking moment she handed Jane a small square of fabric with an ornate emblem drawn on it. "Use tent stitches," she instructed.

Soon, with Lady Sleaford's guidance in the selection of colors, the motif began to emerge, and Jane's mentor nodded approvingly.

"You will do," she declared, "and when you complete enough of these pieces I will teach you how to cut them out and apply them to a large velvet panel."

"What will the panel be made into?" Jane was bold enough to ask.

Lady Sleaford did not seem to mind her question. "Hangings," she replied, "or bed curtains or coverlets or cushions."

The sound of a ringing phone brought Lauren back to the present in a rush. She stumbled to her feet, overturning the heavy frame.

She'd been wrong.

The dreams weren't going to stop.

Worse, she was no longer so sure that she was strong enough to face them on her own.

8

"I've already been told to mind my own business," Sandra admitted as she handed Lauren a cup of freshly perked coffee and motioned her toward the only chair not occupied by a sleeping cat, "but you know me."

Before Lauren could reply, Sandra dashed off again, her long legs eating up the distance to the kitchen in energetic strides. The house in Lumberton Falls was well over a hundred years old and furnished in an eclectic fashion that scattered quality country antiques through a decor best described as early garage sale. At this time of year, during daylight hours, Sandra entertained on the small glassed-in back porch. Insulated windows captured the heat of the midday sun, keeping the area comfortably warm.

Lauren took the seat Sandra had indicated, one of two pulled up to a circular wrought-iron table, and stared bleakly out at the lawn as she sipped the steaming brew from an oversized mug. Leaves blew across the rapidly browning grass with restless abandon, scattered by a chill wind. She felt a bit storm-tossed herself.

First Adam had badgered her. Now his whole family was going to get into the act. There was no doubt in her mind about what had prompted Sandra's mid-morning phone call and the invitation to lunch. The part Lauren couldn't figure out was why she'd accepted.

Her sister-in-law's return with a large tray loaded with finger sandwiches was heralded by a flurry of activity from previously inert felines. Zip, the long-haired Maine coon cat, had been sound asleep on the comfortably padded porch swing, but at the first whiff of tuna her head shot up, quickly followed by the rest of her. The second cat, Boing, expended less effort. Only her eyes moved until Sandra, in one continuous movement, plunked the tray down on the table and swept the calico off the seat of the chair.

"That," Sandra said, indicating Boing's baleful look as she plopped herself down in the cat's place, "is what is popularly known as the hairy eyeball."

Sandra snagged a sandwich from the plate for herself and took a bite. "I suppose Adam told you what Dad said? About locking you up?"

Lauren's sandwich trembled in suddenly nerveless fingers.

"Oh, Lord. Adam didn't tell you that. Open mouth. Insert foot. I'm sorry, Lauren. It wasn't as bad as I just made it sound. I come by my bad habits honestly.

Dad spoke off the top of his head, before he knew who it was Adam was talking about. He didn't mean it. Honest."

"It was a mistake to come here."

Lauren started to rise but her movements were jerky. The sudden lurch of her chair startled Boing. The calico did a back flip and kept going, fleeing toward the farthest corner of the porch. Lauren stared after the cat, her own heart beating like a jackhammer.

Abruptly she sat back down. "Maybe I am cracking up. I can't ever remember feeling this fragile."

"You've had a rough time of it lately. Here, hold Zip." Sandra seized the gray and white cat and pushed her into Lauren's unresisting arms. "There's nothing like a warm fuzzy to soothe the shattered nerves."

Lauren automatically clutched the cat, hugging her close. It didn't surprise her when Sandra told her she already knew about Lauren's refusal to keep the appointment with Dr. Beaumont. Adam had told Dan. Dan had phoned Sandra. That was when Sandra had phoned her.

"In a way I'm glad you know what's been happening to me," Lauren said carefully, "but—"

"You also wish Adam had kept his big mouth shut."

Lauren nodded. It was tempting to confide in her sister-in-law. After all, they had been friends long before they became relatives, and Sandra would not have to be told the background. Better than a therapist, Lauren assured herself, but still she hesitated.

"I wish he'd waited before he talked to your father."

"He meant well."

"Somehow that only makes things worse. We haven't quarreled often, and always before we managed not to go to bed still mad at each other. This time . . ."

Sandra looked sympathetic, but her words weren't the ones Lauren wanted to hear. "You're sure you couldn't bring yourself to go to a therapist? Not Beaumont, necessarily. There are plenty to choose from. You might find it easier to talk to a woman, especially if you're talking about sex. Adam didn't give you any choice, did he?"

"You can guess the answer to that."

"Men!" Sandra leaned closer, propping her elbows on the table and waving her hands as she talked. "Now, I did a little checking for you on my own yesterday."

"That wasn't necessary, Sandra."

Her sister-in-law waved off further protest. She wasn't oblivious to Lauren's objections, but had obviously decided to discount them. "I was glad to do it. What's the use of my being town librarian if I can't use the resources for my own inquiries?"

Lauren helped herself to a second cup of coffee and held it in both hands as she stared at Sandra over the rim. In her own way Sandra was as unstoppable as Adam, and Lauren doubted she had the wherewithal to convince either of them to cease and desist. She might as well, she decided, ask the inevitable question. "What kind of inquiries?"

"About Dr. Andrews."

"The one who uses crystals?"

"The one who is open-minded enough to consider

that reincarnation might be a possible key to her client's problems."

"I don't—"

"You really ought to reconsider the possibility of a past life," Sandra interrupted. "These days a lot of reputable people, intelligent people, believe in that sort of thing."

"I don't doubt it," Lauren conceded. "I'll admit the possibility exists, but I'm pretty sure that reincarnation is not the explanation for what's been happening to me."

"How can you be so certain?"

"Well, for one thing, how many people who claim to remember their past lives think they spent one as a servant? Adam and your father were right not to contact Dr. Andrews."

"Dad couldn't have gotten you an appointment earlier than January even if he'd wanted to. She's booked solid for months."

"You called her?"

"Mmmm."

"Sandra, I appreciate your concern, but—"

"Butt out? Get real?"

It was hard to be angry with someone who meant well, especially when she admitted she was wrong to meddle, but Lauren's annoyance was growing.

"I wouldn't have gone even if she had been taking new, ah, clients. If I decide I need therapy, and that's still very iffy, then I'd just as soon see someone more . . . conservative."

"Well," Sandra said, sounding unconvinced, "if you change your mind, there may be another alternative."

"Forget it, Sandra. I've heard quite enough about past lives."

"Be glad I haven't suggested that you were dropped off by the Tardis." She gave a snort of disgust when her sarcasm garnered only a blank look. "The machine Dr. Who uses to travel through time."

"Ah." If only the solution were that simple. "I think we can rule out the Tardis, Sandra, right along with reincarnation."

A little silence fell and then Lauren said, "You have books on psychology in that library of yours, right?"

"Sure do, but I thought you didn't think that was the answer, either."

"I was positive it wasn't until right before you called."

"Oh, Lord! You had another dream."

Lauren nodded. "I was hoping one good long sleep would put an end to them." Quickly she described that morning's vision.

"That's it? No sex? No violence?"

"It isn't a soap opera!"

"It's not real, either."

Very carefully Lauren put down her empty coffee mug as she felt her irritation increase. She gave Sandra a fulminating glance. "Now it really is time I went home."

"And then?"

"And then I think I'll ask Adam to stop telling his brother every little thing that goes on in our lives."

Sandra's brown eyes widened as she recognized the tightly leashed anger behind Lauren's words. She began to sputter an apology.

Lauren stood, impatient now to take her leave, but the sound of a car pulling into Sandra's driveway stopped her. She groaned inwardly as she realized her escape route had just been blocked.

A door slammed with considerable force, and a moment later Karen Doucette appeared around the corner of the house. She was a tall, broad-shouldered blonde in her late twenties, possessed of a kind of rangy beauty and large teeth. At the moment she was breathing fire.

"I'm going to kill him," she said as soon as she came through the door of Sandra's sunporch. "I swear I'm going to take a shotgun and blow his unfaithful carcass to kingdom come!"

"And you think you've got domestic problems," Sandra muttered under her breath.

All at once, Lauren felt a little better. Whatever else plagued them, she and Adam truly loved each other. That made all the difference.

"Here, Karen," she said, bending down and coming up with Boing in her arms. "Sit down and hold a cat. It will do wonders for your peace of mind."

She deposited the calico in Karen's arms and looked around for Zip. She could do with another dose of unrestrained affection herself.

Jarvis Beaumont was a round man. His cheeks were plump and rosy; his curly beard was trimmed to frame the great circle of his face. A rotund chest and abdomen bowed out all around the circumference of his belt, ballooning amiably inside a striped shirt, knit vest, and tweed jacket as he came out from behind his massive oak desk. His legs were short and stubby beneath loose wool trousers, and short, fat feet turned up their ends.

"Mr. Ryder?" Plump sausage-shaped fingers were immediately extended toward Adam, accompanied by an assessing glance.

"I appreciate your making time to see me, Dr. Beaumont."

"No trouble at all. Doc Brinkwood has done me a few favors in the past, but I understood it was Mrs. Ryder who wished to talk to me."

"Mrs. Ryder isn't convinced she needs to talk to anyone."

A glint of rueful amusement showed briefly in sharp eyes that were only partly concealed behind glasses with perfectly round frames. "And you, Mr. Ryder? Are you uncomfortable with the idea that she might need my sort of help?"

Beaumont resumed his seat in an oversized and deeply padded swivel chair and indicated that Adam should take the armchair situated on the opposite side of the desk. It was, in fact, the only other place to sit in the small office, but it was extremely comfortable and Adam felt himself begin to relax as soon as he sank into it. All Beaumont's furniture was solid, like the man himself. The impression of permanence, of traditionalism, added to Adam's sense that this was a professional who knew what he was doing.

"I think she could benefit from seeing you. I took the liberty of making some inquiries this morning among some of my colleagues in the law enforcement field." He'd discovered that Dr. Beaumont was frequently called upon by local judges to do pre-sentence forensic evaluations of convicted criminals. "You have an extremely good reputation. They tell me your usual procedure is to administer a battery of tests first."

"That's frequently a good starting point, but it is not a prerequisite for therapy. You think your wife would object?"

"I don't know if she would or not, but my sources tell me such tests take a while to evaluate. If she'll see you at all I feel she needs to start telling you about her problem right away. Delay could cause more complications." Not to mention what it would do to exacerbate the growing tension in their marriage.

Beaumont nodded. "I pride myself on my flexibility, Mr. Ryder. It is the court system which insists on statistical analysis as part of the evaluation. I can certainly forego testing and move directly to an initial interview if that would ease the situation."

"If my wife will agree to see you I have the feeling she'd rather just talk."

Beaumont didn't seem unduly disturbed by the news that Lauren was reluctant to come in. His expression gave little away and yet managed to convey sympathy and understanding. "It isn't uncommon to resist the idea of counseling. Pride plays a role. We like to think we can solve our own problems, especially those of us who grew up with old-fashioned New England values. Many people will deny they need any outside help at first."

Denial, Adam thought. Yes, that was the word for

it. Like the alcoholic who refused to admit he had a drinking problem. Lauren was trying to pretend that her dreams weren't affecting other aspects of her life.

"She isn't even willing to discuss coming here." Their quarrel had been at the back of his mind all day. He'd come close to giving in himself and canceling the appointment, just to resolve the conflict between them.

"It's possible your wife is right," Beaumont conceded. "She may not need the kind of treatment I offer. Why don't you try to give me some idea of the nature of her problem?"

"Lauren has started having very vivid nightmares in which she kills her husband and is later executed for that crime."

"Is this a recurrent dream?"

"No. More like a continuing drama. At various times she's dreamed of the murder, her trial, and her first meeting with a lover." Adam shifted uncomfortably in the chair, beset by reluctance to continue. If Beaumont started jumping to the wrong conclusions . . .

"Was there any event in your wife's life, some stressful incident, that preceded the onset of the dreams?"

"A trip to New York."

"Nothing more specific than that?"

"She visited a museum. Shopped. We celebrated our fifth wedding anniversary. If anything, she had a very pleasant day. The only thing at all out of the ordinary was an old painting she saw. She thought she detected a resemblance between one of the women in it and herself."

"How long has Mrs. Ryder been having these dreams?" Beaumont asked.

"The first nightmare was just thirteen days ago."

The psychologist made a note on the yellow legal pad in front of him on the desk. "Doc mentioned a sleep disorder. Insomnia?"

Adam scraped one hand across his brow, shoving the dark blond strands away from his forehead. "For a while there she got so she didn't want to sleep, for fear of having more dreams. That problem seems to have resolved itself. She's sleeping again."

"How many nights in a row?"

"Two."

"Hardly definitive."

"There's something else."

"Yes?"

"Apparently she's suffered from amnesia since she was eighteen."

A flicker of surprise appeared on Beaumont's face before he could control it. "She's never recovered her memory?"

Adam recounted everything Lauren had told him about her memory loss. It didn't take long.

"Well," Beaumont said. "I certainly hope she'll agree to talk to me. I'll be perfectly frank with you and say that what you've said intrigues me. I don't think I've ever heard of a case quite like your wife's."

Adam's eyes narrowed. "I suppose you think you can get an article out of her."

Beaumont's smile was meant to convey reassurance but didn't quite succeed. "You say that as if it were a bad thing."

The candid remark did nothing to alleviate Adam's doubts. "She's not some guinea pig."

"Don't worry. My patients' files are completely confidential. I do, however, have a certain reputation for my case studies. No real names are used." He held up a hand to forestall Adam's objections. "Didn't Doc tell me that you write about the situations you encounter in your profession?"

Adam cautiously adjusted his estimation of Beaumont upward. "Can you help Lauren, assuming she agrees to see you?"

"You must understand that there are no guarantees, but I believe that I can. It seems fairly clear to me that these dreams are linked to events during the years she can no longer remember. With careful probing I can reach those buried memories." He paused to make a note on his desk calendar. "I'll pencil her in for next Tuesday at one. That's the earliest I can manage with the Columbus Day weekend already upon us."

"I appreciate that." Now all he had to do was convince Lauren to show up. Easier said than done, especially if she was free of her nightmares now.

Could he charm her into agreeing? Adam wondered. He had every intention of settling their differences before this evening was over. If all went well they'd make up their quarrel in the age-old way of married couples.

Was he actually desperate enough to consider using sex to control Lauren's actions? The idea shocked Adam when he realized the direction his thoughts had taken.

Dr. Beaumont was watching him intently. "You

could assist in this business of recalling Mrs. Ryder's early life."

"How?"

"It would be useful for me to know something about Mrs. Ryder's background, beyond what you say she'll be able to tell me. With your connections in law enforcement you should be able to find out as much as a private detective could. Anything might help. School records. Obituaries of her parents. You know the sort of thing. The more I learn about all that the better I can direct her treatment."

Adam immediately saw the sense in Beaumont's suggestion. He did have enough contacts to make it feasible. He could call in a few favors, offer to trade some expertise. There were sure to be extant records somewhere on Lauren and her parents. Only one thing troubled him about the project. "She won't be pleased to learn I'm having her investigated."

"There's no need for you to mention it to her. In fact, it might be better if you didn't insist on talking about her past with her at all. Let her volunteer information. Naturally I shan't reveal my source of information to her, either." The jovial image he projected jarred on Adam's nerves. "Can't betray a confidence now, can I?"

Adam thought about Beaumont's words as he drove back to Lumberton, and new doubts surfaced about the therapist's character. Beaumont's suggestion amounted to lying to Lauren. He'd been upset with her because she'd lied to him by omission. How could he even contemplate doing the same thing himself?

Aware that such moral dilemmas wouldn't faze most men in his position, still Adam debated with himself right up to the moment when he turned into their tree-lined driveway. Reluctantly, he decided to give Beaumont's way a chance. The man was an expert, after all, and Adam expected he'd have a hell of a struggle on his hands just convincing Lauren to talk to a shrink in the first place. He'd be a fool to complicate the issue by telling her more than she needed to know.

When he came in from the porch Lauren looked up from the pot of chowder she was stirring on top of the stove and sent him a bright, loving smile. "I've decided you were right," she said before he could open his mouth.

"About what?" he asked suspiciously. She was making one of his favorite dishes from scratch. The steamy fragrances of cooking onions, corn, and potatoes gave a sweet hominess to the scene, but he was still wary. Lauren playing June Cleaver didn't quite mesh with the angry, stubborn woman he'd faced the previous night.

"About therapy. If you still think I'd benefit from seeing Dr. Beaumont, I'll go talk to him. If he's not too expensive, that is."

Always practical, he thought with a touch of humor. Lauren kidded him about being a frugal Yankee, but she had him beat all hallow. "He's not overpriced," he assured her. "Besides, our health insurance should pick up most of the tab."

"Well, then. That wasn't so bad, after all."

"I don't get it, Lauren. Last night you wouldn't even consider therapy."

"You'd made a decision for me. I resented that,

but now that I've had time to think things over—"

"What really changed your mind? Another dream?"

Lauren sighed as she switched the burner off and carefully removed the chowder from the stove, placing the pot on a hot pad inscribed with the words Lauren's Kitchen. "I never could fool you, could I?"

"I hope you won't try. How bad was it?"

She turned and walked into his arms. "It didn't have to be bad. It only had to be."

He cradled her close, searching for the words to tell her he understood, but he didn't. Not really. He could only offer comfort.

"I really thought the dreams were gone for good."

"I know, sweetheart. I'd hoped so, too." He stroked her silky hair, curling a lock of the soft brown stuff around one finger and tugging gently until she looked up at him. "Do you want to tell me about it?"

"I might as well. It looks as if I'm going to tell your Dr. Beaumont." She drew in a steadying breath, then blurted, "I met Lady Sleaford up close and personal this morning. It seems she's the one who taught me all I know about embroidery."

Well before she walked into his office, Lauren had decided to be completely honest with Dr. Beaumont. She'd cooperate in her own treatment because she'd promised Adam she would. Maybe Beaumont would even be able to help, but what she really hoped to get from this session was some professional advice on how to drop a bombshell on her husband.

The scene in the solar was still vivid in her mind on Tuesday, right down to the colorful design on the arraswork that had been hanging against the inner wall. It had been four days since she envisioned it, four days during which there had been no more strange daydreams. She'd been able to resume her normal routine, sleeping an average of eight nightmare-free hours a night. By mutual agreement she and Adam had avoided sensitive topics over the long weekend and simply enjoyed being together.

Lauren's first impression of Jarvis Beaumont's office was that it was impersonal. She'd heard somewhere that couches were out, along with Freudian analysis, but she found his immense desk equally off-putting. A female therapist, Lauren suspected, would opt for a conversation pit or a circular sofa. In fact, now that she thought about it, she was certain she'd seen something just like that in a scene in a recent television drama.

Beaumont himself seemed less formidable than his environment, and even with the barrier of his enormous desk between them, she began to relax as he explained a bit about how they would proceed. The client's chair was well padded, and in spite of the remnants of nervousness her body succumbed to the lure of soft cushions.

"I've been given a brief synopsis of the content of your dreams," he told her, "but I'd like to hear the details in your own words."

"In the order I dreamed them or in the order they happened historically?"

Sounding slightly perplexed, he said, "Whichever is easier for you, Mrs. Ryder."

Suddenly hesitant, she delayed answering his question to ask another of her own. "Is it unusual to have dreams that, well, seem to tell a story?"

"On the contrary, it's fairly common. You're seeing a drama in your head, one that will hopefully, in time, provide a catharsis for you. Think of it as a play being enacted by your subconscious, one that will eventually allow you to face whatever the dream actually represents."

"Can't you just hypnotize me and get to the root of the trouble?"

"There aren't any shortcuts to successful therapy," he cautioned her. "You could fantasize just as easily under hypnosis as you do when you're dreaming."

"You mean I'd probably just conjure up another costume drama instead of recalling a real memory?"

The bewildered look returned as Beaumont leaned back in his chair and peered at her through lowered lashes. His round glasses glinted in the fluorescent light. "Costume drama, Mrs. Ryder?"

For some reason his attempt at nonchalance amused her. "You mean Adam didn't tell you that part? All my dreams have been set in the middle of the sixteenth century. In England."

A frown turned his plump features jowly. "Your husband didn't think to include that little detail." He brightened visibly after a moment's thought. "Still, it's not an uncommon occurrence. As you say, costume drama."

"Well, here's the plot." Attempting a cheerful casualness of her own, Lauren began with the girl in the apple tree.

He let her talk without interruption, and the time he had scheduled for her had almost expired before Lauren finished describing the sensation of flames licking at her feet. By then her air of determined optimism was wearing thin. "My hands were tied above my head, to a stake, and brush and sticks were piled in a circle around me. I was barefoot, so I could feel the sharp twigs, the rough bark. The stake wasn't much smoother, just a log sturdy enough to keep me upright so that all the ghouls in the crowd could witness my agony."

Dr. Beaumont made no comment. He scribbled a few lines at the bottom of the page of notes he'd taken while she spoke, glanced at his watch, then lifted his head to look at her. His expression was controlled, his voice carefully neutral. "Your husband also told me you suffer from amnesia. In the few minutes we have left I'd like to address what you can recall about its onset. Will you tell me about your earliest memory?"

Lauren took a deep breath. She'd come prepared to answer that very question. She meant to hold nothing back, neither the tawdry details of her relationship with Rob nor her uneasiness about revealing them to Adam. After all, Beaumont had to know what the facts were before he could advise her.

Instead she heard herself say, "My earliest memory is of being soundly beaten when I was four years old."

"Why were you punished?"

"I let the roast burn."

"Can you remember any more about the incident? Who beat you?"

"My mother."

She could smell the charred flesh. They didn't get meat very often and this had been an entire haunch of venison, given to her father by Sir Randall. She frowned, wondering what special service he'd done to earn it. The knight was not known for his generosity.

"I were told to turn the spit and not stop for naught," Lauren said in a small, scared voice, "but it were hot by the fire." She lifted beseeching eyes. "I did but think to get a breath of air, sirrah, and then the flames did flare up most horrible."

The picture in her mind was clear. The cottage had only one room, with a dirt floor. A tired, haggard-looking woman, her mother, heaped verbal and physical abuse upon her. Lauren winced as the blows began to fall, feeling the weight and rough texture of the work-worn hands. Coarse dorneck linen abraded her own fingers as she twisted them into the folds of her apron.

"Mrs. Ryder?"

Lauren stared at Jarvis Beaumont for a long moment without recognizing him. Such a burly fellow must be rich indeed, she thought, able to afford the finest fare at board.

"Mrs. Ryder?" Beaumont had so far forgot himself as to have leaned across the desk and seized her arm. "Sit down, please. There's no cause for alarm."

When had she risen to her feet? Embarrassed, Lauren obeyed. "Sorry," she mumbled. "For a moment there the memory was very vivid."

Beaumont hid behind formality, and the desk. "You said you were four years old when this took place?"

Still caught up in the intensity of her experience, Lauren spoke without thinking. "It was in the autumn. Fifteen Henry."

"I beg your pardon?"

Lauren realized what she'd just said and favored the flabbergasted therapist with an apologetic half smile. She really had intended to cooperate.

"That would be 1524," she told him, "the fifteenth year in the reign of King Henry VIII."

9

Dr. Beaumont stabbed the intercom button with one pudgy finger and spoke softly to his secretary. "This session will run a little long, Maggie. Please make the necessary arrangements."

Since it was only a fifty-minute hour anyway, Lauren didn't feel the least bit guilty. He could finish making notes about her case on his own time.

The small eyes behind the glasses seemed a few degrees colder when his full attention returned to his client. Lauren felt as if the barrier between them had just expanded to include more than the oversized desk.

"Perhaps you'd like to tell me about your real first memory now?"

"Why not?" Deliberately choosing her words to shock, she told him exactly what she and Rob Seton had been doing.

His reaction was disappointingly matter-of-fact.

He asked questions. She answered, but when she asked one of her own the psychologist declined to offer advice. He asked yet another question instead. The obvious evasion annoyed her immeasurably.

"Can you tell me, then," she interrupted, shifting the subject to suit herself, "why my dreams are so vivid? Why don't they just fade away after I wake up? It isn't as if I'm having the same dream, over and over. Each segment adds more details and I remember them all."

"Do you read a great deal of historical fiction, Mrs. Ryder?"

"Do you always answer a question with another question, Dr. Beaumont?"

"No." He leaned toward her, fingering the curls in his beard. "Shall I tell you what I think, Mrs. Ryder? I believe you enjoy reading what are popularly called bodice rippers."

She winced at the sobriquet but could not completely deny the charge. "I like historical mysteries and Regencies as well, but, yes, I suppose I am a fan of that genre. You needn't sneer at it."

"I think you'll find that your taste in literature accounts for a large part of your problem. You are extrapolating details from books you've read into a situation which reflects some conflict in the part of your own life which has temporarily been lost to you. Be patient, Mrs. Ryder. It will all make sense before we're through. I've instructed Maggie to set up regular appointments for you, on Mondays from now on. We'll go into greater depth next time."

Lauren left the office feeling unsettled. Dr. Beaumont had said nothing she hadn't already thought of all by herself. That wasn't particularly surprising, since she prided herself on having a good deal of common sense. What troubled her was her own reaction to hearing an expert agree with her. She should feel reassured. Instead she was beset by the nagging suspicion that they were both wrong.

By the time she'd driven back to Lumberton, Lauren's unease had blossomed into full-blown frustration. Beaumont's explanation was too pat, his pronouncement too casual. If she was remembering the plot of some novel, then she ought to be able to identify that source. Instead of taking the turn toward home at Lumberton's only traffic signal, she headed in the opposite direction, into the center of town.

Lumberton's public library had been built well before the turn of the century, constructed of local stone with an exterior designed to resemble a Greek temple. It was only open twenty-five hours a week, but that was far more than any other library in Jefferson County. Fortunately for Lauren, Tuesday was the one day on which patrons could browse from ten in the morning until seven in the evening.

Parking anywhere nearby was almost impossible. What wasn't reserved for the church across the street had been commandeered by students and staff of the Lumberton branch of the state university, whose red brick buildings encroached on three sides of the little library. Lauren eased her car into an illegal space beneath a sign that read NO PARKING: DANGER OF FALLING SNOW.

Sandra had been town librarian for the last twenty years and was in her accustomed place behind the circulation desk when her sister-in-law came in. Her red-brown hair had been neatly pinned on top of her head at some point but was now in imminent danger of tumbling down. Ten to eleven Tuesday morning, Lauren remembered, was children's story hour.

"How did it go?" Sandra asked.

"I'm not ready to face a postmortem on my session with the shrink," Lauren warned.

"No problem." She looked as if she wanted to say more, but at that moment a woman appeared with a stack of books to check out and the opportunity for private conversation was abruptly gone.

Just as well, Lauren thought, as she hurried up the stairs that led to the hard-cover fiction collection on the top floor. She made her way up and down the rows, pulling out any title that seemed familiar. She'd exhausted the small library's supply of historical fiction years ago and started buying her own books at the local Mr. Paperback, but she found she still remembered much of what she'd read. Not one of the plots was at all similar to the content of her dreams, though some of the novels were certainly set in the right era. It was a great temptation to check out a few of her old favorites and reread them.

Downstairs again, Lauren made a cursory study of the tattered paperback romances Sandra kept shelved near the door on a four-sided metal rack. Sandra didn't bother to catalog them, insisting that any patron who wanted to keep one was more than welcome to do so as long as she brought in another in exchange.

"Looking for something in particular?" Sandra called from her perch behind the circular oak barrier.

Lauren stifled a sigh. She'd known she couldn't avoid Sandra's curiosity forever, not here on her own turf. She wasn't sure she wanted to. For all her earlier resentment, it was comforting to know that someone cared enough about her to meddle.

"My plot," she muttered disgustedly.

"No luck?"

"Not a bit. I'm not sure whether to be disappointed or relieved."

"Come downstairs and have a nice hot cup of tea. That'll make the whole situation look a hundred percent better."

"I look that bad, huh?"

The other woman's silence spoke volumes. When Sandra signaled her assistant to take over the desk and collected her oversized tote bag from beneath it, Lauren gave in and followed her through the wooden gate that guarded a narrow, winding flight of steps.

The library basement held a rest room and one large conference room. Two sections of the latter had been partitioned off. The first wall concealed a tiny kitchen. The other formed an area to house Lumberton's genealogy and local history collection. Comfortable armchairs and a large, round oak table had been donated to lend the space an illusion of being a private reading room. The highly polished wooden surface of the table held microfilm readers and card files, but one end had been kept free of clutter. There Sandra put down a placemat and soon set two steaming cups on top of it.

"So Dr. Beaumont is convinced it's all a plot, is he?" Sandra mused when Lauren had explained her quest.

"He is. I'm not. Oh, I know I suggested the same thing myself at first, but it won't wash."

"Ever read much straight history?"

"Some. Mostly looking for designs. I was interested in the Regency and Edwardian and Victorian periods, though, not the sixteenth century."

"What about this? You've taken the plot from a novel, but you've changed the century?"

"I could make *Romeo and Juliet* into *West Side Story*, but I didn't. The technique's been used successfully lots of times, but it's not what I'm doing." Lauren took a sip of her herbal tea and suddenly remembered how much she disliked the stuff. Without comment she set the cup aside.

"You know," Sandra said with suspicious casualness, "Karen was telling me after you left the other day that one of her cousins married a woman who has documented ability as a conscious channel."

"A what?"

"She can sense things about a person's past lives without going into a trance."

"Hold it right there."

"Have you got any better ideas?"

"In fact, I do. One came to me just sitting here." She'd been looking idly about, unconsciously absorbing the fact that the nearest shelves were full of volumes on family history, Lumberton history, and Maine history. Her gaze came to rest on the row of standard reference books designed to help amateur genealogists in their efforts to trace English ancestors. "Pass me that copy of Burke's *Peerage,*" she said impulsively.

"This edition only has dormant peerages," Sandra warned, hoisting a two-volume set. "Sir Bernard Burke's *Dormant, Abeyant, Forfeited and Extinct Peerages,* published in London in 1883."

"I don't expect to find anything anyway." Lauren searched quickly for an entry under Sleaford. The old book smelled a bit musty and its pages were thin and fragile with age, crinkling as she turned them. "Well, I'm not disappointed. Nothing."

"Wasn't this Sir Randall just a knight?"

"Right. Oh, I see. No title."

"Maybe not when you knew him, but what about later?"

Lauren grimaced at her sister-in-law's choice of words. Obviously Sandra had not yet abandoned the reincarnation theory. She closed the volume and started to hand it back. "It was just a long shot."

"Don't give up so soon. If he did get elevated to the peerage later, or if some descendent did, the entry would be under the title, not the surname. Generally those came from landholdings. Come on, Lauren. Think. What was the estate called?"

"I don't remember."

Sandra pushed the book back into her hands. "See if anything rings a bell. Wouldn't it be a kicker if you found something?"

Lauren was curious herself. Slowly she flipped through the pages, working backward from the S's in case she'd missed an entry the first time. Nothing looked familiar, though the title Baron Ogle triggered a faint smile. She continued into the M's, turned another page, and abruptly encountered Thomas

Sleaford, 1st Baron Morwell. Shock made her utter a small sound that attracted Sandra's attention.

"Find something?"

"The date is much too late," Lauren murmured as she skimmed the entry.

Thomas was Sir Randall's grandson.

"This is surreal," Lauren whispered as she read the paragraphs a second time. Each fact confirmed what she'd learned from her dreams.

Sir Randall Sleaford (1488–1540) had married Anne Roundsey in 1509. They had both been at the Court of Henry VIII at the beginning of his reign. Anne had stayed, part of the queen's household, but her husband had left in 1510, returning only for brief visits in the years that followed.

Lauren knew why. Anne had entered into an illicit liaison with one of Henry's favorite courtiers. Sir Randall had tried to spirit her off to a nunnery and confine her there, but her lover had been more powerful than her husband and he'd arranged her rescue. In an era when divorces were almost impossible to obtain, unless you happened to be the king, Sleaford had eventually reconciled with his wife.

Burke listed two children, a boy born in 1514 and named Henry for the king, and an unnamed girl. Girls weren't important enough to identify, but Lauren knew she'd been called Catherine, after Henry's first queen. She was born seven years after her brother.

"According to this, the family estate is in Yorkshire," Sandra remarked as she read over Lauren's shoulder. "Morwell Hall."

"The manor," Lauren murmured. "It was called the manor."

In her mind she saw herself standing in the shadow of the gatehouse. A high wall, constructed partly of stone and partly of dirt, surrounded the house. The oaken gate, with its two sturdy locks, was set in a stone arch with a room above for the porter. The morning sun behind her picked out the words Sir Randall had caused to be inscribed there. She could not read them for herself but she had been told they said "This gateway was begun in the year of our Lord 1511, the second year of the reign of King Henry VIII, by me, Randall Sleaford, Knight."

Lauren blinked. A new picture replaced the first.

Morwell Hall was a half-timbered, gabled manor house. It sat on a low, stone base and sported a multitude of chimneys. A portion of the yard was fenced off with rails that it might be used for cattle, and there was other livestock, too. Ewes and wethers were fattening on the rich pasture, and she saw steers, oxen, and runts about. A hayrick stood in the open section of the yard, but the harvest had already been stored in various outbuildings. There were two barns, one for wheat and one for spring corn. The granary, strawhouse, and hayhouse had all been freshly thatched, as had the smaller buildings. A pigsty, stable, and byre were flanked by dog kennels and a henhouse on one side and a carthouse, bakehouse, and brewhouse on the other.

"Lauren?"

Sandra was standing across the room, a small red-covered volume in her hands. If she was aware that Lauren's attention had wandered she gave no sign of it.

"What have you found?"

"This is a book on the Field of Cloth of Gold, an account of all the courtiers and ladies who attended that famous meeting between Henry VIII and Francis I of France. Sir Randall and Lady Sleaford are both on the list."

"What year?"

"Fifteen twenty."

Lauren did some quick mental calculations. "Jane Malte was born in fifteen twenty."

Sandra took that in stride and plucked a plain, tan book from the shelf. "This one's on sixteenth-century women," she explained, "and arranged by maiden name since women so often went through three or four husbands and had a couple of elevations in the peerage to add to the confusion of multiple surnames. Drat. Nothing under Roundsey. We need more information. Will you let me look for it?"

"You're asking my permission?"

"I'm turning over a new leaf. Of course I may go quietly crazy if you say no. I don't deal well with frustration."

Lauren sighed. "Go ahead. I can't imagine you'll find much more. I'm astonished that there was this much."

"Never underestimate the power of a librarian. We don't have all the answers but we know where to go to get them."

"Where will you start?"

"A catalog of that exhibit we went to in New York."

"I'm way ahead of you. I've already sent for one."

"Then with that retired history professor we met at the museum. Professor Markham. And I'll use the interlibrary loan system to borrow books on artists of the period."

"What good will that do?"

Sandra frowned. "I'm not sure, but it stands to reason that painting we saw has some significance. I want to find out more about the person who painted it."

"He's unknown. Remember? It was done 'in the manner of' Hans Holbein."

"It can't hurt to check. They're always turning up new data, you know. Rewriting history. If nothing else, the doctoral candidates have to find original topics for their dissertations."

Lauren gave in. "How can I help, other than by agreeing to visit a channeler?"

Sandra laughed outright. "I have a much more palatable suggestion. The college library is all of two blocks from here, and their card catalog is on a computer that links into the rest of the university system and then some. If you find a title that's at another campus, I can borrow it for you through this library. If the book's at Lumberton, you can take it out yourself—if you pay them five bucks for a library card."

About to agree, Lauren suddenly came to her senses. "This isn't real, Sandra. It can't be. There's no sense wasting your time—"

"Intellectual inquiry is never a waste." Sandra gathered up her empty teacup and Lauren's nearly full one and headed for the kitchen. "What have you got to lose?"

"My sanity?"

Sandra chuckled.

Lauren wasn't entirely sure she'd been joking.

* * *

Tuesday was Adam's night to teach. At Lauren's suggestion he'd had supper in town, giving her all evening alone to compose herself after her session with Beaumont. As matters had fallen out, he'd needed some time to think as well.

Lauren met him at the door. "I'm glad you're home."

As she came up on tiptoes to kiss him, he tensed, then berated himself for the reaction. Why should he be suspicious just because she was happy to see him? A month ago he wouldn't have thought twice about her state of mind if she'd been waiting for him like this. He'd have been able to relax and enjoy the fact that she'd missed him.

"How did it go today?"

She put a little distance between them, so that she could study his face. "I could ask you the same thing. You're getting new worry lines."

"I mean with Beaumont."

Lauren's artful carelessness told him more than she knew. He waited, hoping she'd open up, but she said only, "I don't think I'm taking the details from some novel I read years ago. I stopped at the library on my way home and Sandra and I did some research. That theory won't fly."

"Will you go back to Beaumont?" he asked cautiously.

"I have an appointment next Monday."

"Come here." He tugged her down beside him on the comfortable sofa in their living room. Against the opposite wall, on top of an oak lowboy, were the television and VCR but neither had been turned on.

Lauren sat obediently enough, but she stared straight ahead, her eyes on the framed lithograph of

Lumberton in 1853 that hung above the lowboy. They both started to speak at the same time.

"I have something to tell—"

"I wanted to tell you—"

"You first," Lauren insisted. She swung round to face him, her eyes wider than usual, and he had the uncomfortable sensation that neither one of them was going to be happy with the result of this night's exchange of confidences.

"Beaumont made a suggestion when I met with him," Adam said carefully. "I thought it was a good one, so I've gone ahead with it. I've been having you investigated."

Lauren said nothing, absorbing the implications. When she moved away from him he let her go, watching as she crossed to the sliding glass doors, pushed aside one end of the insulating draperies, and stared out into the starlit night. For a moment he thought she might open the door and go out onto the deck, but she stayed where she was. Without turning she finally spoke, her voice thready and hesitant.

"How bad is it?"

She expected something terrible.

That conclusion shouldn't have come as a surprise, but it did. Taken aback, Adam didn't answer right away, and by the time he'd regrouped his thoughts Lauren had returned to his side. She stood next to the couch, tension radiating from her small frame in palpable waves. "What did you find out?"

"Sit," he ordered.

A flash of dark humor caused her smile. "That bad?"

"No, not that bad. Sit down, Lauren." By the time she was tucked snugly against his side, he was the one staring at the lithograph. "The worst thing either of us can do to the other is try to soft-peddle the truth. Agreed?"

Her murmur of assent was barely audible. She had something to tell him and he wasn't going to like hearing it. He was certain of that now, but it didn't change anything. He'd always believed honesty was essential in a marriage, and today he'd come to the conclusion that there had been enough evasion.

"Okay. Here's what I've done so far. I contacted a friend of a friend who used to be on the police force in Darien, Connecticut. Dave started checking into records for the years you and your parents lived there."

"Was I ever arrested?"

"Where did you get that idea? Never mind. No. As far as we can tell you weren't."

"What do you mean, as far as you can tell? Didn't your friend check the police records?"

"Honey, before 1975 there wasn't any standardized crime reporting in this country. I don't know about Darien, but in the sheriff's department here things were damned informal. When I first started working as a corrections officer we had one particular family of troublemakers in this county. One brother or another was always in jail. The paperwork for all of them was filed in one big manila folder with their surname on the front."

Lauren seemed fascinated by the knots her fingers were making in the long fringe at the bottom of her loose pullover sweater.

"There are other places for Dave to check. Newspapers. Land transfers. Vital records. City directories. It's a cold trail but not impossible to follow. I already have a fax of your mother's obituary from the newspaper."

The fingers stilled.

"It would help if I knew exactly when your father died."

"I'm not sure." He felt her hesitation before she blurted, "I was told I hated him and that he was dead. I had the impression that he hadn't been dead long when I lost my memory, but those months are . . . blurry. I know it was summer. That's about all I do know."

Adam suspected his man in Darien probably hadn't checked into records that recent. He had himself mistakenly assumed that Hugh Kendall's death had taken place much earlier than the onset of Lauren's amnesia. The oversight was easily rectified. Less simple to handle was Lauren's increasing nervousness.

"Dave's found out very little so far. Nothing terrible, just puzzling."

"Why puzzling?"

"You didn't stay in any one school long. A phone call to Todham Academy in Massachusetts, which is apparently the last place you were a student before you went to England, turned up the fact that they have transcripts from previous schools . . . five of them."

"Five? Why so many? Was I expelled? Did I run away?"

"I don't know. Yet. There are limits to what a registrar will give out, even to someone with a badge, without a court order, but there's another way to get the information. You could visit the campus in person. They'd have to turn over all your records to you.

You might also be able to find someone still there who remembers you from your stint as a student."

"No."

"It's not impossible. A teacher. An administrator."

"I mean no, I don't want to go there."

"Why are you so reluctant to find out more about your past?"

"You're supposed to be trained as a detective. Can't you guess? I'm afraid I won't like what I find."

First she expected a jail record; now she seemed certain there would be only negative reports from Todham Academy. The assumption disturbed Adam. "Don't you want to know how you ended up in an English boarding school?"

"Miss Cogswell's? No."

"Do you remember where, exactly, this Miss Cogswell's is?"

"I only know what I was told, and that was that it was in Yorkshire. James Herriot country. Oh."

"What?"

"Nothing. I thought . . . never mind. I'll tell you when I sort it out myself." Very carefully she disentangled herself from his arms and moved to the far end of the sofa. "This isn't easy for me, Adam. I'm not proud of those years right before I came here to Maine."

Annoyance coupled with disappointment made his voice gritty. "Something else you never intended to tell me?" Was this going to be another secret she felt pressured into confiding only because she realized he might find out on his own? "I always thought we could tell each other anything, that we had no secrets between us."

Guilt flitted across what he could still see of her

expressive features, but was quickly replaced by a desperate determination as she lifted her head and met his hostile gaze. "Shut up and listen, Adam."

In hesitant, broken sentences, she told him she'd lived with a man named Rob Seton for three years. He was the "friend" who'd been with her when she lost her memory.

As the story unfolded, Adam's anger heated rapidly, but all that scalding, mindless rage was directed at Rob, not Lauren. "Damn it, Lauren. He used you!"

Her primary attraction had obviously been her trust fund. Rob Seton had taken advantage of her amnesia for his own gain and compounded the crime by pushing her into using drugs.

"I was totally dependent on Rob," she admitted, "even after we returned to the U.S."

Adam surged to his feet, too infuriated to sit still. Lauren let out a little squeak of startled surprise. Arms wrapped about herself, she looked vulnerable huddled on one end of the sofa, as if she had given up hope. As furious as he was, her desolation moved Adam. He strode back across the room, intent on offering comfort, but Lauren took one look at his grim expression and the threat implicit in his body language and seemed to expect the worst. She cringed when he reached for her.

Her mistrust hurt. The pain of her rejection shafted through him, leaving behind a tight, cramped feeling in the area of his heart. He withdrew a step, his arms at his sides. "Lauren," he said in his gentlest voice, "I love you."

"How can you, after everything I've done? I used drugs. I broke the law. Even if you can forgive me for living with someone like Rob, how can you condone that?"

He went down on his knees beside the sofa and put one hand over hers, relieved when she didn't try to pull away. That fine line between right and wrong, which had always seemed so clear to him, abruptly blurred. He couldn't condemn Lauren, no matter what she'd done, and he wasn't convinced she'd had any choice in her actions. It had been Rob's fault she'd broken the law, not Lauren's.

"Sweetheart, I'm surprised that you experimented with drugs, but so did a lot of other kids who didn't know any better. You smartened up, and the statute of limitations ran out on any of those misdemeanors years ago. Besides, from what you've said, I don't believe you knew you were doing anything illegal."

"Ignorance of the law is no excuse," she quoted. "You've said that often enough."

"Your case is an exception."

"You can overlook what I've told you? Change your mind about how a person is responsible for knowing the difference between right and wrong just like that?"

"Yes. Just like that." He planted a gentle kiss on the hand he still held, but Lauren didn't seem to notice.

"What if I did know I was committing a crime? I think I must have known, Adam. Even while we were still in England, we seemed to be . . . hiding. I can't explain it exactly, but Rob never went out during the daytime. We never saw anyone else. And there was an endless supply of marijuana in the flat."

"Will it make you feel better if I check into it? See if there are any outstanding warrants? I'm pretty sure England has a statute of limitations, but—"

"I can't believe this. You should be furious at me. I kept all this secret from you. I broke the law!"

He wasn't sure he understood his attitude himself, but Adam was certain of one thing. He loved his wife, no matter what she'd done while under the influence of Rob Seton. "I'm not upset with you, Lauren." He hesitated, then added, "It's always better to know the truth."

"You're going to keep investigating, aren't you?"

"I have to. And I have to ask you more about Rob."

His jaw clenched involuntarily as he spoke the other man's name. Raw rage coiled in the pit of his stomach. He meant to track down Rob Seton. If he was still up to his old tricks it wouldn't be hard to find proof of it. Adam hoped he was. He wanted to uncover grounds to lock him away for a long time. Hell, he wanted an excuse to thrash Rob Seton within an inch of his life. He'd settle for putting him in jail.

"Where was that flat, Lauren? You've never said what city you were in. Was it London?"

"No. Leeds."

"Why Leeds?"

A testy note came into her voice. "How do you expect me to know? I lost my memory, remember?"

"You must have some idea."

She tugged her fingers free and used them to massage the bridge of her nose. "There's a university in Leeds. A big one. I think Rob may have been a student there before I met him. Junior year abroad or some such. But I've told you the literal truth. I never went out of that apartment until the day we started for home."

"But you didn't go home, did you? Not back to Darien, Connecticut."

"No. I've already told you. Rob and I lived in Boston."

"No contact at all with people in your old hometown?"

"We hung out with Rob's friends. I don't think any of them knew me before we came back from England, and no one ever used last names. Things were very . . . informal."

"Why Boston?"

"I wish you'd stop snapping out questions. I feel as if I'm being interrogated."

"Sorry. Old habits die hard. Why Boston?"

"I imagine because that's where the bank with the trust fund was based."

"You caught on after a while?"

"Figured out he was using me to get the money? Oh, yes." The bitterness in her voice was tinged with sadness.

"And, after that, you left Boston and came to Maine to start over?"

She nodded, confirming what she'd told him a little earlier. She hadn't given many details but he could see how exhausted she was. He wouldn't press for more tonight.

"Then Boston is the place I'll start looking for him," Adam muttered.

Lauren paled visibly.

Adam's reaction was both violent and uncontrollable. The corrosive acid of jealousy had been gnawing at his guts ever since she first mentioned Rob Seton. "Are you worried that I won't find him?" he taunted. "Or worried that I will?"

"I know you won't find him."

He shot to his feet and stood at her side, glowering down at her. "I'm very good at finding people. Don't forget that I spent two years as an investigator before we met."

She sent him a sad little smile, faintly apologetic. "You don't understand, Adam. You won't find him because Rob is dead. He was killed by a hit-and-run driver fourteen years ago."

10

Lauren had long since gone to bed. Adam stood by the sliding glass doors in the dark, staring morosely out into the night as he downed the last of a can of beer. A few well-chosen phone calls had confirmed Robert Seton's death at the age of twenty-three. His car had been forced off the road and over an embankment by some unidentified hit-and-run driver, probably drunk. There had been no witnesses, but the man was unquestionably dead.

He'd been dead for nearly fourteen years.

Adam's fingers curled into fists, crushing the now empty can in one hand. Damn it. A part of him had wanted Seton alive, so that he could turn that life into a living hell.

Frustration warred with indecision. There was an aspect to Seton's death that bothered him even more than being thwarted in his quest for vengeance. Lauren's revelation meant that she hadn't chosen to leave her lover and his life-style behind. She'd been forced to start over after his death.

"Adam?"

She'd come halfway down the stairs so silently that he'd had no warning of her presence until she spoke. He turned to look at her and his body reacted instantly to the sight of a light in the upstairs hall shining through the fine fabric of her white nightgown. It turned the high-necked, long-sleeved garment into a dangerous instrument of seduction.

Hesitant, her voice wavering, she clung to the handrail and looked down at him. He couldn't see her eyes, but he could hear her uncertainty. "Are you coming to bed?"

"Soon."

"I . . . I know you're . . . disappointed in me, but I'd hoped—"

He was beside her in three quick strides, dropping the crushed can to the carpeted treads as he caught her close. "Lauren, no. It's not that."

Her smile was tremulous, as if she scarcely dared hope they had a future left now that she'd confessed her sins. "I knew you were going to be angry when I told you about Rob and . . . everything."

His anger was at himself. He'd behaved like an insensitive jerk, first telling her he wasn't upset with her and then giving every indication that just the opposite was true. He'd badgered her, for God's sake, when any fool could tell that she was already at the end of her emotional rope.

"Sweetheart, there's no excuse for the way I carried on."

He was still baffled by the intensity of his own reaction. All his life, decisions about what was good or evil, right or wrong, had been clear-cut and unemotional for him. Only once before had he faced a crisis of comparable complexity.

He'd been burned out then, the result of too many years of dealing with criminals, but he'd still believed himself capable of telling the difference between actions that fell within the law and those that were against it. It had taken a near tragedy to wake him up. He'd gotten out of active police work rather than risk a repetition of the incident.

He'd abandoned a career rather than face the loss of his ability to make the "right" choices, but he could not abandon his marriage. The ease with which he seemed to be able to accept Lauren's past was almost frightening when he thought about it, but he refused to dwell on that further tonight. Right now she needed his support, his love, his reassurance. There was no room for anything else.

She filled his arms and his thoughts. The pure misery in her voice nearly broke his heart. "I hurt you."

"No man likes to hear about his wife's old lover, but that was a long time ago, before we met. If it wasn't to help you in your therapy, believe me, I wouldn't want to know more."

"You were the first in all the ways that really matter," she whispered.

"That's how I felt about you, too."

She'd come to him so sweetly, as if their joining had been preordained. They'd meshed, body and soul and mind, fulfilling the promise of the spark that had flared between them the night they'd met. No other woman had ever affected him the way Lauren had, the way Lauren did. No other woman had ever made him think of marriage, but with her the next step had been inevitable. He'd never regretted it, not for an instant, and he didn't regret it now.

She was the other half of himself.

"I thought—"

"You thought wrong." He could see her eyes now, bright as sapphires and overflowing with love.

They made their way slowly up the remaining stairs, clinging together like shipwreck survivors.

"How can you forgive me? You'd argue against anyone else getting away with breaking the law. I knew, Adam. I knew what we were doing was wrong. We were selling drugs, too. You have to understand that I could read by then. I knew it was illegal to—"

"No more. It's over. Long past the point where anyone could prosecute even if they wanted to." He didn't intend to talk about it anymore tonight. His overwhelming desire was to make love to her, to give her concrete proof that nothing had changed between them.

If anything he felt more protective toward her, for in spite of her futile attempts to accept blame, he believed absolutely in two things, her fundamental innocence and Rob Seton's guilt.

"Rob—"

"Rob's dead. You were right to try to forget all about him and the things he made you do."

He stopped further conversation with a long, lingering kiss. They stood at the top of the stairs, only a few steps away from the bedroom where their massive, sinfully comfortable bed awaited them.

"I love you, Lauren," he whispered huskily, and with one smooth movement lifted her high into his arms, just the way he had in New York before all this craziness started. "I will always love you. There is nothing you can tell me that will make any difference in the way I feel about you."

After that passionate declaration no more words were necessary.

Lauren entered her psychologist's inner sanctum with great reluctance. She'd seriously considered canceling her second appointment, but Adam had put an end to that cowardly impulse by announcing at breakfast that he had business of his own in Twin Cities and would give her a lift to Beaumont's office.

"Be right with you, Mrs. Ryder," Beaumont assured her as she settled herself in the comfortable client's chair, but he didn't look up from the notes he was inscribing in a precise and rounded hand on one of his omnipresent yellow legal pads.

While she waited, Lauren's thoughts turned to Adam and she stifled a sigh. She'd hoped things really would return to normal after the exquisite, passionate lovemaking that had followed her confession. Instead, at least outside their bedroom, he'd begun to treat her like a piece of fragile statuary. He was too cautious around her, as if he thought she might break, and that, in turn, had made her wary. He had sworn nothing would change the way he felt about her, and yet neither of them could predict what might come out next about her mysterious past.

"Well, Mrs. Ryder, how are you today?"

Lauren's head snapped up at Beaumont's jovial greeting. There was an avid expression in his beady eyes. He was looking at her, she decided, the same way a biologist might regard some odd new species.

"You were wrong about the historical novels."

Lauren plunged into an account of what she and Sandra had found in Burke's *Peerage* about the Sleafords. As she related the details, she realized with sudden dismay that she'd completely forgotten to share the discovery with Adam. She'd meant to, but his reaction to her revelations about Rob and the years in Boston had driven all thought of events of the sixteenth century right out of her mind.

Beaumont nodded sagely. "Perhaps you read a great deal of nonfiction, Mrs. Ryder?"

"Don't you think I'd remember such a . . . scholarly pursuit?"

"Not necessarily. It could be that you were interested in the period some time ago. Tell me, can you remember every single thing you've done in the last seventeen years?"

"Of course not, and I'm sure I have read some books that included sections on the domestic arts of the sixteenth century, but I never did serious research into that period. I couldn't have forgotten something like that."

She hadn't even known how to use a library properly until the previous week and her first visit to the college's ultramodern facility. On Friday afternoon she'd braved the unknown. Now a stack of books sat in one corner of her workshop, and Sandra had promised there would be more when the inter-library loans she'd requested came through.

Still convinced he was right, Beaumont began to ask about the dreams. "Have you kept to a normal routine, as I advised? Stopped fighting your subconscious?"

"I've spent a great deal of time this last week thinking about the past." He didn't seem to catch the wry note in her voice. She'd opened herself up all right, to both the past she'd shared with Rob and the life Jane Malte had lived over four hundred and fifty years earlier.

"Any more nightmares?"

"No. I get occasional vivid glimpses of the sixteenth century. New bits and pieces. Day or night, it makes no difference." At least she'd been sleeping normally.

"And these . . . glimpses. Have any of them been frightening?"

"No."

"Pleasant little scenes, then?"

She grimaced. "All but one."

He waited, pen poised.

Lauren hesitated, nibbling delicately on her lower lip, then gave in. This was, after all, why she was coming to him in the first place. She was supposed to tell him about her dreams and he was supposed to figure out what they meant.

"It was the day of the annual rush bearing. Everyone was very excited, racing along the street toward the common near the mill."

"Can you describe this village?"

"Beyond the church, near the forge, a rough wooden bridge crosses a stream that runs for a bit down the very center of the western end of the street. There are four tenements on the far side. Each one contains a house with a yard, one or two outbuildings, a garden, and an arable strip of land to the rear."

Beaumont should have been scribbling furiously, getting all those details down on paper. Instead his note taking continued at a sedate pace. Lauren wondered absently if he was secretly recording the session. It didn't matter, she supposed, but it did seem a trifle underhanded.

She was aware of Beaumont's growing interest as she talked about the village, evidenced by the fact that he'd stopped taking notes entirely, and yet a part of her was back at that open space she'd seen so clearly on Saturday morning when she'd gone into town for groceries.

The vision had come out of the blue, and faded again with as little fuss. Still, while it had lasted, the specifics had impressed themselves upon her with considerable force. She'd felt herself part of that brutal scene, participating in something she'd never have enjoyed in real life. As briefly as she could she described the badger baiting.

Beaumont cleared his throat. "Bloodthirsty lot. I've been told that spectators used to flock to Smithfield, to attend the executions, in those days, too. Most modern men and women wouldn't have the stomach for it."

"My burning was well attended," Lauren agreed bitterly. "Just another blood sport."

Without warning, another scene appeared in her mind's eye. She was looking at a half-finished portrait of Sir Randall Sleaford. "He's splendidly dressed," she murmured aloud. "The doublet is wine red, and the trunk hose of gold cloth paned in scarlet, and the knitted hose are of a fashionable color known as maiden's blush."

She blinked and, for the first time since she'd begun to describe the badger baiting, she met Beaumont's hooded gaze head on. She was startled by the hostility she saw there.

"Clarify something for me, Mrs. Ryder. You've dreamed all these scenes in color?"

The request surprised her, but she answered honestly. "I must have. How else would I know what colors things were?"

"That is a very good question. You see, most people only dream in black and white."

"You think I'm making all this up?" Was that why he'd stopped taking notes? "Why on earth would I want to do that?"

"You can answer that question better than I."

"The dreams were in color," she insisted. "Every single one of them. There is no other way I could know the details of Lady Sleaford's embroidery, or the—"

"Certainly there is another way. You even admit to reading about the domestic arts of that period."

"But—"

"I apologize for suggesting you might be making all this up simply to test my patience. Obviously you'd have no reason to do something like that. However, you must see how important it is for you to accept certain facts. For the most part, your dreams cannot have been in color. Dreaming in color is exceedingly rare."

"But—"

"Now, if you wish to progress in your therapy, you must make an effort to distinguish between fact and fantasy. You've simply supplied the color afterward, to enhance the drama as it were."

"But—"

"I cannot stress enough how important it is that you not make such additions." He glanced at his watch. "Next time we talk you will tell me only what you have actually dreamed. No more details you've added later. You have an excellent imagination, Mrs. Ryder, but this is not the place to exercise it."

His arrogance was exceeded only by his pomposity. If it hadn't been for the fact that she'd promised Adam she'd give therapy a fair chance, Lauren would have told Beaumont exactly what he could do with his next appointment.

Adam was waiting for her when she came out. He knew before she'd said a word that the session had upset her. "Let's get an early lunch before we head back," he suggested.

"I do dream in color," she muttered as he escorted her out into the bright October sunlight.

Ten minutes later they were seated in the privacy of a restaurant booth. Over club sandwiches and fries she filled Adam in, adding the details she'd neglected to share with him earlier. "Sandra seems to think we can find out more about the Sleaford family, and perhaps something about the person who painted the group portrait we saw in that museum in New York."

He reached across the small table to take her hands in his. "Do me a favor and give Beaumont the benefit of the doubt. I'm sure you do dream in color, but if that's as uncommon as he says then you can't really blame him for being skeptical."

"He was confrontational, Adam. You know I don't like confrontations."

"Maybe he's had success with that technique in other cases. I think . . . I think that we both need to go on with what we've started. We need to get everything out into the open, put an end to the mystery, an end to all these secrets."

An uncomfortable, wary sensation prickled along the surface of Lauren's skin at his words. She'd known that he would continue his investigation into her background, but she could not like the situation. She disengaged one hand and put another french fry into her mouth to block impetuous words. Lauren knew her husband well enough to be certain she could not change his mind, not about this.

"I wish I didn't have to be out of town the rest of the week," Adam said.

"I wish you could stay home, too, but you'll only be gone from Wednesday through Sunday."

"Come with me."

"You'll be too busy to spend time with me."

"I was busy on the last trip and we still managed to have fun."

Memories of the visit to New York alternately warmed and chilled her, but aloud she said only, "The town you're going to this time is too small to have much to interest me. Besides," she added brightly when he started to speak, "I have the rest of the week all planned. Aside from my regular work I'm going to go back to the library, and then there's that home shopping party Sandra has planned."

"If you came with me . . ." Adam let his words trail off as he cast a thoughtful look her way. "It isn't an ordinary party, is it?"

"No."

It was Sandra's none-too-subtle way of helping Karen Doucette get out of the funk she'd been in ever since she uncovered proof of Clubber's infidelity. There was no formal law-enforcement wives support group in Jefferson County, but the nature of the profession had long ago prompted Sandra to make certain efforts on behalf of the wives of her husband's officers and on behalf of the one husband of a Lumberton officer, too. Since her marriage to Adam, who continued to be sworn in as a part-time officer year after year, even though he never put on a uniform or a gun, Lauren had been included in all of Sandra's efforts.

Adam's hands suddenly clenched on hers, betraying the strength of his feelings. "Marriage vows should mean something, damn it."

To her own amazement, Lauren suddenly felt much more optimistic. Adam would stick by her through the "worse" and just maybe, after a few more sessions with Beaumont, the "better" would return.

"I'll be fine while you're away," she assured him. A way to lighten his mood suggested itself and she seized on it with enthusiasm. "I've been thinking there may be a simple explanation for all my dreams, after all."

"That would be nice."

"Mmmm. How does this sound? The dreams are an indication that I should consider a career change. My subconscious is telling me that I have the potential to become the next great historical novelist of our generation."

"I like it," Adam said. "Work on that while I'm away."

It was Friday afternoon before Adam could escape from his consulting job for a few hours and drive to Todham Academy. He'd managed to make arrangements by phone, however, to talk to a former classmate of Lauren's. Melanie Fairchild had gone back to her alma mater as a teacher.

"Do you recognize her?" he asked, handing the attractive blond a recent snapshot of Lauren. It was the same photograph he'd faxed to Dave in Darien, showing her in a relaxed pose, playing with Hassle. She looked beautiful, he thought, her soft brown hair falling in gentle waves around her face. Those big blue eyes were laughing up at the camera, full of life and love.

"To be truthful, I wouldn't have." Melanie Fairchild returned the photo and studied Adam instead. "It's been a long time and I didn't know her particularly well."

He wasn't sure why, but Adam had not told Melanie that Lauren was his wife. He'd allowed her to jump to the conclusion that he was some sort of private detective tracking down a missing person.

"This isn't a very big school."

Tree-shaded sidewalks connected four handsome red brick buildings, but only one housed students. The total enrollment was held at three hundred, assuring exclusivity. Adam and his companion left the administration building, with its tall bell tower, and strolled in the late afternoon sun toward the path that circled a man-made lake at one side of the small, perfectly groomed campus.

"If you were to think very hard," he suggested, "perhaps something might come back to you."

"Perhaps. Food stimulates the brain, you know." When he failed to respond to her hint that he offer her dinner, she tried another angle. "Was your high school large?"

"Not especially." The surrounding towns fed their grade-school pupils into a regional secondary program, but there was no comparison to the typical enrollment of an urban high school.

"Still live in the same area?" She smiled slightly when he nodded. "Try looking at your high-school yearbook sometime and see how many of those people still bear much resemblance to themselves."

"Point taken. I had hoped someone would be able to help, though. It's important I find out everything I can about her early life. I realize she wasn't here long, only about six months. She left a month before the end of the term, but—"

"Wait a minute. Kendall?"

"You've remembered something?"

"Maybe I have." For a moment Melanie seemed ill-at-ease with that thought. She stopped walking to stare out over the still waters of the pond.

A wrought iron and wood bench had been placed nearby, in the shelter of a leafless elm, and when she turned Adam gestured toward it. "Why don't we sit down while you tell me all about it?"

Her voice a trifle breathless, she asked, "Is Lauren Kendall in some kind of trouble?"

"Not that I know of." Adam sat, waiting patiently. After a moment Melanie sank down beside him, but she was wary now, wondering if she'd made a mistake by agreeing to talk to him.

"It's essential that I learn all I can of her life here," he said quietly. "Was she expelled? Is that why she left so abruptly?"

"Surely the records in the registrar's office can tell you that?"

One lifted eyebrow spoke volumes. "A school like this is very careful never to document scandal." It was a shot in the dark but he hit the bull's eye.

"You were fishing," Melanie accused. "You've already heard the rumors."

"Why don't you tell me what you know? I wouldn't want to be accused of leading the witness."

"This is just gossip," she warned as she leaned closer, one hand creeping along the bench to brush against his leg. "I can't swear to any of it. In fact, I'd probably deny I said it if anyone else were to ask me."

She hesitated until Adam produced his warmest smile. He made himself reach over and pat the hand that was now hovering near his thigh. He found her actions more annoying than provocative, but he needed the information she had. "I'd appreciate anything you can tell me. More than you can imagine."

"I've got a pretty good imagination," she assured him. Her nostrils flared slightly and her pupils dilated. Adam found himself hoping she'd spill the beans before he was forced to dump her hot little body in the lake to cool it down.

"Tell me."

Suddenly coy, she lowered her eyelashes. Her fingers smoothed the fabric of his gray slacks, but the contact had precisely the opposite effect from the one she obviously intended. Her flagrant behavior was beginning to repulse him.

"You do realize that I could lose my job if it got back to the administration that I'd been spreading rumors about the school?"

"I'd appreciate your candor, Melanie, and I can assure you that the details of this conversation will be kept confidential." He would definitely not describe to Lauren what he was going through to get them. "Nothing you say will be used against you." She didn't seem to notice the omission of the words "in a court of law" that usually came next.

"I really shouldn't be telling you any of this."

"But . . ."

"It can scarcely matter now. After all, it was years ago. We were girls of fifteen."

Adam endured the frank appraisal she put him through next, determined to let her think whatever she wanted about his availability. He had to find out what she'd remembered even though he could tell already that it was not something he was going to like hearing.

"She wasn't very friendly," Melanie began. "Arrived with a chip on her shoulder. Pretty soon there were rumors going around that she had drugs stashed in her room. Not just pot but the hard stuff. She'd sell it if you asked, if you had cash."

"That's why she was expelled?" Adam listened in stunned disbelief, careful to let none of his seething emotions show on his face or in his voice. If there was more, he wanted to hear it, no matter how bad it was.

"Not entirely." Melanie was very willing to talk now that she'd started. Adam wondered what the young Lauren had done to her in the brief time they'd lived in the same dormitory. "As I've told you, I have no proof of anything, but there was another sudden departure at about the same time Lauren Kendall left. A young mathematics teacher. A man. The story was going around that they were lovers and that she was pregnant. After she left here she probably had an abortion."

"She was seduced by her teacher?"

"More likely the other way around."

Grimly Adam demanded details. It didn't take him long to get the man's name, or to confirm that he had been fired for "moral turpitude" on the same day that Lauren Kendall left Todham.

Adam arrived home late Sunday night. He spotted Lauren as soon as he came through the door. She was sound asleep on the living room sofa.

He stared at her for a long moment, wondering how he was going to keep her from guessing something was wrong. She knew him too well.

He'd thought he knew her.

Grimly, he hung his coat in the closet and moved toward her still form. No nightmares. She slept the sleep of the innocent.

But she wasn't innocent. Not by a long shot.

He was no closer to sorting out his own emotions than he had been when he drove away from Todham on Friday afternoon. The canker of mistrust, of her and of his own judgment, had been festering ever since.

Maybe Beaumont was right. He shouldn't try to talk to Lauren about this new information himself. His phone conversation with the psychologist had almost convinced him to put off that particular confrontation, but it had done nothing to ease his nagging doubts.

On Saturday, in addition to consulting Beaumont, he'd called the other schools Lauren had attended. She'd been thrown out of at least one for smuggling beer and marijuana into the dormitory and talking other students into joining her to get stoned.

He'd caught up with the mathematics teacher only this morning. The man hadn't gone far, though he'd given up teaching in favor of running a small computer store. He'd readily confessed to knowing Lauren, though he, too, had said he wouldn't have recognized her from the picture. She'd been a sullen kid when he knew her, he'd said. Sexy as hell, but sulky, resentful of her parents for neglecting her, always trying to do something outrageous to get attention.

Adam had been hard-pressed to refrain from punching the guy out. He'd taken advantage of Lauren every bit as much as Rob Seton had. Restraining himself with difficulty, in the interest of maintaining his hired investigator pose, Adam had hit him with questions instead. None of the answers had brought any relief. If she'd been pregnant, her ex-teacher, ex-lover swore she'd never told him. He wouldn't have married her. He already had a wife. He wouldn't have given her any money for an abortion, either. Why should he? She was a rich little bitch. He'd been more concerned at the time about being brought up on charges of statutory rape.

Asleep, Lauren looked innocent, Adam thought again. She was curled in a ball, her hands tucked under her cheek.

Had she been pregnant? Did a botched abortion account for her sterility? The gynecologist had told them an infection had damaged Lauren's reproductive organs, but the doctor had been unable to pinpoint its cause or say with certainty how many years earlier it had occurred. Lauren had been upset by the news, and when she'd claimed not to remember any illness that could account for her condition Adam had not pressed her. At the time it had not seemed all that important.

He ran agitated fingers through his hair as he stared at his sleeping wife. What kind of woman had he married? Could he have been completely wrong about her character?

One irrational belief kept hammering at his tired brain. He could not accept that anyone who had been that wild as a girl could change so completely, almost taking on a new identity. The only way the scenario made sense was if she'd lied about having amnesia—which meant that their entire life together had been a lie.

Beaumont had cautioned him about jumping to conclusions. He'd warned him to say nothing about any of her early life to Lauren until after she'd kept her third appointment with him tomorrow morning.

It probably was better to let a professional handle such a potentially volatile situation. Adam had been telling himself that, on and off, all the way home.

Lauren stirred in her sleep, and his body tightened in automatic response. This close to his wife it was hard to remember she might be guilty of all Melanie Fairchild claimed. There had to be some mistake. Some reasonable explanation. He could not have fallen in love with a woman that depraved.

He was still struggling to come to terms with his conflicting emotions when Lauren opened her eyes and blinked sleepily up at him. "Adam. You're home." There was love in her voice, and barely leashed excitement as she added, "I didn't mean to fall asleep. I wanted to wait up for you to show you what we found."

His face was in shadow, since she'd left only one light on, burning low. She couldn't see his strained expression and didn't seem to sense his lack of enthusiasm as she reached for the oversized, well-thumbed book she'd left on the end table.

"Sandra sent for some things and the very first one came yesterday. Look. It's a self-portrait of the artist whose painting I saw in New York. He was an official Court painter by the time he did that one, but in the blurb under his picture it says he started his career by doing portraits of the Sleaford family of Morwell Hall."

The sixteenth century again. Adam took the book and stared down at a bland and rather heavy face. His question sounded testy, even to his own ears. "What's the big deal?"

"This artist is Edward Teerlinck." Lauren's eyes were bright, reflecting her unadulterated delight at the news she was about to impart. "At Morwell Hall he was called Ned and he was my lover."

11

"Your lover?"

"Well, Jane Malte's lover." Lauren stopped herself just short of adding "same thing."

One glance at Adam told her that he was coldly furious. She didn't understand why he was angry now. He'd surprised her by calming down so quickly and being so reasonable after she told him about Rob and the drugs. Since he'd seemed willing to overlook that period of her life, she'd begun to hope that he'd be able to handle whatever she threw at him next. It had never occurred to her that he might not share her excitement about the discoveries she and Sandra had made during his absence.

With excessively quiet, careful movements that hinted at just how tightly he must be holding his temper in check, Adam closed the art book and returned it to the end table. "You're confusing fantasy and reality again, Lauren." The warning was issued in a low, almost threatening voice.

"Ned Teerlinck was real, Adam." She'd recognized his self-portrait instantly as the lover in her dreams. "So were the Sleafords. History is backing up what I've been seeing in my mind."

"Damn it, Lauren. Forget about the sixteenth century. It's recent history you'd better work at remembering. That's what's important here. The dreams are nothing more than symbols of—"

"I'm not so sure of that anymore," she said. He seemed irritated by her inability to face reality, but from her point of view she was simply seeking the truth. The key was in the distant past, and the discovery of a name for her lover had been an important clue. She tried to explain, but Adam impatiently cut her short.

"You've been hanging out with Sandra," he accused, "and listening to her go on and on about that past-life crap."

"I've been hanging out with Sandra, yes, but she hasn't mentioned reincarnation for days. We're looking for facts, Adam. Solving a mystery. Just like cops do."

If he noticed that sarcasm had crept into her voice he gave no sign of it, and his annoyance did not abate. The undercurrent of real anger in his mood confused Lauren, as did the mockery in his voice.

"Let me know when you find proof in writing that Jane Malte ever existed."

Her own temper flared. "I wish I could uncover a record of the trial, just to wipe that sneer off your face!" She knew already that it was highly unlikely she would.

"Lauren—"

"Don't you think it's significant that it turns out I've populated my dreams with real people when I'd never read anything about the Sleafords or Ned Teerlinck before we went to New York?"

The arching of one sardonic brow answered for him.

"Of course I haven't found any evidence that there was a girl named Jane Malte in that household. Servants were pretty unimportant back then, especially female servants. Noblewomen were lucky to get a mention in contemporary records and when they did it was usually only as so-and-so's wife or such-and-such's daughter."

"Lauren, I really don't—"

She cut him off without a qualm, caught up once more in the excitement of her discoveries. "We were very lucky to find as much as we did on Lady Sleaford, you know. If she hadn't been in Queen Catherine of Aragon's household when it was broken up by the king in 1531 we wouldn't have gotten nearly as much. You see, the queen, about to be replaced by Anne Boleyn, was packed off to a small country house, and her ladies were dispersed to their own homes."

Adam's carefully blank expression began to annoy Lauren halfway through her discussion of Lady Sleaford's history. He wasn't even listening. Lauren lowered her gaze to her lap, frowning. She'd been about to mention the small chronology problem they'd encountered, but changed her mind. Adam wouldn't care whether Lady Sleaford had been at Morwell Hall several years prior to 1531 or not.

Lauren had given the matter a great deal of thought and had decided that the queen's ladies must have paid occasional visits to their homes and that Lady Sleaford had met the girl Jane Malte and authorized adding her to the household during one of them.

Her head snapped up again at the sound of Adam picking up his suitcase. He was already stalking toward the stairwell by the time she recovered from her surprise and uncurled from her position on the sofa.

"Where are you going?"

He disappeared around the corner but his disembodied voice drifted back to her. "It's late, Lauren. I'm going to bed."

She scurried after him, alarmed by his behavior. The sudden complete lack of interest in her did not bode well. He didn't want to talk; he didn't even want to argue. He preferred to avoid her altogether. A horrible, hollow feeling settled into her chest. Something was very wrong, and she was almost afraid to find out what it was.

Adam was stripping by the time she reached their bedroom. His bare, muscular chest appeared as he pulled a garnet-colored turtleneck over his head. Sensing her arrival, he froze, letting the garment drop to the carpet. Hostility radiated from him. His stance was aggressive, almost primitive, his legs braced wide apart. His eyes glittered dangerously in the low light, filling her with a uniquely feminine wariness. Why was Adam acting so strangely? She racked her brain for an answer, and in desperation seized on the only possibility that occurred to her.

"You're jealous," she whispered.

The taut, menacing look on his face convinced her she was right.

"It's Ned, isn't it? You're jealous because I dreamed I had a lover."

His hands clenched into fists and it was a long moment before he spoke. Even then his voice sounded odd, almost strangled. "Should I be?" he asked. "Do you dream of what it was like to make love to him?"

A guilty flush gave her away before she could deny the charge. "It's not what you think. It's just sex, not love."

The utter disgust in the flashing gold of his eyes was like an arrow through her heart.

"Sexual fantasies, Lauren? A little erotic day-dreaming to jazz up your boring life?" He turned away from her, flicking a window curtain aside and pretending great interest in the dark landscape below.

He couldn't even bear to look at her, Lauren thought wildly. Desperate to convince him that the meanderings of her subconscious meant nothing compared to what they had between them, she threw herself at him, wrapping her arms around him and pressing her cheek against the hollow between his shoulder blades. She could feel heat as well as tension where their bare skin touched. He absorbed the impact of her body colliding with his but did not move or speak.

"I can't control my dreams, Adam." The fact that she was pleading for understanding would have appalled Lauren under any other circumstances, but at that moment she'd have gotten down on her knees and begged if that could have convinced him that he was the only man she'd ever loved.

"Tell me what it was like."

The hoarse demand shocked her into releasing him. "You can't mean that you want me to describe making love to another man?"

He took a step away from her and turned. His face was a stranger's, hard and flushed with barely suppressed rage. His words lashed out, cruel and wounding, but his fists remained curled at his sides. "What's the matter Lauren? Memory not that good?"

Goaded, she burst into speech, her own anger momentarily wiping out any thought of appeasing his male pride. "My memory of my nightmares and dreams is excellent. I wish it weren't."

"Then tell me. What were your old lovers like? How do I compare?"

"There *is* no comparison." She wanted to throttle him, wanted to hurt him for taunting her this way, and he'd given her the perfect opportunity, but the truth was that he was the only man to completely satisfy her, in bed and out of it. She drew a deep breath, marshaling her thoughts.

"I want to know everything, Lauren. Now. No more evasions. No more lies."

"Fine. You want details, I'll give you details. I don't have that many. I only dreamed of making love with Ned once, and I wasn't comparing him to you. I was comparing him to my husband." He winced at that, but she hurried on. "Ned was gentle and kind, and in my dream I was aware that those qualities were a wonderful change from the brutality I'd been accustomed to from Will Malte. For all that, Adam, Ned Teerlinck didn't know much about pleasing a woman. He was a tender lover, but he was a man of his times."

In those days, Lauren suspected, ordinary working

men like Ned hadn't been aware of the ways a man could pleasure a woman. It had been the good old missionary position, though they probably hadn't called it that in the sixteenth century. Just slam, bam, thank you ma'am, with no thought for the woman's satisfaction.

There was a difference in Adam's voice when he spoke again. Some of the anger had faded, though there was still an uncertain undertone. "Before I left," he said slowly, "you weren't having this much difficulty keeping your life separate from Jane's."

She didn't reply. She couldn't. Lauren felt the color leech from her face as she realized he was right. At some point she'd accepted the fact that Will Malte was her own former husband and that Ned was her former lover.

The glance Lauren sent Adam's way was filled with tense expectancy. She longed for the comfort of his embrace, but he had folded his arms across his chest and was studying her with a baleful expression. She felt like a butterfly, about to be carefully murdered, pinned in place, and put on display.

A saying she'd read somewhere years before drifted into her mind, disturbing and strangely apropos. She couldn't remember the writer's name or the title of the book, but she did recall the unanswerable question he'd been pondering. Was he, he'd wondered, a man dreaming he was a butterfly or a butterfly dreaming he was a man?

Echoes of the past kept assaulting her, Lauren realized, despairing; illusions of reality tormented her. She no longer knew what was real and what wasn't.

Adam's stark voice broke in on her bleak thoughts.

"Let's deal with Lauren Kendall's lovers instead of Jane's. Tell me about those men."

She blinked at him in confusion. "You know I don't remember anyone before Rob. I don't know if he was the first or not."

"Tell me what a great lover Rob was, then. He must have been. You stayed with him nearly as long as you've been married to me."

"Adam!" For one horrible moment she wondered if Dr. Beaumont had betrayed her confidentiality.

"The truth, Lauren."

"The truth is that Rob Seton was skilled in the mechanics of sex but never let himself get emotionally involved. All right? Does that tell you what you wanted to know?"

She saw the flicker of pain in his eyes before he could hide his reaction, and at once she was filled with remorse. She was at his side in an instant, terrified he'd push her away but driven to touch him all the same. Her hand caught his forearm and she waited.

"Look at me, Adam," she whispered. "Please."

The muscles beneath her fingers knotted, but slowly, as if he could not stop himself, his head turned and his tormented gaze scanned her uplifted face. Lauren's tension began to dissipate. He was listening. He wanted to be convinced.

"It was not until you and I made love that I first knew true physical and emotional satisfaction. A few seconds of sensation by themselves are worth nothing. I could give myself that fleeting pleasure if I chose to. You and I don't just have great sex together. We . . . mate."

"For life?"

Relief flooded through her veins. "For life," she vowed. She sensed that he was still deeply disturbed by something, but when he reached for her she stopped trying to analyze his strange mood and gave herself to him willingly.

"You are an obsession," he murmured against her lips as he began to kiss her with ever-increasing passion. "I'm addicted to you, Lauren. I can't resist you, no matter what may have happened in your past."

Jarvis Beaumont's short, pudgy fingers smoothed over his neatly trimmed beard, then shoved his glasses more firmly into place on the bridge of his bulbous nose. He'd just finished telling Lauren of the charges made against her by someone at Todham Academy. With bated breath he waited for her reaction.

Lauren met his intensely interested gaze across the massive desk with the contempt it deserved. "What you've just told me is impossible."

"These details sparked no memories at all?"

"Don't be absurd. How could they when none of that ever happened?"

"There's no point in denying facts, Mrs. Ryder."

"What facts? You've repeated gossip. Unattributed gossip, at that."

"The source is reliable."

"Who? Who went to Todham Academy? Who could have talked to . . . ?" Lauren's voice trailed off as the obvious answer hit her. Todham was in Massachusetts and Adam had just spent five days in that state.

Stung by the realization that Adam had listened

to these slanders and, worse, believed they might be true, Lauren suddenly understood his combative mood the previous night. She had no patience with Beaumont once she came to that conclusion. If he expected shock tactics to jolt her into remembering life before Rob Seton, he deserved to be disappointed.

"Why didn't my husband just tell me about his discoveries at Todham when he came home last night?" she demanded.

No wonder he'd been hung up on lovers in her past, and because she hadn't known what was upsetting him, she had blundered along, causing him more pain before they'd finally resolved their differences in bed.

"I advised him to let me tell you," Beaumont admitted.

"Where do you get off interfering between me and my husband?" She was furious with Beaumont and ridiculously happy at the same time. Adam's instincts must have been urging him to confide in her. She felt certain of it. That meant he hadn't really believed the lies.

"It was my professional opinion that—"

"You're a worse meddler than my sister-in-law, Dr. Beaumont. I'll thank you not to butt in again. My marriage—"

"Mrs. Ryder, you are missing the point."

"Am I?" It felt remarkably good to challenge him.

"There are certain obvious connections between your dream about murdering your husband and the fact that you aborted a pregnancy when you were fifteen."

Incensed, Lauren rose to her feet. "I did not kill

my own baby," she informed him in her coldest, haughtiest voice. "I may not remember specifics of my early years but I can assure you that if I'd seduced a teacher and had an abortion I would remember it."

"There's no reason to suppose so, Mrs. Ryder. That's exactly the kind of thing people do forget. Your amnesia—"

"Didn't start until some three years later." Still on her feet she planted both hands on his desk and leaned forward until her face was only inches away from his. "What took me so long? Or maybe you think I got pregnant a second time? Killed another baby? Went off the deep end over that?"

She could see the effort it took for him to retain his composure. For a moment she almost felt sorry for him. She didn't fit into any of his neat psychological profiles. That was the problem. Hoping she'd made her point, Lauren backed off, but Beaumont seemed to misinterpret her withdrawal, viewing it as a sign of weakness, a retreat. He promptly launched a new attack.

"Do you have strong opinions about a woman's right to abortion, Mrs. Ryder?"

"Going to analyze that now, are we?" Disgusted with his lack of perception, Lauren flung his own words back at him. "You're missing the point, Dr. Beaumont."

"Humor me, Mrs. Ryder."

"I don't think so."

Beaumont's voice buzzed in her ears, persistent and annoying as a mosquito. Without warning, what he was saying not only landed but drew blood. "It's quite possible the enormity of your actions did not hit home until several years later. It could be quite traumatic to discover that, as a result of an earlier abortion, you could never bear children."

Lauren squeezed her eyes tightly shut, anticipating a wave of pain and guilt, but it did not materialize. Instead, quite suddenly, she knew that whatever had happened at a posh girl's school twenty years earlier, it had not been the cause of her barrenness.

"I was married at thirteen," she said in a subdued voice. "I was fourteen when I gave birth to a stillborn child. Afterward I was very ill with childbed fever. The white leg, they called it."

Jarvis Beaumont's round face started out pink and progressed through several successive shades to a purplish hue that gave new meaning to the term beet red. Fascinated, Lauren stared at him. He seemed to be having trouble taking in enough air to speak, but at last he succeeded.

"This has gone far enough."

"What has, Dr. Beaumont?"

"This historical nonsense. It's time to do some testing." He was rifling papers on his desk, muttering to himself. "I should have done it the first time you came in. We'll start with the M.M.P.I."

"I have no intention of looking at ink blots."

Beaumont's beady little eyes bulged with affronted indignation. "This is the Minnesota Multiphasic Personality Inventory, a highly sophisticated evaluation tool. It is scored by computer. The results will take about two weeks to get back, and then—"

"You'll know what kind of fruitcake I am? Thank you, no."

"I'm afraid I must insist, Mrs. Ryder." His stiff formality was a defense, she realized. She guessed that there was a great deal he wanted to say to her but his professionalism forbade it.

She tried again. After all, she had promised Adam.

"There's something I want you to see. It came in today's mail. I would have shown it to you right away if you hadn't been so anxious to dish the dirt from Todham Academy. It's the catalog from that exhibit in New York. You see, I think I'm beginning to understand what really has been happening. These dreams that take place in the fifteen hundreds are—"

She stopped, astonished. She'd never before actually seen anyone's nostrils flare in anger.

"Mrs. Ryder," Beaumont said in a strangled voice, "you will stop talking about the sixteenth century. It's time for you to face reality."

"Yes, it is, and the reality is that you can't help me if you won't listen to what I think."

"I'm listening, Mrs. Ryder." Beaumont's face had become more mottled than red and his breathing had slowed. He straightened his vest with a forceful tug and waited.

Lauren sighed. The words were right but Beaumont was still regarding her with the gravest suspicion. "It's no use." She stood and gathered up her black leather shoulder bag and her coat. "You won't understand."

"Mrs. Ryder, if you don't want to be helped, then perhaps we are wasting our time, but think very carefully before you walk out of here."

"I am thinking, Dr. Beaumont." Her earlier anger returned with a force that surprised her and she leveled a final, fulminating glare in his direction as she reached the door. "I don't need or want help from a man who'd advise a husband to keep secrets from his wife."

* * *

Adam's office was on the third floor of an old brick building in downtown Lumberton. He was supposed to be compiling statistics from the previous week's study but his mind kept wandering. He was worried about Lauren. She should be through with her session by now. How had she reacted to Beaumont's news?

Finally he put his notes back in the file drawer. He'd done nothing more productive than doodle all over the margins. Sketches of Lauren, he noticed absently. He was rarely conscious of what he was drawing, but it hardly came as a surprise to discover she'd been his subject.

He turned to overdue correspondence which, since he didn't employ a secretary, tended to pile up. His powers of concentration were still under a strain, but he managed to finish one letter and start a second before Lauren's softly spoken accusation floated across the small room.

"There was more going on last night than I realized, wasn't there?"

Damn, Adam thought, swiveling his chair around to stare at her. So much for Beaumont's ability to protect his sources. "Lauren, I—"

"You've always been such a stickler for honesty." Her quiet condemnation cut far deeper than any shouted words could have. "You were upset about what you'd been told I did in my past. How could you take me to bed with such horrible suspicions in your heart?"

"The Lauren Kendall I married is innocent of those charges."

"Because I can't remember?" She came across the room in a rush, berating him with her eyes as well as her words. "After Beaumont told me what you found out I thought it hadn't mattered to you. I thought you'd automatically believed in me. But you didn't, did you? There was another meaning in every word you spoke last night. What were you hoping for, Adam? A list of former lovers? A confession that I really did remember everything? That I was a horrible person? Well, I can't give you that. I don't know what a fifteen-year-old girl did at Todham Academy. Or what happened to her at the school before that, or the ones that came earlier. I don't remember. I may never remember."

"Lauren, calm down." There was an edge in her voice now that alarmed him. She'd obviously been brooding during the entire forty-five-minute drive back from Twin Cities, drawing unpalatable conclusions that, unfortunately, were accurate. He *had* doubted her.

"Why should I calm down? Don't you think I have good reason to be upset with you?"

His fingers tore through the dark blond pelt of his hair as he tried to find the right words. "Look, Lauren, I'm trying my damnedest to accept the unsavory facts I uncovered."

"I could not have been that kind of person and not remember it."

In front of his eyes she went perfectly still, as if arrested by a sudden, startling thought.

"Lauren? Is something coming back to you?" He was torn between wanting her to remember and hoping she never did, not if the recollections confirmed what he suspected they would.

"If I'd been into drugs as a young teenager, why would Rob have had to teach me how to smoke pot?" She rushed on before he could begin to answer. "I mean it, Adam. I didn't even know how to inhale. I remembered how to chew food, how to swallow a drink. Why didn't I know how—"

"Lauren, none of that is important. No matter what you did, we can get past it."

"Because you're willing to forgive me?"

He didn't like the challenging light that had come into her eyes and wisely remained silent.

"Listen to me, Adam. I could not have been that kind of person and not remember it, not show it in some subliminal way."

Let her deny it, he told himself. It really didn't matter. He circled the battered old metal desk toward her. She took a step closer, too, as if some invisible magnet drew her toward him, but she stopped when they were still several feet apart.

"There are some unanswered questions about your past," he said carefully. "You will admit that."

With equal caution she nodded.

"I realized something after I got home last night. You are the woman I married. Our life together began when we met. I fell in love with an adult female who loves me in return, and even if she was once an amoral adolescent with too much money and no common sense, *that does not matter.* I did not marry that girl, I married this woman."

He held out his arms and she came into them in a rush, propelling them both backward until the edge of the desk stopped them.

"Oh, Adam, I was so afraid," she murmured. "If I lost you I wouldn't want to live."

"You won't lose me. You're stuck with me, lady."

She drew in a shuddering breath. "If I did have an abortion at fifteen, and I'm not saying that I did, that could account for the infection. That girl may have denied you children, Adam."

Her convoluted wording was more disturbing than what she was suggesting. There were times when she seemed confused about her own identity, times when he feared he might still lose her to the dream world she'd been creating.

"I thought we worked that out four years ago. I never planned on a family. Dan has two sons. The Ryder clan isn't about to die out."

"Doesn't every man, deep down, want sons of his own?"

Her question took him aback and he lifted her chin with one finger to force her to meet his eyes as he answered. "Sweetheart, it's your turn to listen. Until I met you I hadn't planned to marry, let alone have kids, and the only reason I went along with that fertility testing business at the end of our first year together was that you seemed so disappointed that you hadn't gotten pregnant. If we'd had children, I'd have done my best to be a good father, but I'm just as content to have a family that only consists of the two of us. I love you, Lauren. I didn't marry you to make babies with. I married you because I couldn't imagine life without you."

She couldn't doubt his sincerity, and she was blinking back tears before he finally released her. Sniffling and almost laughing at the same time, she bent toward her purse and began to rifle through it. "I never have a tissue when I need one."

"Here." He reached back across the top of his desk

and tugged the top drawer open to pull out an entire box of them. When he handed it to her she passed him a padded mailer. "What's this?"

"Something I got in this morning's mail. I was going to show it to Dr. Beaumont but I never had a chance." She swiped at the last of the tears, then met Adam's questioning gaze head on. "I'm not going back to him. He may do very well with most problems but he can't explain that."

The postmark was New York. Adam knew even before he opened the package what he would find inside. It was the catalog from the exhibit where Lauren had seen her own likeness in a painting.

She took the glossy-covered volume back from him long enough to find the page she wanted. Then she perched on one corner of his desk while he resumed possession of his chair. The catalog lay open on the blotter between them.

The reproduction was in color but it was small, too small to see much of the figure in the corner. Adam felt a vague sense of familiarity as he stared at it, but he shrugged off the import of that impression. He'd heard the thing described often enough. He dug out a magnifying glass, but soon found it wasn't much help.

"It's difficult to make out any details of this face, Lauren. It might resemble you, and any similarity might also be your imagination." He thought of the fashion prints in their bedroom and decided that the latter explanation was far more likely to be the right one.

"Look at the other faces, Adam. Each one of them is distinctive. He was a good portrait painter."

"Ned Teerlinck?"

"Yes."

"It says here the artist was unknown."

"It was Ned," she said confidently. "He was at Court at the right time to have painted this picture, and he put me in it because we were lovers."

Adam looked at the blurb under the picture again. "In 1545. I thought you said Jane Malte died in 1535?"

Lauren blinked in confusion. That increasingly frequent occurrence, together with her tendency to jump to conclusions about people who had lived hundreds of years ago, was beginning to scare him. She seemed so convinced that all she knew of the sixteenth century was real.

"I guess it must have been some kind of memorial. He loved deeply. Unless . . . Adam, do you think it's possible that someone could survive a fire? Could a dummy have been substituted at the last minute or something?"

"You're really stretching, Lauren. Maybe you should consider writing fiction as a career. You certainly have the imagination for it."

"Now you sound like Dr. Beaumont."

"I'm only telling you what I think. You did ask my opinion, you know."

"Sorry. You're right. I just can't help speculating. What if Jane escaped somehow?"

"I don't think it's likely." Adam told himself he was willing to humor Lauren up to a point. "I've heard of rare cases where hangings failed because the knot came loose or the trapdoor didn't work, but burning's pretty final. It wouldn't have been the flames that caused Jane Malte's death. Smoke inhalation would have proved fatal first."

Lauren's sudden pallor made him wish he'd taken more care in his choice of words. He kept forgetting how closely she identified with Jane.

"It's a horrible way to die." She shook herself, and managed a small smile to let him know she was okay.

"Those were cruel times." He glanced at the catalog again. "It seems to me that there's another inconsistency here, aside from the dating. How do you explain that this is a scene at Court? From everything you've told me, all your dreams take place in rural England."

"Yes. In Yorkshire." Lauren's tenuous smile widened a little more. "One other thing has occurred to me recently. Burke's *Peerage* wasn't very specific, but it did indicate that Morwell Hall was in Yorkshire. I've been thinking that the site could be part of the present city of Leeds. In the sixteenth century Leeds wouldn't have been much more than a market town, but during the Industrial Revolution it must have grown by leaps and bounds."

"Then is it possible you did visit Morwell Hall? Before you lost your memory? If so, that could be the reason you've used it in your dreams." He'd suggested something of the sort before and it still seemed an obvious answer.

"Sorry, Adam. It won't wash. Burke's also says that Morwell Hall burned to the ground in 1726 and was never rebuilt. From then on the family seat was a small, unpretentious castle in Kent."

They stared at each other in silence for a long moment. "What next, then? You say you won't go back to Beaumont, but we can't just leave things as they are."

"I agree."

"I'm almost afraid to ask what you have in mind." There was a stubborn tilt to her chin and a determined gleam in her eyes.

"It's simple enough," Lauren told him. "I think the time has come to investigate the possibility that I was Jane Malte in a past life."

12

Her optimism, as she entered Adam's office on Wednesday afternoon, was completely different from the uncertainty she'd felt the last time she'd dropped in on him. Thank God, Lauren thought. Two days earlier she'd been convinced their marriage was in mortal danger. Since then Adam had gone out of his way to prove that he meant what he'd said. Her past didn't matter. Their present did.

He looked up from his reports and smiled at her. "Hi, hon. Good day at the library?"

"Terrific day at the library." Her enthusiasm made her bubbly and she practically danced across the room. "I keep finding out such odd little facts about life in the sixteenth century. It's all perfectly useless information, but it's fun."

"Anything more on the Sleafords?"

"Well, no. That's frustrating, I'll admit." She chuckled as she sat carefully on the lumpy piece of furniture Adam had designated as a client's chair. He rarely needed to offer it to a visitor. He went out to meet with people who hired him. "I can find out that in 1686 Leeds had stabling for 454 horses and guest beds for 294, but I can't discover any reference to Morwell Hall."

"Sixteen eighty-six? That's too late anyway. More than a hundred years after the period you're interested in."

"Mmmm. I did find out that the population of the parish of Leeds in the sixteenth century was about three thousand souls. In 1982, which was the last year we could find records for in the college library, it hit 716,100."

"Grown a bit, you say." His overt display of interest was beginning to show unmistakable signs of strain. Lauren knew that deep down Adam couldn't have cared less about English history.

"That fact adds strength to the theory that Morwell Hall was absorbed into the metropolis," she informed him loftily. "I just can't prove it yet."

Neither could she prove that the fatal quarrel between Will Malte and his wife had ever taken place, but she had come across a definition of one of the unfamiliar epithets Malte had hurled at her. He'd accused her of being a Winchester goose. Lauren's research had just revealed that in the sixteenth century one of the most notorious areas for brothels, called stews in the popular parlance, was Southwark, which was under the jurisdiction of the Bishop of Winchester. His "geese" were the local prostitutes.

Adam scribbled a note to himself in the margin of one of the already messy, typed pages littering his desk and asked, with halfhearted interest, "How about your other research? What are you and Sandra uncovering about reincarnation?"

Lauren hesitated over that answer. She didn't often try to manipulate Adam, but today she had little choice in the matter. If she wanted him to go with her tomorrow night, she had to make him see a visit to a conscious channel as the lesser of two evils.

"Sandra came across one possibility we hadn't thought of before. She thinks I may be a wishy-washy sort of walk-in. The term refers to what happens when a person is so troubled by his own life that he wants no more to do with it. At that point, if both parties agree, another spiritual entity simply takes over. Walks in. The person wakes up feeling very odd. He's stuck with all the same karma to live out, but he also has a whole new set of attitudes with which to do it."

His pencil snapped in his fingers as Adam looked up sharply. "Are you trying to tell me that now Sandra thinks you're possessed?"

"Not quite." She had to smile at his consternation. This might work, after all. "You, ah, aren't buying that explanation, I take it?" His tolerance, as she'd suspected, had limits.

"Not in a million years." Disgusted with himself and, no doubt, with the farfetched scenario she'd just suggested, he tossed the two pieces of number-two pencil into the trash and reached into his top desk drawer for a replacement.

"Good. I didn't like it, either." She smiled brightly at him.

"I don't suppose that means you're willing to give up all of this cockamamie past-life business?"

"Not quite. You don't have any plans for tomorrow evening, do you?"

His eyes narrowed suspiciously. "Why?"

"We have an invitation for drinks at Mary Lee Marley's house. She's married to one of Karen Doucette's cousins."

"And?" He was toying with the second pencil in a way that made Lauren fear for its safety, but she soldiered on.

"Mary Lee Marley is reputed to have some rather . . . extraordinary abilities."

"Yeah?" He tossed the pencil aside before it could share the fate of its fellow. "Tell me, what does Karen think of these . . . abilities?"

"Karen thinks Mary Lee is weird, of course." Lauren leaned forward eagerly, her smile quite genuine now. "I really have to hand it to Sandra. She convinced Karen to vouch for me without spilling a single bean. Karen probably thinks we've got a few marital problems, but—"

"Vouch for *you*? Shouldn't that be the other way around? How do you know this Marley woman isn't some crackpot trying to make a fast buck with phony seances?"

"For one thing she doesn't charge, and for another it's a cocktail party we've been invited to, an informal opportunity to meet with her and let her decide if she wants to work with me or not."

Skepticism radiated from him as he leaned back in his chair. She could almost see him turning the idea over in his head, balancing his distrust of something that smacked of the occult against his desire to do anything that would help ease Lauren's mind. Compared to her description of walk-ins, this shouldn't sound too bad.

"I don't know, Lauren. Do you really think this woman can explain your dreams?"

"I can only hope so. At first I felt certain reincarnation wasn't the answer. Now I'm not sure of anything anymore. But I do know that, in a way, it would be a relief to discover that I've lived a past life as Jane Malte. Then I could forget about figuring out what the dreams mean and get on with my life. There would be . . . closure."

"There can't be complete closure until we know the details of your early life in this century," he reminded her. "You need answers to those questions, too. We both do."

"Not as much as I need to know the truth about Jane Malte. Will you go with me, Adam? I'm not sure why, but I think it's important that you meet Mary Lee Marley."

His bleak expression told her he was resigned to his fate. "I'll go," Adam promised, "but don't expect me to enjoy the experience."

"All I ask is that you try to keep an open mind." She hopped up and circled the desk to kiss him goodbye. She was already thinking that she'd go straight home now that her mission had been accomplished, but as she playfully tweaked one end of Adam's soft, thick mustache she happened to glance down at the papers scattered across his desk. A drawing in the margin of one of them seemed to leap off the page at her, capturing all her attention.

"That's me!"

He picked up the sheet of paper in question and held it so that they could both study the small caricature. "I've been doodling pictures of you quite a lot lately. I guess you've been on my mind."

"But, Adam, you've drawn me standing the exact same way I'm posed in Ned Teerlinck's portrait. Did you do that on purpose?"

"Don't be ridiculous. I sketched this one before I ever saw that reproduction in the catalog."

"Really?"

"Really. Earlier that morning, in fact, when I was worrying about how things were going between you and Beaumont."

She didn't doubt him, but the news filled her with a vague sense of unease.

"Go on home," Adam told her gruffly. "Get out of here so I can get some work done. I'll see you at the house in a couple of hours."

Lauren went, but the pencil sketch stayed in her mind. When she arrived back home she immediately dug out the catalog and stared at the maid's figure until her eyes blurred with the effort. She wasn't at all sure they should brush the coincidence aside. If Adam hadn't copied the portrait, then was this proof of what Sandra had suggested in New York? Was Jane's pose one characteristic of Lauren? If it was, did that support the theory that she and Jane were the same person? Was she Jane, reincarnated as Lauren?

Frowning, Lauren finally put the catalog aside and headed for her workshop to execute a long-neglected needlepoint commission. This past-life business seemed to get more complicated with each passing day.

Would a visit to Mary Lee Marley clarify things . . . or just create more confusion?

* * *

Nothing was as he'd expected. If he hadn't known the purpose of this evening's gathering, and if there had been alcohol in the fruit punch, he might have believed he *was* at an ordinary cocktail party. It felt a lot like the last one he'd been to, in fact. He'd felt out of place then, too.

That reception had been given by the president of the University of Maine at Lumberton, and Adam had been one of five guests of honor, much to the chagrin of the other four. The event had been planned to honor faculty members with new publications. Adam's textbook, *Evaluating Policy and Procedures For the Small Jail,* had been displayed next to scholarly tomes by three Ph.D.'s and the newest volume of poetry by the college's artist in residence.

"Interesting decor," Lauren whispered.

He answered with a noncommittal grunt. Interesting wasn't the word for it. Stark, maybe. Futuristic? Damned uncomfortable to live with, of that he was certain.

The large living room contained a minimum of furniture, every sharp-angled stick of it either black or white or, in the case of tables, glass. The walls were white, too, and bare, except for the one with the fireplace. A fire blazed merrily in the hearth and Adam and Lauren stood a few feet away, enjoying the warmth and the scent of applewood. Above the mantle, incongruous and yet somehow fitting, a large watercolor of a sand castle had been hung.

Mary Lee Marley herself circulated among her

invited guests, dispensing charm and "readings." She was a mouse of a woman, so incredibly ordinary that in other circumstances she'd have passed unnoticed. Even now she did not stand out. She wore a black pants suit of some dressy material, the lace blouse and the jacket cut long and loose to conceal the normal bulges of middle age. Her only jewelry was a single small crystal on a chain.

Adam's eyes narrowed as she approached them, the skeptical cop in him still looking for an angle. He'd checked her out. Lauren's information had been accurate. She never took money from those who sought her advice. She didn't advertise her services, either, or reap any benefits from dispensing them—at least none that anyone in local law enforcement knew about. Dan had suggested that Adam accept that Mary Lee Marley might just be sharing her much vaunted talent out of the goodness of her heart.

Adam was having trouble with that, just as he was finding it difficult to believe she possessed any kind of special perception. Any psychic link to the distant past, especially other people's pasts, had to be a hoax.

Mary Lee stopped just before she reached Lauren to gaze at the painted sand castle Lauren was still studying. "It's a lovely thing, isn't it?" she murmured.

"Yes, it is," Lauren agreed politely. "I wouldn't mind having a slightly smaller version of that subject in my living room."

"The artist lives only a short distance from here, in Oakland. I'd be happy to give you her name and address."

"Do you get a kickback if we buy something from her?" Adam asked.

"Adam!"

"Your husband is a suspicious man, Lauren Ryder."

"Did you see that in your crystal ball?"

Lauren poked him in the ribs, coloring with profound embarrassment that he'd level such sarcastic jibes at their hostess. "Adam, you promised. Remember—you were going to keep an open mind?"

"Sorry."

For her sake he silently vowed to stop sniping at Mary Lee Marley, but he held on to what he considered a healthy skepticism. He told himself that he had to. Lauren was credulous enough for them both.

"His comments cannot hurt my feelings," Mary Lee assured Lauren. "I am accustomed to disbelief. To answer your question, Mr. Ryder, I get nothing but my own satisfaction from promoting local talent. I also tell people they should see plays at the Theater at Monmouth, during their season every summer, and in the past I even recommended your wife's work to a client who was interested in tapestry designs."

Before Adam could bring himself to apologize a second time, Mary Lee Marley lost all interest in him. She turned the full force of her awareness on Lauren. One hand fluttered a moment, then came to rest on Lauren's forearm. Other than that Mary Lee did not make any physical contact. Her eyes drifted closed and immediately snapped open again. She smiled.

"What is it?" Lauren asked. "Do you sense something about me?"

"You've an old soul. Very old. The most recent thing I can see—Heavens! Rome, and not even a century into the A.D.'s. You were a laundress." Her nose wrinkled. "Dreadful job in those days. They bleached with urine, you know. Kept it in great huge vats."

Adam started to interrupt, but Lauren spoke first. "You may be right." A puzzled frown came over her face, and her voice dropped lower. "I remember that we removed spots and stains by dampening them and rubbing them with a ball made of bull's gall, white of egg, burnt alum, salt, orris root, and soap."

"How interesting," Mary Lee murmured. "Do go on."

A faraway look on her face, Lauren obeyed. "You're wrong, though. I wasn't a laundress. I didn't have much to do with laundering at all, but I can tell you that washing wasn't done very often."

"You aren't speaking of Rome, are you?"

Lauren's voice was as dreamy as her expression. "Of course not. This was at Morwell Hall and now I do remember there was one discolored sheet we were bidden to make clean again. It was soaked from Saturday through Monday in a thick green mixture of soft water and sheep's dung."

Adam grimaced and struggled to keep silent. A glance at Mary Lee Marley's face told him she was utterly fascinated by the turn the conversation had taken.

"Sheep's dung!" she exclaimed, in raptures at the idea. "Just think of that."

"Only summer dung will do," Lauren said. Her eyes were unfocused. "Monday through Wednesday the sheet must be dipped repeatedly into the pond. On Wednesday it is beaten out and left to soak until Thursday afternoon, and then it is allowed to dry."

"Summer dung," Mary Lee repeated with a little trill of pleasure. "Do go on."

Lauren freed herself from Mary Lee's grip and rubbed her arms with her hands as if she felt a chill. "On Friday the dry sheet is put into a tub and a buck sheet is spread over it. A thin paste of dog's mercury, mallow, and wormwood is spread over the buck sheet and then strong, boiling lye is poured over all."

"And that did it?" In spite of himself, Adam was curious. "That finally made the sheet white?"

"Not yet."

A wan smile surfaced. Adam thought the blue of his wife's eyes seemed closer to that of flowers painted on a glazed plate than to living forget-me-nots but her next words reassured him that she still knew who and where she was.

"I'm certainly glad we have a washer and dryer and good old Clorox. The next step was to cover the whole mess and let it stand overnight. You can imagine the smell. Then the sheet was spread out on the grass and watered all the next morning, and then the business with the buck sheet was repeated all over again. And again the next day. Then the sheet was dropped into straight lye and soaked until Monday morning, after which it was laid out and watered daily until the head laundress deemed it white enough."

"No wonder they didn't do laundry very often."

The voice was unfamiliar to Adam, and for the first time since Lauren had begun to speak he realized that everyone else at Mary Lee's party had been listening to her, too. Now they had questions and Lauren, remarkably, seemed to know the answers. When she began to discuss the best way to turn dog's mercury into a bright yellow dye, Adam knew he was in grave danger of breaking his promise. He moved away from the group before he yielded to the impulse to pick Lauren up and carry her off, to rescue her from whatever strange things were happening to her here.

Something wasn't right, but he couldn't quite put his finger on what was wrong. He didn't trust Mary Lee Marley. He knew that. Lauren's absolute assurance as she chatted casually about the domestic duties of Tudor laundresses made him uneasy, too. Had she read about the bull's gall and summer dung, or dreamed those details?

Restless and increasingly disturbed by what was going on in Mary Lee Marley's living room, Adam wandered out of doors. He stood, lost in contemplation, in the middle of an herb garden behind the Marley house. There were no answers in the delicate fragrances that wafted up to him from the cold earth, nor in the late October sky above. That only reminded him that Halloween was almost upon them.

There were no witches or ghosts.

There were no former lives to remember, either.

Whatever was causing Lauren to dream of the past, it had nothing to do with reincarnation.

You died and went to heaven, damn it. Maybe you got hell, instead, but you didn't come back as a dog, or as another person. This nonsense had gone far enough, he decided. It was time to get Lauren and leave.

"I'm uncertain that hypnosis would help you," Mary Lee Marley was saying to Lauren as Adam came back into the too white living room. "I'd be willing to give it a try, of course. I'm always happy to oblige, and I have had some success in the past. If I tape the session you can listen to it for yourself afterward, but I can't guarantee there will be any results. Frankly, you puzzle me. I get no sense of a former life in the sixteenth century from you at all. Just that Roman one."

"That's because she didn't have a former life," Adam interrupted, "but I do agree with you that hypnosis would be a waste of time." He took Lauren firmly by the arm. "Ready to leave, sweetheart?"

Mary Lee Marley held out her hand, forcing him to shake it with his free one in farewell. Her eyes assessed him in that single, brief moment of linkage, full of curiosity and strangely free of resentment. "Odd," she murmured. "I'd have thought you'd be more in tune with your wife."

"And why is that?"

Irritation that this woman would presume to give him advice made Adam's voice harsher than usual. He was determined to hang on to his temper, but it was taking almost superhuman effort.

His hostess smiled enigmatically. "Because it took you so long to find her, of course."

"You were very rude to Mrs. Marley," Lauren said as they walked into their own house a short time later.

"Mrs. Marley is lucky I didn't denounce her in front of all her guests."

"What do you mean?"

"I mean that all that Roman laundress business was a con job."

"And my laundress business? Where did that come from?"

"Lauren—"

"Oh! Never mind! There *is* no explanation. That's just the problem."

"Does that mean you've rejected reincarnation as the answer?"

"I was afraid all along that it wouldn't be that simple. I'd hoped. It's the lack of any explanation of what's happening to me, reasonable or otherwise, that's so hard to endure."

"Well that's something," Adam said.

His relief that she hadn't been taken in by Mary Lee Marley was so obvious, she had to smile. Her own opinion was that the woman was perfectly sincere, but she wasn't going to argue with Adam about the matter. It simply wasn't that important.

"Now what?" he asked as he opened the refrigerator and pulled out a can of beer. He leaned against the kitchen counter, popped the top, and took a long swallow.

"I'm not sure." She'd gotten so she could almost regard the glimpses into the sixteenth century as a normal part of her daily routine, so regularly did they come to her. She'd ruled out psychological symbolism as the reason behind the dreams. Now she had to abandon all hope that a past life as Jane Malte could account for them. "I suppose I'll continue the historical research."

She also intended to look seriously into the possibility that being hypnotized might be useful. Even the police occasionally used that technique to jog the memories of witnesses. Lauren started to broach the subject with Adam, but before she could get a word out the phone rang.

Adam answered it, and as soon as Lauren heard him say Dave's name she left the room. Dave. Our man in Darien. She had no desire to hear any more unpleasant details from the lost years and only mild curiosity as to whether he'd learned any more about the minor mystery he'd stumbled on just before his last report.

It seemed that Dave was not the first person to ask questions about Lauren Kendall. Some years earlier, maybe five or six, two middle-aged women had been looking for her in Darien. One of them, Dave had reported, might have been English.

Adam found her in his upstairs office a short time later. "My P.I. has come up with a new wrinkle."

"Something about those two women?"

"No such luck. Tell me again what Rob told you about your rift with your father."

Lauren kicked off her shoes. There was a comfortable armchair tucked into one corner of the room and she sank into it and curled both feet up beneath her. "There wasn't much to tell. Apparently he washed his hands of me when I was about sixteen, at the same time I was shipped off to finishing school in England."

"It looks as if your father might have died shortly *after* you lost your memory."

"What difference does it make when he died? He's dead now, just as my mother is. Neither one can give us any answers."

"But your stepmother is alive and well and still living in Darien, Connecticut."

"I never had a stepmother."

"How can you be so sure?"

"All right, Rob never told me that I'd told him that I had a stepmother. Satisfied? Surely it's something I'd have mentioned." Her lips twitched as a question slipped out. "Is she a wicked stepmother?"

"Looks that way."

Abruptly sobering, Lauren went very still. "Exactly what did Dave find out?"

Adam turned the swivel chair in front of his computer work station around and sank into it, stretching his legs out toward her. He contemplated the toes of his black dress shoes, then shifted his gaze to encompass her pale face. "We may be in for some legal problems. It seems my investigation has opened up a real can of worms."

"Go on."

"Dave finally located your father's obituary in the newspaper and discovered that there were two relatives listed, not one. You were named, identified as currently abroad as part of a student-exchange program. The other survivor was the dead man's widow, one Fiona Kendall. It took Dave a couple of days to track her down. She'd remarried. Twice. At first she wasn't very cooperative. Then Dave showed her a photo of you. Suddenly she was extremely interested in everything about you, including your trust fund."

"What does the trust fund have to do with her? That money came from my mother, not my father."

"Yes, but apparently your father stood to inherit if you predeceased him."

Bewildered, Lauren blurted, "But, obviously, I didn't."

"That's not what your stepmother is claiming." Adam's words brought an icy chill into the cozy little upstairs room. "Dave says she waved that photo of you in his face and declared that you couldn't have changed *that* much. She says you're an impostor."

"Ryder, Lauren," Lauren told the woman seated at the long table adjacent to the curtained voting booths. She watched as her name was checked off on the computer printout and accepted three paper ballots from the Lumberton warden seated at the far end of the same table.

"My sister gave me one of your scarves for my birthday," the checker said, recognizing Lauren's name. "It's a beautiful thing."

"Thank you."

Lauren thought fleetingly of her last attempt at a new design. Adam had been right. Deer guts trailing down a scarf would not have appealed to her customers, not even during hunting season. She shut herself into one of the dozens of cubicles at the polling place and regarded the referendum issues with dismay. There were far too many, and not one of them was couched in understandable language.

By the time she'd finished voting, stopped at the grocery store, and driven home, Lauren's active imagination had eliminated the dead deer from the design but kept the hunters' picnic that had also been depicted in the tapestry in the great hall of the

Sleafords' Yorkshire manor. She'd mentally updated the costumes, adding blaze orange vests and ballcaps. She was still smiling at the image as she turned off the two-lane highway into their long, curving drive.

Sugar maples bordered the first stretch, leafless now, and the mountain ash around the next bend had lost all their bright berries. Three apple trees in a row marked the last turn, and two weeping willows flanked the opening into a blacktopped dooryard. Everything was just as it had been when she'd left, except for the silver BMW parked in front of the house.

Definitely not a hunter.

Lauren got out of her own rather pedestrian vehicle, leaving the groceries where they were. It was cold enough that she didn't worry about the frozen food melting. There had been frost on the ground for four mornings running, and snow was in the forecast for the weekend.

A woman emerged from the other car, a bosomy, fur-wrapped, black-haired woman whose age was somewhere between fifty and seventy. Lauren experienced no sense of recognition, had no feeling that she'd ever laid eyes on the woman before, and yet she had no difficulty guessing her identity.

"Mrs. Innes, I presume?" Adam had told her that Innes was the name of husband number three.

With one disdainful glance the woman surveyed and dismissed Lauren. "That is correct. I was here once before. You've made improvements in the place."

"Thank you."

"It was the least you could do." The accent was

Connecticut Gold Coast and went well with the hoity-toity demeanor.

With scathing politeness, Lauren asked, "Did I address you as Mama when my father was your husband?"

"So, you're going to insist you're Lauren Kendall? It won't work. Lauren had a crooked tooth, right in front."

"These are caps," Lauren informed her. "Nice job, isn't it?" She'd had all her teeth capped in Boston. Rob had insisted, and she'd never thought to question why—until now.

Since Dave's phone call five days earlier there had been several developments. Mrs. Innes seemed bent on making trouble. Adam theorized it was in the hope of getting a cut of Lauren's trust fund in an out-of-court settlement. Dave had done some checking and discovered that Fiona Innes apparently needed money, a lot of it, soon, in order to sustain her opulent life-style. Whether she genuinely thought Lauren was an impostor or not was a moot point. She had taken a look at the photo of Lauren and remembered how difficult it had been to contact her stepdaughter at the time of Hugh Kendall's death. Dave had let slip that Lauren had suffered memory loss. The next thing anyone knew, Mrs. Innes was accusing Lauren of fraud. If she could convince a district attorney they had a case, formal charges might soon be filed.

"You'd do well to take me seriously, Mrs. Ryder. In seventeen years you've taken a great deal of money from Lauren Kendall's trust fund, and you've had the use of this house as well." She cast a pointed glance that way, but Lauren decided she'd rather risk frostbite than invite this vulture into her home.

"And what, exactly, makes you think I don't have every right to both?"

"The cat," Mrs. Innes said succinctly, a Cheshire grin of her own momentarily in evidence. "The photograph I was shown pictured you holding a large, hairy cat. You, my dear, are obviously not Lauren Kendall. My stepdaughter was allergic to cats."

"Do you have proof of that alleged allergy? Childhood medical records?"

Just that morning Adam had asked about medical and dental records. She hadn't been able to tell him much, and the first time she could remember having had her blood typed was when they were applying for their marriage license.

Lauren held her breath, but if Mrs. Innes could produce anything to back up her claim she wasn't prepared to do so on the spot. Adam had warned she'd rely on threats and intimidation, and it looked as if he'd been right.

Lauren regarded her opponent steadily, her face grim. "I must confess I'm curious," she finally admitted. "Let's say, for the sake of argument, that I am an impostor. How would that help you? The real Lauren would be the only beneficiary."

"I should think that would be obvious," she said, her voice as cold as she, apparently, was becoming. She tugged her coat closer about her and favored Lauren with an icy stare. "It's unlikely she's still alive. How else would you have gotten away with this for so long? First I'll prove you aren't Lauren

Kendall. Then I'll have the real Lauren declared dead."

"And if you claim she died before her father did, then he'd have inherited the trust fund and this house and you'd have subsequently inherited both from him. I have to admire your gall, Mrs. Innes."

"Justice will prevail," the odious woman said in a smug voice. She waved a hand holding a white fur muff toward the acres surrounding the house. "All this will soon be mine. It should bring a good price, even in this depressed economy. Perhaps you'd like to buy it back yourself . . . if you aren't in jail."

"If you keep waving that muff around that way you may not live to enjoy your victory."

"Threats, Mrs. Ryder?" She looked hopeful, sensing weakness.

"Common sense. You're in the middle of the woods and it happens to be hunting season. Perhaps you should consider leaving before someone mistakes that flash of white for the back end of a deer."

Mrs. Innes looked as if she'd like to argue but thought better of it. She settled for muttering "You haven't heard the last of me," as she climbed back into the car.

Lauren watched her drive off, then unloaded and put away her groceries. She did not want to think about Mrs. Innes and her threats, let alone the possibility that the woman might be telling the truth.

Hassle wandered into the kitchen, demanding dinner.

"Allergic to cats," Lauren grumbled. "And people think I have an overactive imagination!"

She opened a can of cat food, wrinkling her nose at the pungent smell. The worse the odor, the better Hassle seemed to like the flavor. Then she bent to put the bowl on the Garfield placemat. She was unprepared to see a tear land in the middle of the chunks of chicken and egg. Angrily Lauren swiped at her damp cheeks with the backs of her hands. Mrs. Innes's lies weren't worth crying over.

"I'd just as soon not be Lauren Kendall," she whispered defiantly. She didn't care for any of the things they'd learned about her past, and if Hugh Kendall's choice of a second wife was any indication, he hadn't been any prize, either.

She sat down at the dinette table and tried to think logically about the situation. Would it really be so bad if she wasn't Lauren Kendall? With a sinking sensation she realized that it might well be worse than anything she'd thus far imagined.

If she wasn't Lauren, then they'd have to give up this house, and they'd have to pay back all the money she'd taken out of the trust fund over the years. She and Adam did well enough with their two businesses, but they were hardly wealthy. Making reparations on that scale would be far beyond anything they could afford.

"Can't get blood from a stone," Lauren muttered.

Stricken, she looked down at her hands, half expecting to find them spattered with red. She'd dreamed she'd killed her husband, she reminded herself. Not a woman. A man.

There couldn't be any connection, and yet two

terrible, unanswerable questions now tormented her, both born of Mrs. Innes's insistence that her stepdaughter must be dead.

If she wasn't Lauren, who was she?

And what had happened to the real Lauren?

13

"*I don't like* it, Dan. Not one bit."

He felt as if he'd been going around in circles for months, though in fact it had been barely a week since this latest development, only seven days since he'd begun to contemplate the horrible possibility that his wife was an imposter, or worse.

"Keep digging," his brother advised. "We'll come up with something eventually."

Adam's bleak expression didn't change. "Such as?"

To their utter frustration, every lead they'd followed had been a dead end. While Mrs. Innes had not been able to produce fingerprints or medical or dental records to prove Lauren was an impostor, neither had Adam been able to establish that she was unquestionably Lauren Kendall.

Virtually no early photographs existed. Those which had turned up were inconclusive. Hair and eye color were right. Height was irrelevant in a growing girl. Facial features were distorted by a variety of scowls, smirks, and hairstyles. The young Lauren had not liked having her picture taken and apparently no one had cared enough about her to insist she do it often. She'd never stayed at any one school long enough to make close friends who would have wanted snapshots. Her parents' total lack of interest in their daughter meant there had been none of the usual family portraits, either.

"What about checking her blood type against those of the parents?" Dan suggested. "Don't they advise that in paternity cases?"

"Already done, but the results were inconclusive. She could have been their kid, but that doesn't prove she is."

"This is nothing more than a nuisance suit," Dan said. "Hang tough and the old battle-ax will give it up."

"Meanwhile, Lauren goes through hell."

They had managed to get a few answers from Mrs. Innes. She claimed she didn't know why Lauren had left Todham Academy, but did reveal that she'd disappeared for several weeks afterward. Hugh and Fiona Kendall hadn't started looking for her right away. They'd been in Las Vegas on an extended honeymoon at the time and couldn't be bothered.

Fiona had met Lauren for the first time just after that episode. They'd spent one month together in the house in Darien, avoiding each other for the most part. On that brief acquaintance, some twenty years ago, Fiona based her certainty that Lauren wasn't Lauren. Right afterward, Lauren had been shipped off to England and more or less disowned by Hugh. He'd agreed to pay her bills until the day she turned eighteen. He'd died a week after that birthday.

Fiona's story was that she'd never talked directly to Lauren after Hugh Kendall's death. She'd left a message with some boy named Rob who'd promised to tell Lauren her "old man had croaked" and had added that he "didn't figure she'd care."

"What a mess," Dan said. "What a mess. You'd think there'd be something someone could do to bring her memory back."

"Apparently there isn't. The only thing everyone agrees on is that it must have been some kind of trauma that made her forget everything." Adam hesitated, then blurted out what had been on his mind for days. "Killing another person could sure do that!"

"Come on, Adam. You can't believe she's a murderer. Not Lauren."

"Are you sure you're Lumberton's chief of police? Anybody can kill, given the right set of circumstances. Have you forgotten why I got out of police work?"

"That was an accident."

"I think we have to consider the possibility that my Lauren isn't Lauren Kendall at all," Adam said. He didn't look at his brother, but continued to stand at the window, staring out at the parking lot. "Let's be generous and assume that she genuinely has amnesia but accept that she may still be a ringer."

"Could be. Could be. Go on."

"From what Lauren's told me of this Rob Seton,

his primary concern was getting access to that trust fund. She was barely eighteen when she lost her memory, and eighteen was the age at which she could start drawing on the interest without interference from a trustee."

"Wait a minute. If your wife isn't Lauren Kendall, she could be any age."

"That's irrelevant. Lauren Kendall, if she lived that long, would have just turned eighteen when her father died. That's the important part of this, that and the fact that she had some connection with Seton."

"Okay. Then what? Seton kills her? That doesn't make sense. Better to keep her alive and get his hands on the money."

"Maybe she wasn't willing to cooperate. Hell, Dan, I don't know. I'm speculating here."

"Go on."

"Seton kills the real Lauren, possibly with help from his girlfriend, *my* Lauren, in order to take her identity and her inheritance. She certainly left all her possessions behind, including her passport."

"Which argues that no switch took place at all."

"Or that Lauren Kendall is dead."

"This all happened in England, right?"

Adam nodded. "Somewhere in the city of Leeds."

"So, how about we see what I can get from the local authorities?"

Adam wondered why he hadn't thought of that himself. "I'd appreciate it, but how are you going to explain your interest? This isn't exactly official police business."

"I'm making it official. You're one of my part-time

officers, aren't you? On the other hand . . ." Dan's voice trailed off suggestively.

"What?"

"I was just thinking, there's really no point in speculating from thousands of miles away."

"So?"

"So, how about you go there in person and see what you can find out? If the real Lauren Kendall was murdered, there has to be a body. Besides, going back to the scene of the crime might jog Lauren's memory."

Adam stared at him. His suggestion made sense, and yet with it came yet another small problem. "Damn."

"What?"

"Passports."

"No big deal. No big deal. Takes about two weeks. You can get an application at one of the bigger post offices. Lumberton's too small. Then you have pictures taken. Send them in with your fee and proof of—"

"Identity," Adam finished for him.

"Until proven otherwise, she's Lauren Kendall. If she's still got her old passport, she can send that in instead of a birth certificate. Hell, if I understand the law right, she could just send in an old driver's license with a picture on it."

"I'm familiar with the law!" Adam didn't mean to snap at his brother, but his temper was suddenly uncertain. All she needed, in fact, was a letter from someone claiming they'd known her for two years or more.

It was the principle of the thing that upset him. If they applied for a passport knowing she might not be who she said she was, they would be breaking the law. It was a little law, an unimportant law, even a stupid law, considering how easy the government made it for people to get around it, but it was still a law. Once again Adam Ryder, who had always been straight-laced and proud of it, was going to betray the philosophy he'd lived by all his life.

"Come on, Adam. Go home," Dan advised. "Go home and talk to Lauren. See what she thinks about making a trip to England."

"Home? You mean that house that may not even belong to us?"

A commotion in the outer office distracted both men before Dan could answer. "Damn it. Now what?" Leaving Adam at the window, Dan left the room, only to return a moment later with a stricken expression on his face.

"What's happened?"

"I don't believe this. I really don't believe this. You know how you were saying only a few minutes ago that anyone could commit murder given the right circumstances?"

Adam waited.

"Karen Doucette has just turned herself in. She says she shot Clubber with his own gun."

"What's the latest on Clubber?" Lauren asked as Adam hung up after a long telephone conversation with Dan. It was two days after the incident but she was still having difficulty believing what had happened.

"He's sticking to the story that he accidentally shot

himself." Adam joined her at the table and picked up one of the ham-and-cheese sandwiches she'd prepared for their lunch. "Karen's been released."

The bullet had passed through Clubber's upper thigh, but as soon as he heard Karen was confessing to attempted murder he apparently convinced himself that his wife had shot him because she couldn't stand losing him to another woman. Now he wanted her back, and was willing to lie to get her.

"Dan also had news on your case."

Lauren stiffened. For a moment it seemed to her that Adam must be drawing parallels between their situation and that of Clubber and Karen, but she could find no censure in his steady gaze. His voice, too, was matter-of-fact, though what he was saying brought her no comfort.

"He got a reply to the fax he sent to England. The police department there was very cooperative. They didn't give a lot of details, naturally, but they did tell Dan that Miss Cogswell's School for Girls closed down in 1978 and that Miss Cogswell herself died in 1980. I imagine the teachers are pretty scattered by now, but we may be able to track one of them down. Chances are it was someone from there who was looking for you back in '85 or '86."

"I'd certainly like to find someone who remembers me from before I lost my memory. It will drive me crazy if I never find out who I am."

"The rest of the report was negative, too. There is no record of any unidentified female turning up dead seventeen years or so ago. Neither are there any reports of a missing teenage girl at around that time. The only thing that seems to connect to you at all is the drug-overdose death of a young man."

"American?"

"No, a local lad. Jonathan Harwood. He was a student at the University of Leeds and apparently hung out with Rob Seton's crowd." Adam chewed slowly on his sandwich and just as carefully chewed over these new facts in his mind.

Lauren tried to finish her lunch, but the whole-wheat bread now tasted like cardboard. Jonathan Harwood. Should that name sound familiar to her? "Did the authorities in Leeds know any more about Rob?"

"Nothing new." He went on eating, but Lauren gave up.

Adam had already found out that Rob Seton had been at the University of Leeds on a junior-year abroad program, just as she'd suspected. Less expected was the information that prior to his trip to England he'd gotten good grades at a small American college. He'd apparently planned to go back to school in the U.S. for his senior year. Instead, he disappeared into the counterculture.

"Adam? An unpleasant possibility occurs to me. If Rob was clean before he went abroad, is it possible that Lauren Kendall might have introduced him to drugs, rather than the other way around?"

He wouldn't meet her eyes. "It's possible but there's certainly no proof of that."

"Did this Jonathan Harwood know me, I wonder?"

"Your name didn't turn up, and according to the files of the West Yorkshire Police, Seton was only questioned because Harwood's mother insisted that 'those Americans' were to blame for his death." Adam seemed to lose his appetite at last, holding the last bite of his sandwich suspended halfway to his mouth. "You said Seton seemed to be keeping a low profile while the two of you were in Leeds. Maybe that's why."

"If the local cops were watching him why didn't he just get out of town?"

"No money?" With a disgusted gesture, Adam tossed the food back onto his plate and shoved it away from him. "Who knows? Maybe we'll be able to find out when we get over there."

At first Lauren was certain she'd misunderstood him. "What did you say?"

"We're going to Leeds." He shoved his chair away from the table and stood, grabbing his plate to take with him to the kitchen.

"Don't be ridiculous. We can't afford a trip like that."

"We can't afford not to go."

"You have too many commitments here." She followed him, taking her own plate. She dumped all their leftovers into the garbage with abrupt, somewhat clumsy movements. The empty plates clattered back down onto the countertop as Adam ignored her reaction and began to outline his plans.

"I can get someone to cover my class for me, and I had a cancellation on a consulting job. I've called a travel agent. She's going to book seats for us on the first available flight to London."

"I can't do it, Adam. Just the thought of that many hours in an airplane makes me nauseous."

"Are you telling me that you'd rather never know the truth than make one overseas flight?"

"It's not *one* flight. It's a flight to Boston, and then London, and then Leeds. And as many takeoffs and landings coming back. If they let me come back. If I'm not rotting in some British jail, charged with murder." In growing panic, she grasped at straws. "I can't go, anyway. How could I get a passport? I'm not at all sure who I am."

"How do you get one? You lie."

The moment Adam snapped at her, Lauren realized that the straw she'd grasped at so desperately was also, from Adam's point of view, the last straw.

"Oh, Adam." She reached for him, but he backed away.

"No. Not this time. That way's too easy, and too hard to bear."

She didn't understand what he meant, but there was no mistaking the implacable look on his face.

"I need to get away from you, go someplace where you don't dominate my every thought. I've got to think this through without being tempted to take you to bed and forget my doubts."

Lauren stared at him in utter disbelief. Adam looked stricken himself as he grabbed a ski jacket from the closet. Without another word to her, he fled. A moment later she heard the car start, then the sound of her husband driving away.

Adam had left her.

He'll be back, she told herself. He'd drive around a bit, and then he'd return. They'd both be calm, and they'd talk this through. He hadn't gone because he didn't love her, she reasoned. If anything, he'd left because he loved her too much.

She knew now that what she'd seen in his eyes so often when he looked at her lately was pain. How much time, she wondered, had he spent thinking about all those terrible things she was supposed to have done, wondering if they could possibly be true?

Several hours later Lauren heard a car door slam and ran out onto the porch, sure it would be Adam returning, but it was Dan Ryder who'd arrived on her doorstep, Dan who cleared his throat, obviously ill at ease, and tried to explain his brother's absence.

"Adam phoned me," he said. "He isn't sure how long he'll be gone. I'm supposed to keep an eye on you for him while he's away."

"Why, Dan? Why did he go?"

Dan looked even more uncomfortable. "I don't know, Lauren. I just don't know." They stared at each other in troubled silence for a long moment. Then Dan cleared his throat once more. "So, is there anything you need?"

"I need Adam."

"Come on, Lauren. He'll be back. I'm sure he will." He'd turned to go, his duty done, then belatedly recalled a second errand. He fished a long white envelope, folded once, out of a pocket. "I almost forgot. Sandra sent this along for you. It came in today's mail."

Lauren took the proffered letter, but without any interest in its contents.

"Come on, Lauren. Look on the bright side. Adam will be back eventually. In the meantime you can keep busy with this. You remember that retired professor you and Sandra met in New York? This is the answer to the letter she wrote him. He's sent you a list of all the research libraries in the Leeds area."

As soon as Dan left Lauren put the letter down and forgot all about it. She couldn't focus on anything but how much she missed Adam. If such a thing had been possible, she'd have brought him back by sheer force of will.

She felt a sudden, nearly overwhelming urge to pack her own bags and run away. Her life was falling apart around her, and the possibility of Adam's desertion devastated her. What was the point of staying here if she didn't have Adam?

Without Adam, nothing had any meaning. He had to come back. He had to, in spite of everything that was happening, everything that was going wrong in their lives.

If she was not Lauren Kendall, they were going to lose this house, her refuge for so many years. They were going to have to pay back hundreds of thousands of dollars to Lauren Kendall's trust fund, which would bankrupt them. Then she might well be going to jail for fraud if they couldn't prove murder.

Adam kept saying that there was no evidence that she wasn't Lauren, but the more she thought about it, the more certain she became that she was not. There was the matter of the cat, Pounce, for one thing. If Lauren Kendall was allergic to cats, she would not have had such a pet as a child.

With an ease that had become natural over the last weeks, her mind provided a picture of girl and cat. The girl was sitting outside on a cold winter's day, wrapped in a cloak of coarse checked wool. Plodan, the material was called. In her lap she held the cat called Pounce, a scrawny, ugly, cross-eyed tiger.

Lauren drew in a shaky breath.

Pounce had been Jane Malte's pet.

Abruptly Lauren knew that she wasn't going to run anywhere. Whatever had happened seventeen years earlier, she had a life here now. She was not going to give it up without a fight.

She was not going to give Adam up at all. He was the most important part of that life. She could lose everything else, even her freedom, but if she still had Adam's love, she could survive.

He would be back, she told herself. And she would be here waiting for him when he returned.

He drove until he was too tired to see the road, then checked into a motel. The next morning he set out again, still driving aimlessly along the rugged Maine coast. He crossed the causeway to an island without knowing exactly where he was, but when he came to the headland he parked the car and got out. In the early November chill the place was deserted. Summer homes were boarded up and empty. Adam had the rock-strewn shore to himself.

He walked with as little direction as he'd driven, but slowly his surroundings began to impinge on his consciousness. He stopped to study the teeming life in a tidal pool, to smell the salty sea air. He sat on the cold, hard surface of a boulder and watched the tide come in.

It was a harsh environment, peopled by hardy settlers, the kind who did not give up no matter how bleak the future appeared to be. How many others, he wondered, had sat in this exact spot and stared out at the broad Atlantic, thinking of the green and pleasant land on the other side?

Something had happened to Lauren in England. That much was a given. The more he thought about it, the more certain he became that by going there they could solve the mystery. The problem lay in the nature of that solution. What would they find, and how would it affect them?

He'd needed to separate himself physically from Lauren in order to be sure he was thinking rationally. Even after five years of marriage she could still weave a sensual spell around him. She wielded a uniquely feminine power she probably didn't even know she possessed, but he knew. He'd known from the first.

It had begun as an overwhelming compulsion to be with her every second he could spare from his fledgling business. Then, from the first time they'd made love, he'd been addicted to her, knowing with an absolute certainty that no other woman would ever satisfy him. He'd become obsessed with the idea of marrying her and had run roughshod over her mild objections. They'd barely met, she argued. He pointed out that he felt as if he'd known her forever.

Now she was his lover, his best friend, the most important person in his life. In a way, she was still his obsession. It was both his privilege and his responsibility to protect her.

She'd made a big deal out of the way that Ned had

offered Jane Malte a potion to ease her out of life, to spare her the pain of burning. She felt sorry for him because he'd been powerless to save the woman he loved.

Adam knew himself to be far from powerless. He could work within the law . . . or around it. There would be no trial for murder, no execution, for *his* woman, even if it did turn out that she'd helped do away with the real Lauren Kendall.

If Lauren was guilty of murder, or if she had been an accessory, before or after the fact, did it make a difference in the way he felt about her? It should have, to a man who preached law and order and devoted his life to writing rules for those who administered correctional facilities.

The thing that had driven him from Lauren's side had not been the suspicion that she was a murderer but the fear that she'd lied to him. She'd been so set against going to England that his earlier doubts had surfaced again. He'd wondered if she was lying about the amnesia.

That was why he left her. It would have been too easy to be convinced of her honesty in her presence, in her bed. He had to go over it all again when he was certain he was thinking clearly. Now that he'd had that opportunity he came to the conclusion that she had never lied to him, that she could not lie to him. She knew no more about her past than he did.

And if she had done murder? Adam had told Dan that anyone could kill, and he had the best of reasons for knowing that was true.

He did not like to think about the night he almost caused a man's death, but it did give him a certain unique perspective on Lauren's situation.

Adam sat on the rock for a long time, staring blindly at the sea, thinking, before he rose and walked back to the place where he had left his car. His mind was clear. No matter what the outcome, no matter how many petty rules they had to break to find the answers, he and Lauren were going to pursue the truth. Together, no matter how horrible the discoveries they made, they would face the future. They would draw strength from each other.

The mouth-watering smell of freshly baked apple loaf met him when he got home. Lauren wasn't far behind.

He'd never doubted that she'd be there waiting, but her bleak, uncertain expression unnerved him. He hadn't meant to hurt her.

Adam didn't give her a chance to speak. Taking her arm, he led her to the sofa and sat, his arm looped loosely over her shoulders. There was no easy way to begin. He opted for bluntness.

"I very nearly killed a man once. I'd like to tell you about it, Lauren."

She tensed, then relaxed against him. "I've heard some of the details, from Sandra. It wasn't your fault."

"Yes, it was. Neither the newspapers nor my brother's wife knew everything. Will you let me tell you what really happened?"

"Of course I will, if it's important to you."

"It is important, to both of us." Again he saw no way to get through the story except to plunge right into it. "The incident happened not too long before we met. I was chief deputy then, but we were always shorthanded. I was frequently called out. I answered a call for backup from one of my deputies. He needed help to break up a brawl at a party. The participants weren't ready to make peace, and when one of them took a swing at me, I swung back. I didn't knock him out, just stunned him. I'd gotten the handcuffs on him and started to maneuver him into the back of the cruiser when he decided to resist arrest."

Sensing his growing tension, Lauren offered silent comfort by resting one hand on his chest. She was listening carefully to every word. Her steady gaze never wavered as she watched his face.

"The guy was wound up. Abusive. Said some choice words about cops in general and me in particular. After fourteen years in the business I should have been immune, but I wasn't. All the years I'd kept my temper in check had built up an anger, one I'd tried to ignore even when it started eating me up inside."

"You were burned out," Lauren said softly. That was about all he'd been willing to say about the incident before, and she'd never pressed him for details.

"That term doesn't begin to describe it. Don't you understand, Lauren? I totally lost it. I wanted to shut that scumbag up and I didn't care how I did it. Oh, I used a standard choke hold, something designed to encourage his cooperation, but I was so enraged that I applied too much pressure. It wasn't until I saw that I had a handcuffed man lying at my feet, not breathing, that I realized how out of control I was."

It had been touch and go for the next hour, Adam remembered. He'd started CPR, brought him back, lost him, brought him back a second time.

"It turned out the prisoner had a heart condition. In the ambulance they finally managed to stabilize him, but the paramedics told me that if I'd taken even a few more seconds to start CPR it would have been a wasted effort."

Lauren didn't say anything, but she didn't move away from him either. She stayed at his side, offering silent support. Did she understand why he was telling her this? Adam wasn't sure, but he knew he had to go on with the story.

"I got out of active police work right after that. I'd come too close to killing a man once to risk it happening again. Cops know going in that they may have to kill or be killed at some point in their careers, but if that man had died, I'd have been guilty of manslaughter."

He stopped speaking and turned Lauren in his arms so that she was facing him. "Civilians don't have the advantage of years of police training to help them deal with a thing like that. A woman like you would have had trouble handling it. It could easily have been enough of a shock to you to cause you to lose all memory of the act."

"All memory of murder. You may as well use the right word, Adam. We're talking about me deliberately killing the real Lauren Kendall."

"Perhaps. I'm not convinced of that, not by a long shot, but I want to be sure you understand that it won't matter to me if you turn out to be responsible for her death."

"I do understand, Adam."

"We need to go to England and find out what really happened. Whatever we discover, we'll deal with it."

"All right, Adam." She attempted a smile. "I guess I can stand anything, even a trans-Atlantic flight, as long as you're at my side."

"I'll keep you safe, Lauren. I swear it. We'll get through this together."

The next two weeks seemed to fly by. They got their passports in record time. They booked seats on a flight to London that left from Portland on the day before Thanksgiving.

In spite of the rush of packing and other preparations, Lauren was determined to find time to try one other method of unlocking the secrets of her past. She told Adam where she was going and why only a few hours before her appointment and refused to let him talk her out of keeping it. Neither would she let him come along.

She was nervous going in, only sleepy when it was over.

She blinked at Mary Lee Marley and asked, "Did it work?"

The other women shrugged. "We got something, all right. I wish I had some idea what it was."

"Play the tape."

It had been a risk, letting herself be hypnotized. Lauren remembered Dr. Beaumont's warnings about weaving fantasies. She'd also considered the possibility that her subconscious memories included a very modern murder.

Mary Lee rewound the tape without comment. After a moment, Lauren heard the other woman's soft, soothing voice, counting backward. Then Mary Lee asked, as Lauren had requested, for the first words she could remember upon waking up in that flat in Leeds.

Her own voice, quoting Rob, whispered, "Much better. Gonna keep you, honey."

"What did you say to him?" Mary Lee's voice asked.

Lauren listened to herself, thinking how odd one's own voice always sounded in recordings, as she spoke of being in pain. She quoted Rob again, telling her to try something. A salve, she thought. Probably some kind of antibiotic cream, or maybe one of the cortisones, or a product with aloe. "Got to take care of those feet, honey," her voice said. Still Rob's words. Then his chuckle and, "I like my women well heeled as well as roundheeled."

"He really was a pig," Lauren muttered, glancing at Mary Lee for confirmation.

The other woman's face was a mask of confusion. "Lauren," she said cautiously, "can you understand what you're saying?"

They both listened. The conversation she was repeating between her younger self and Rob Seton was strangely inconsequential. It wasn't even true dialogue. It was full of non sequiturs and incomprehensible comments which, Lauren supposed, just confirmed what she'd already guessed, that Rob had been stoned and that she'd been half out of her mind with some kind of fever. None of what she was hearing provided any new information, but at least it wasn't incriminating.

"Not exactly a revelation, is it?"

"What did you just say?" Mary Lee stopped the tape, ran it back, and played the last bit again. "Just then. Tell me what you said."

Puzzled but willing to oblige, Lauren repeated the words of her taped voice: "I'm hungry. May I have some bread?"

"Listen again," Mary Lee insisted, and repeated her maneuver with the tape. The third time through, Lauren caught on. Her translating had been so automatic that she hadn't been aware she was doing it.

The voice on the tape continued. It sounded American when it was quoting Rob, but when it was quoting her younger self it spoke with a broad accent. The words should have been almost totally incomprehensible to her.

Rattled, Lauren stopped the tape and jerked it from the recorder. She scarcely took time to thank Mary Lee as she rushed from the other woman's house.

Adam was waiting for her at home. "I think you'd better listen to this," she said as she pulled Mary Lee's tape out of her shoulder bag.

Twenty minutes later they sat across from each other at the dinette table with the tape player between them. "What do you think?"

"I take it that's a rural Yorkshire dialect? I seem to remember something that sounded similar from an episode of 'All Creatures Great and Small.' I couldn't make head nor tail of what the farmers were saying, but you didn't seem to have a bit of trouble understanding them."

"Now we know why."

"Do you think you're from the Yorkshire dales? A local girl and not an American at all?"

"That's one possibility."

"Meaning?"

Instead of answering, she took both his hands in hers and met his gaze directly. "Interrogate me," she ordered.

"About what?"

"Anything. I don't have any secrets from you now. You know every detail of every dream, and everything I remember of the three years with Rob, but there is probably more—information I've had no reason to think about. There must be questions that have been raised in your mind. If you were investigating this case, what would you ask me, as a suspect, or a witness, or whatever?"

"You're sure about this?"

"Yes." A vague sort of idea had been forming at the back of her mind for some time now. She hoped this exercise would cause it to solidify.

With a brusque nod, he released her hands. She let them fall to the table, folded in front of her. A tingle of anticipation raced through her veins. There was an answer, and they were on the right track to find it now. She was certain of that.

"Tell me about your injury, the one to your foot that he was putting salve on."

It was not a question she'd expected, but she answered before she thought. "My foot was burned."

"How?"

"Rob said I scalded it with boiling water. A kitchen accident."

"Do you believe that?"

Rob had told her a lot of things, and more than one of his statements was now suspect. "Not necessarily."

Lauren frowned. She did not like to recall this particular memory, fuzzy though it was. She'd felt so helpless tied to that stake, her hands jerked painfully above her head and slightly behind it. There had been flames licking at her bare feet and then she had mercifully lost consciousness.

No wonder there had been a scar! She reached down and removed her shoe. "It's barely visible now."

Adam's firm grip captured her ankle, lifting her foot onto his knee. His thumb caressed the long-ago injury. "This was too severe to have been caused by boiling water. Did he . . . do you remember that Seton mistreated you in any way?"

"The man was selfish but he wasn't a sadist." Amusement flared briefly in her eyes. Trust Adam's police background to cause him to come up with the most gruesome scenario.

His hands still cradled her foot as he shook his head. "The more we learn, the less we know. I'm beginning to wonder if we'll ever have an explanation for everything we've found out."

"I think we already do," she said softly.

His brow arched and he waited.

"It would explain everything. Lauren Kendall's disappearance. My accent on that tape. The dreams."

"Go on."

She took a deep breath. "What if that really was my portrait? What if, somehow, the real Lauren and I switched places? What if Lauren Kendall was the one burned to death as a murderess . . . in my place?"

14

"Lauren, this is Detective-Constable Jenny Barnes," Adam said, presenting a young woman with a cheeky grin and an abundance of carrot-colored hair.

D/C Barnes had been assigned by her superiors to assist the visiting American and, Adam suspected, keep him from bothering the other officers, but from the first she'd been enthusiastic about helping him, intrigued by the complex story he'd told. Her repeated assurances that Lauren Kendall could not have been murdered in Leeds without a body having turned up by now had been comforting to hear even though they hadn't completely convinced him. Stranger things had happened in the annals of crime.

Today Jenny Barnes was on her own time, pursuing their quest with Adam and Lauren because of her own lively curiosity. She was casually dressed in trim, tan wool slacks and a white sweater.

Lauren greeted the young police officer warmly. "It's nice of you to help us out this way."

Adam could detect no trace of the nervousness he thought his wife ought to be feeling.

In the past week Adam had come to envy, and despair of, Lauren's serene self-confidence. Ever since she'd come up with that completely preposterous idea—what she insisted on referring to as a "time swap"—she'd been eager to get to Leeds and look for evidence to back up her theory.

She'd scarcely been bothered by the long overseas flight, helped in overcoming her usual mild phobia by the fact that the airplane was huge. She'd been so buoyed up by that success that she'd announced herself willing to fly from London to Leeds if that would save them some travel time. Adam had talked her out of the idea, reminding her that the entire country wasn't all that big. By rail the 185-mile journey had taken less than three hours.

On their first full day in Leeds Lauren had headed straight for the university's impressive campus. She'd been reading up on that, too, since she couldn't remember if she'd ever visited it when she was in England seventeen years earlier. Unfortunately the only book she'd found at home that described it in any detail was twice that old.

Adam had found he had little interest in the city's sights. They hadn't come to England to play tourist. He left Lauren on campus that first day and went to police headquarters.

He was still amazed at the degree of cooperation

and the promptness of the assistance he'd been given. He'd simply introduced himself to the desk duty sergeant, clarifying that he was what they referred to here as a friend of the police. That meant, apparently, that he wasn't a tabloid journalist looking for a scandalous story. A few minutes later he'd been explaining the situation to D/C Barnes.

After that brief, initial meeting Jenny had promised to find the file on Jonathan Harwood's death and then call him at his hotel. Adam had filled the afternoon doing some research of his own, consulting the press-cutting books and the newspapers on microfilm at the Leeds Central Reference Library.

He'd read every account he could find on Jonathan Harwood's death. The *Evening Post* had printed full details of the coroner's inquest. The obituary had listed as survivors his mother, Mrs. Agnes Harwood, of Leeds, an aunt, Mrs. Sharon Wilks, of Manchester, and several unnamed cousins.

Since then, Adam had been busy. He'd tracked down the inspector who'd been in charge of the investigation seventeen years earlier. He was retired now, and working in private security. He'd been willing enough to talk, but had turned out to have little to offer that hadn't been in the file Jenny Barnes had produced. She'd gone through it with Adam, all the statements, all the reports, even the details of the postmortem. Their best hope of new information seemed the interview planned for today, a talk with Mrs. Agnes Harwood, the dead boy's mother.

"Have you checked into the resources of the

Thoresby Society?" Jenny Barnes asked Lauren as she led the way out of the modern high-rise hotel Adam had insisted they stay in. Her car was parked nearby, since she'd offered to drive them to the Harwood house.

"That's next on my list," Lauren told her. "The nicest retired history professor gave me letters of introduction to pave my way."

Adam glanced assessingly in Lauren's direction as she got into the backseat of Jenny's compact car. Lately her interests centered almost exclusively in the dead past. Living with that had begun to make him uneasy, and he was concerned, too, about the outcome of this morning's meeting.

Their destination was a forty-year-old council house in a working-class area of Leeds. Riding in a car and on streets in which the normal order of things was reversed added to Adam's growing tension. If for no other reason than that, he was glad Jenny had volunteered to play chauffeur.

It didn't hurt, either, that she let the woman who answered her knock assume their visit was official. "Detective-Constable Barnes, Mrs. Harwood. I wonder if you'd mind answering a few questions?"

Jonathan Harwood's mother was a widow in her early sixties, slightly dumpy, but with enough semblance of a figure left that she could wear jeans and a loose pullover. Behind thick glasses her eyes had the bulgy look of someone with cataracts, and Adam wondered just how well she could see.

She seemed neither wary nor eager at the idea of helping the police, but responded politely to Jenny Barnes's request. She spared a curious glance for the couple with the young D/C, but evidenced no signs of recognition when her gaze came to rest, briefly, on Lauren's face.

The interior of the Harwood house was clean and neat but had little personality. Newspapers and magazines were arranged in tidy piles, all their edges aligned. The walls were decorated with a busy wallpaper and a multitude of framed photographs, most of them featuring a young man with long hair. The smell of furniture polish pervaded the air.

Mrs. Harwood offered her unexpected visitors chairs but no refreshments. In fact, as she noticed Adam's interest in the pictures Agnes Harwood's bulbous eyes narrowed fractionally.

"We're trying to locate a young woman who lived in Leeds about seventeen years ago," Jenny Barnes explained, whipping out a notepad and a pen.

Adam hoped she wasn't going to get into trouble over this charade, but he wasn't about to object to her methods. Any means that produced results was fine with him. If Mrs. Harwood had ever met Lauren Kendall, she could have the answers they needed.

"Is this your son?" he inquired, cutting in before Mrs. Harwood could ask who it was they were seeking. He tapped the glass over the largest photograph. "His name was Jonathan, is that right?"

Agnes Harwood stiffened perceptibly at the sound of his easily identifiable accent and her next words were not a question but an accusation. "You're American."

"I'm Adam Ryder and this is my wife." Lauren was seated right next to Mrs. Harwood, a polite smile on her face. If nothing else, it was obvious that meeting

Mrs. Harwood had sparked no memories. In fact, Lauren was acting as if this morning's exercise had nothing to do with her at all.

"What do you want, Mr. Ryder?" Ignoring Jenny Barnes, Mrs. Harwood focused her growing animosity on Adam. Her mistrust was suddenly as obvious as her intense dislike of Americans.

"We've come to England to try to find out what happened to a young woman your son may have known."

"My son knew many girls. Jon was a handsome lad. You can see that for yourselves." She rose to her feet and Lauren followed suit, studying the photographs with quiet intensity as Mrs. Harwood faced off against Adam. Jenny stayed where she was, watching the drama being played out before her avid gaze.

Adam glanced at Lauren. There was no sign of it if she was finding anything familiar about the young man in the pictures.

"The girl we're looking for is an American named Kendall, Mrs. Harwood. Laur—"

"Laurie," Mrs. Harwood finished for him. "Laurie Kendall." Her tone of voice spoke for itself. She not only knew the name, she hated the girl it belonged to with a virulent passion.

"We'd like to find out what happened to her," Adam said.

"If she got what she deserved she's roasting in hell!"

"Are you saying she's dead, Mrs. Harwood?"

"I certainly hope so after what she did to my boy! She didn't deserve to live. She got away with murder!"

Even Lauren seemed unnerved by that accusation, but it was Jenny Barnes who asked the next question. "What happened to your son, Mrs. Harwood?"

The woman seemed to crumple before their eyes, shoulders sagging, eyes filling with tears. Blindly she fumbled for a tissue and then sank down into an overstuffed chair. "My Jon was a good lad. You ask anyone. He was going to make something of himself, he was. Then she came along."

"I understood it was an American named Rob Seton who was Jon's friend." Adam stayed where he was and motioned for Lauren to do the same.

"Friend?" Mrs. Harwood's voice rose sharply. "Friend? He was no friend to my boy. Led him astray, he did."

"And this Laurie?" Jenny prompted.

"That little slut seduced my Jon, she did. After that he wouldn't hear a bad word against her, not even when he found out she was sleeping with the other boy, too."

"Rob?"

"Didn't I just say so? Yes, Rob. I ask you, what kind of girl goes with two men at once? Nothing but a whore, she was."

"Did she ever come here? Did you ever meet her face to face?"

"She wouldn't have a face left if Jon had tried to bring her home, or if she'd turned up on my doorstep after he was dead." Mrs. Harwood's lip curled menacingly. "I'd have scratched her eyes out, I would."

"What about photographs? Did Jon ever show you a picture of her?"

She shook her head and sniffed, then blew her

nose. Her eyes were wary when she lifted her head to return Adam's stare. "What's this all about, then?"

"We've told you, Mrs. Harwood," Jenny Barnes reminded her. "Mr. Ryder is trying to find out what happened to Miss Kendall while she was in Leeds. You're one of a very few people who might be able to help him do that. Do you remember where this Laurie lived?"

"Before or after she killed my son?" The renewed venom in her voice sparked Adam's temper.

"Jonathan Harwood died of a drug overdose, Mrs. Harwood. The coroner's inquest ruled it an accidental death."

"And who got him taking that poison, I ask you? Laurie Kendall, that's who. Convinced him that was the only way to prove he was a real man."

While Mrs. Harwood indulged in a few more self-pitying tears, Adam glanced again in Lauren's direction. She was very quiet, but she seemed to be taking these new revelations well. His mouth twisted into a wry grimace. There was a reason for that, he supposed. Lauren had convinced herself that it was no longer *her* past they were discussing.

Her growing reliance on fantasy annoyed Adam nearly as much as Agnes Harwood's histrionics. At least the boy's mother had some excuse for her imaginings. Her conviction that "those Americans" had been responsible for her son's death relieved her own guilt, and took some of the onus off Jon himself. She was even partly right. Rob and Lauren had undoubtedly provided the means for the boy's destruction. Morally they'd been to blame. Legally there hadn't been enough to warrant an arrest.

Adam's frustration mounted. He'd been accustomed in his years as a police officer to being able to turn up solid evidence admissible in court. This investigation defeated him at every turn. Lauren might be satisfied to weave fantasies, but he needed concrete proof. Somehow, somewhere, he had to find a way to establish her identity. Even proof she was not Lauren Kendall would be easier for him to accept than this last crazy idea she'd come up with. For the sake of her sanity and his peace of mind he had to discover the truth.

"You're sure of these addresses?" D/C Barnes asked as she finished jotting something down on her notepad. Adam realized he hadn't even heard her ask for the information again or any of Mrs. Harwood's answer.

"I'm sure. You don't forget some things, or forgive." An odd look that seemed somehow crafty as well as defiant came over her weathered features. "Those Americans knew they were responsible. Tried to hide out by moving to another flat, they did. But I found out where it was."

Jenny and Adam exchanged a startled look before the young constable asked, "Did you confront them, Mrs. Harwood? Did you meet Lauren Kendall in this second location?"

Agnes Harwood's aggrieved tone made her feelings painfully obvious. "They took off again. They were afraid of me, and well they should have been."

"Why's that, Mrs. Harwood?" Jenny asked in a voice full of sympathy.

She stared at her hands, which were twisted together in her lap. "I could have caused them all kinds of trouble," she muttered, "and they knew it. They still had drugs in their possession. I could have reported them."

"But you didn't?"

"I could have," Mrs. Harwood insisted. "Would have if things had been different. They didn't deserve to get away with leading my boy on, causing his death."

Detective-Constable Barnes flipped her notebook closed, signaling her belief that there was nothing more to be learned from Mrs. Harwood. The older woman was already upset by their questions. Badgering her would serve no practical purpose. Jenny formally thanked the woman for her assistance and they all began to move toward the front door.

Jenny was already on the porch when Lauren spoke for the first time. "Mrs. Harwood, have you and I ever met?"

Meaning to caution her, Adam spoke without thinking. "Lauren, don't—"

Mrs. Harwood's head whipped around, her eyes full of cold fury. "Lauren! Not Laurie. Lauren. *You're* her. Get out of my house you little tramp!"

Her composure shaken by the direct verbal attack, and by the threat of physical violence, Lauren retreated onto the porch. Adam quickly followed, shielding her with his body.

"Slut! Murderer!" Agnes Harwood slammed the door in their faces. Through that wooden barrier they could still hear her plainly. She was raving, a woman in the throes of an incoherent rage. She was crying, and cursing Lauren, and in general carrying on like a mother who'd only just lost her son, rather than one who'd lived with his death for many long years.

"It's unlikely she'll cooperate further." Jenny's wry observation was the only comment she made as they walked back to the car.

"I don't think she actually recognized my wife," Adam said.

"Probably not." Jenny started the engine and pulled away from the curb.

Adam had already told her about Lauren's amnesia, and their difficulties in proving her identity, but he hadn't come right out and said it was possible that she and Rob had killed the real Lauren. He was reasonably certain that Jenny had come to that conclusion on her own, however. She could hardly have avoided it when she had access to all the questions he and Dan had asked.

After a few moments of silence, Jenny glanced into the rearview mirror and addressed Lauren. "What did you hope to gain by asking Mrs. Harwood that question? Did you think it was possible that she'd met you under some other name?"

Lauren sounded calm and composed once more. "I asked because for a moment there I thought she looked familiar to me. I was mistaken, though. It's really highly unlikely that I ever saw that woman before today."

"Why the sense of familiarity, then?" Adam couldn't let the matter drop any more than Jenny could. They had only Agnes Harwood's word that she and Lauren Kendall had never met. If she'd known where Rob and Lauren were holed up, she might well have gone there. The real question was whether it had been before or after Lauren lost her memory.

Lauren bestowed a serene smile on her husband,

one that did little to ease his mind. "The person I was reminded of couldn't possibly have been Mrs. Harwood. I've placed the woman I was thinking of. I saw her just once, at an outdoor craft fair in Maine. It was several years ago, shortly before we first met, in fact, but she stuck in my mind because she seemed so out of place." Lauren chuckled. "She was wearing this voluminous black wool cape, you see, and it was one of our warmest summer days."

Lauren tossed her notebooks onto the small table in their hotel room and went to stare morosely out the window. She suspected she'd found all she was going to in the old records. Accounts of the trial of Jane Malte simply did not exist, nor was there much on the Sleaford family, in spite of their later prominence.

She didn't need documentation to convince herself. With each passing day she became more and more certain her theory was the only one that explained everything. That it was an unheard of phenomenon no longer troubled her. If she remembered her Sherlock Holmes correctly, that great fictional detective had once declared that after one had eliminated the impossible, whatever remained, no matter how unlikely it seemed, had to be the true solution.

If only she could convince Adam of that.

The closest thing she had to proof was an odd coincidence. She'd found references, early on, to what must have been an earthquake in the area in 1535. Today she'd located the record of an "unexplained seismic disturbance" during the summer she'd lost her memory. In the 1970s such things were no longer thought of as acts of God or supernatural manifestations. The peculiarity had garnered barely a mention, but the fact that it had occurred in the right year in the right area gave at least a modicum of support to Lauren's theory.

She wasn't sure whether to be relieved or not that she'd found that "proof," for the discovery had brought with it a brand new worry. If what she'd been imagining as a sort of hole in time had opened up in this location once, could it happen again? Could the process somehow be reversed now that she was back in England? Could she end up being returned to her own time?

Lauren stared blindly out the hotel window, oblivious to the view. Any fate was preferable, even being accused of Lauren Kendall's murder. She'd almost managed to convince herself that her fears were foolish, that such flukes were like lightning, never striking the same place twice, when Adam came in.

"Is she down there again?" he asked when he saw Lauren at the window.

"Who?"

"Agnes Harwood." Adam crossed the room in long, forceful strides, came up beside her, and peered toward the street below. "That woman is starting to annoy me."

Puzzled, Lauren followed the direction of his glare and caught a momentary glimpse of a woman in a dark gray coat just before she rounded a corner and disappeared from view. "That was Mrs. Harwood?"

"Haven't you noticed before? That woman, in that

gray coat, has been like a damned shadow for the last couple of days."

"She's following you?"

"No, Lauren." His patient explanation sounded strained. "I'd say she was following you, and I don't like it. I spotted that coat at several of the places we visited. I thought I recognized her the other day when we toured the museum at Temple Newsam, and I know that woman was outside the restaurant we ate at last night. Did you notice anyone following you when you went to the library this morning?"

"No, but then I wouldn't, would I? I don't keep an eye out for such things, since I don't expect to be tailed."

"She was upset when she found out you were Lauren Kendall. I don't like the idea that she's hanging around you like this."

"Maybe she's trying to work up the courage to apologize for what she said the other day."

"Right. And if you believe that, I've got a nice bridge in—"

"What you have is one of those nasty, suspicious, policeman's minds," Lauren informed him with deliberate lightness. "Forget about her, Adam. You can't even be sure that was Mrs. Harwood. You haven't really gotten close enough to her to tell, have you?"

"Instincts," he said succinctly as he reached for the phone.

"Who are you calling?"

"Jenny Barnes." Both his face and his voice were grim. "I think it's time we found out a little more about what Mrs. Harwood's been up to during the last seventeen years."

A few minutes later, by the time Lauren came out of the bathroom, Adam's good humor had been restored. "What did Jenny say?"

"She's doing a little informal checking for me. She says if the lady's a loony they'll have something on her. She had other news, too. We've got permission to visit the apartment where you and Rob lived."

Lauren took an involuntary step backward, but he didn't notice. Oh, God, she thought. What if there was something . . . supernatural about that location? If anything weird was going to happen to her in England, it would happen in that flat. Everything had started there. Would it end there, too?

Adam didn't seem to notice her reaction to his news. He went on talking about how lucky they were. It seemed the building had been condemned but not yet torn down. Gathering her courage, Lauren plastered a smile on her face and tried to summon up some appearance of enthusiasm for the visit. They had to go. It was a logical place to search for answers to all their questions.

"Jenny said the owner would leave the place unlocked for us this afternoon. We can take a cab over there after lunch. Do you want to go out or order room service?"

"Adam, we need to talk about that."

"Lunch?"

"No. Room service. This hotel." Her gesture encompassed the modern, American-style room. "This place is costing us an arm and a leg."

"Don't sweat the small stuff, sweetheart."

"Adam! It's not small. I mean, it wasn't cheap flying over here, and this is probably the most expensive hotel in the city. We could go somewhere else for half the price."

"No."

"Adam, be sensible. We can't afford this."

"Honey, if worse comes to worst, this expense is only a drop in the bucket, and if things work out well, then we deserve a luxury vacation. Don't worry about it."

"How can I not worry? We don't even know what Fiona Innes has been up to while we've been away."

"Yes, we do. I called home this morning while you were at the library. Everything's fine. Hassle's enjoying her visit with Zip and Boing. No charges have been brought against you by vicious, vindictive stepmothers. To be honest, if it came right down to a trial and her word against yours, even with all the holes in your story, you'd win hands down. Dan says Dave's been hard at work. Seems the woman has a well-documented gambling problem."

Lauren sighed deeply as she sank down on one end of their bed. "Even if there is no legal evidence of fraud, even if I'm not obliged to pay all that money back into the trust fund, I can't keep taking money out of it, not now that I know what Rob was up to."

"We haven't actually used any of the income from it for a couple of years," he reminded her. "We've been having the checks direct deposited into a high-interest account."

"That was supposed to be our nest egg for retirement."

"We'll do all right without it. If we have to. In the last few days I've begun to think there's a good chance you *are* Lauren Kendall, after all."

She wondered if he really believed that, or if he was just trying to cheer her up. "And if I'm not? What do we do then?" Her lips trembled slightly. "I don't see how we can keep the money or the h-h-house then."

"We won't lose the house. Hell, even if Fiona Innes could find proof, she'd just as soon sell it back to us, fast and cheap. She'd take the money and run straight to Vegas. And if she's out of the picture, well then I'm sure we can make some arrangement to buy the house from the bank that handles the trust fund."

He was as worried as she was, Lauren suddenly realized, maybe more so. There was no clear distinction between right and wrong in this instance. They could hardly give in to Fiona's blackmail, but that still left a tangled moral issue to unravel. Did they return money that might, after all, belong to her? They might never find proof, one way or the other. The whole situation had to be driving Adam a little crazy. As he sank down beside her on the bed, Lauren ran loving fingers over his tousled hair, smoothing the silver-streaked strands back into some semblance of order.

"The house isn't the most important thing," she said softly. "We could find another."

"Let's hope we won't have to. Anyway, there's no sense worrying about it. Things will sort themselves out eventually."

Lauren wasn't so sure of that, but she did have one advantage Adam didn't. She was already certain of her own identity. She was not Lauren Kendall, and even though she'd been an unwitting impostor it was obvious to her that some sort of reparations had to be made.

"I've been thinking," she said slowly, drawing patterns with her fingertip on the back of Adam's hand, "that if Fiona has no claim and it turns out that there are no other heirs and we can't prove that I am Lauren Kendall, then I'd like to turn the trust into an endowment fund. I thought I might start a shelter for battered women."

Adam relaxed visibly. "You can do whatever you want with it, sweetheart." He was smiling as he added in husky, teasing tones, "I'll support you, in both senses of the word."

She punched him in the arm, suddenly feeling much more lighthearted than she'd been in days. "I can earn my own way, thank you very much. I will have you know I am a highly regarded artisan. A hungry one, too. Take me to lunch."

"Look familiar?" Adam asked as their cab pulled up in front of a dilapidated brick building a few hours later.

Lauren's shudder was all the answer he got.

Inside it was even worse. The place was a dump, and there was certainly nothing left over from the time, seventeen years earlier, when Lauren Kendall and Rob Seton had shared the flat.

"This isn't jogging any new memories," she said, "and its freezing in here. Can we go now?"

"I'm ready to leave, too," he admitted, but as he moved past a window with one pane broken and boarded up and the others filthy with years of neglect, he glanced down at the street. There she was again. Mrs. Harwood. What the hell was that woman up to? He was tempted to ask Jenny Barnes if she could make that background check official. This was damned close to harassment even if the woman hadn't actually approached them.

He turned to tell Lauren about Mrs. Harwood's lurking presence just outside, but the astonishing sight that met his startled gaze banished any thought of the older woman from his mind. Speechless, he could only gape.

His wife was standing in an open space, her arms lifted so that her hands, the wrists touching, were held in an unnatural position above her head and slightly behind it.

"Lauren?"

Slowly, she brought her arms forward and down. "That's a relief," she said.

"I don't like it," Adam complained when they returned to the hotel room after a late breakfast.

Two days had passed since Jenny Barnes started her inquiry into Agnes Harwood's past. Adam and Lauren had continued the routine they'd established the first day, with Lauren digging for information in libraries and Adam doing a more modern kind of research. He'd talked to dozens of people since arriving in Leeds, even some who had been at Miss Cogswell's, and followed up every lead, but he'd not turned up one single person who remembered Lauren Kendall well enough to identify her after seventeen years.

"I thought you'd be relieved that Mrs. Harwood isn't following us around any longer."

"I'd like the situation better if she hadn't completely disappeared. She hasn't been seen at her home, either."

"You probably scared the poor woman," Lauren said, unconcerned. "Adam, I have something to tell you."

His instant wariness was not encouraging.

"You must have wondered what I was doing the other afternoon in the flat."

He'd asked, of course, in the cab on the way back to the hotel and again later, but he hadn't persisted when she'd put him off. She'd needed time to sort out what she'd felt there, time to assimilate everything in her own mind so that she could explain it properly to him.

"Stretching?"

She managed a weak smile. "Lauren was. She was probably wearing a white slip, or perhaps a nightdress of some sort, though I suppose she could have been naked. She was standing in that spot, stretching, at the exact moment the earthquake hit. Only it wasn't an earthquake." Lauren prevented Adam from interrupting by placing her fingers gently on his lips. "It was a ripple in time. At the same moment, four hundred and forty years earlier, Jane Malte was in the same place in the same pose, only she wasn't stretching. She was tied to the stake, and flames were already licking at her feet."

"Lauren—"

"Let me finish. They were in the same spot, the exact same spot, and they were the same size, the same height, the same weight. One body went back in time; the other came forward."

"Sweetheart, you're losing your grip on reality.

Hell, if nothing else, if someone went back in time, they'd change history. We'd know about it, for God's sake."

"She went back," Lauren insisted. "She went back and burned at the stake in my place. She died almost instantly. She never got a chance to change anything." Lauren sighed. "At least, now that we know she was the cause of Jon Harwood's death, I don't have to feel so guilty about her being put to death for murder in my place."

"Are you listening to yourself? What you're saying is crazy. Lauren, you—"

"I'm certain now that I'm not Lauren Kendall. I haven't wanted to be her for some time. I'd feel more comfortable if you'd start calling me Jane."

"The hell I will."

"It's my name, Adam. My real name. The dreams weren't dreams. They were memories. I've gotten my memory back and what I remember is my life as Jane Malte."

"Your real name is Lauren Ryder." She started to protest, but he cut her off. Her suggestion had infuriated him, and he didn't trouble to lower his voice. "You may not be Lauren Kendall, but you are, legally, Lauren Ryder, and you're going to stay Lauren Ryder."

"Won't you even consider the possibility that—"

"Not a chance. I deal in facts, Lauren, not fantasy. There's an answer out there, and I'm going to find it."

"I've already found it," she insisted, still trying to be reasonable in the face of his stubborn refusal to listen. "Think, Adam. Is my explanation any less likely than believing that I'm a murderess? Didn't one of your scenarios call for me to have done away with

Lauren Kendall, hiding her body so well that it hasn't been found in seventeen years? If you could really believe that your own wife was a cold-blooded killer, then—"

"What's the difference? By your own account you *are* a murderer!" He was yelling at her now, enraged by her stubborn refusal to abandon her theory. "You've insisted all along that you killed your husband!" His hands gripped her shoulders, only inches from her throat.

"Adam! You're hurting me."

She got one glimpse of an appalled expression before he released her, grabbed his coat, and stormed out of the room, slamming the door behind him. For the first time since the night they'd met, she'd seen evidence of the barely contained rage that had convinced him to give up police work.

Shaken, Lauren didn't try to follow or call him back.

She was too close to being out of control herself.

Adam's retreat took him out of the hotel and into a chilly December day. By the time his anger, at Lauren and at himself, had burned itself out, the cold began to penetrate.

He realized he'd walked a considerable distance. He debated returning to the hotel, then opted to pay one more visit to the police station first, since it was closer. He wasn't quite ready to face Lauren again, and there might be more news on Agnes Harwood.

Several officers knew him by now. He had no difficulty getting in to see Jenny Barnes.

"I was about to try to reach you at your hotel," she said when she looked up from a mound of paperwork and caught sight of him. "I don't know if it's important or not, but we've uncovered an odd fact about your Mrs. Harwood. She's made several trips to the U.S., which is a bit unusual for a woman in her financial situation."

"When?"

Jenny handed him a sheet of paper with a list of dates.

Adam read the information with a sense of disbelief that was quickly replaced by growing concern.

"What is it?"

Adam found he had difficulty speaking. "The other day Lauren said she'd seen a woman who looked something like Mrs. Harwood years ago at some craft fair in Maine. Do you recall exactly when she said it was?"

"Shortly before she met you."

"Damn." He reached for the phone on her desk. Moments later Adam's alarm had increased to a fever pitch. Lauren was not answering the ringing telephone in their hotel room.

Jenny was already on her feet, anticipating trouble, as he dropped the receiver back into its cradle.

"I've got to get back to the hotel."

"I'm coming with you. Fill me in on the way."

"Agnes Harwood was in Boston fourteen years ago, the same week that Rob Seton was killed there by a hit-and-run driver, a driver who's never been caught or even identified."

"You don't think—"

"I don't know what to think," he admitted as they raced out of the building. "The next couple of dates mean nothing to me, but the last one, five years ago, certainly does. Agnes Harwood flew back to England the same night Lauren's house was broken into."

15

A light herbal fragrance from the complimentary hotel shampoo clung to Lauren as she came back into the bedroom from the bath. It was a wonder, she decided, that no psychologist had yet made a study of the therapeutic properties inherent in taking a shower, washing one's hair, blowing it dry, and getting into clean, comfortable clothes. She was still upset about her quarrel with Adam, but thanks to that "treatment" she was calmer now, certain she could handle whatever fate threw at her next.

Facing the mirror over the dresser she gave locks that were getting rather long a final fluff, then tugged at the bottom edge of her light blue sweatshirt, forcing the soft fabric down over hips encased in well-worn blue jeans. She wasn't dressed to go out, but she looked and felt . . . normal. When Adam got back they'd talk this over like two rational adults. Somehow, she'd find a way to make him accept the truth.

She sighed and made a face at her image in the mirror. "Who do you think you're kidding?" she asked it. "Adam isn't going to believe such a wild tale. Not in a million years."

Lauren had just started toward the bath to retrieve the too noisy portable hair dryer she'd picked up on her second day in Leeds, when a knock sounded at the door. She wasn't expecting room service and was sure Adam had a key with him, wherever he was, so she took the precaution of looking through the security peephole. She had no trouble recognizing the back of a now familiar uniform. The sight came as no surprise. The maid hadn't been by to clean their room yet. Lauren hurriedly undid the locks.

She was staring down the barrel of a small but deadly looking pistol before she realized that although the uniform was right, the slightly overweight, stoop-shouldered body inside was not that of a hotel employee. The woman in the corridor was Agnes Harwood.

Lauren's first reaction came as the direct result of having married a man in the law-enforcement profession. "I thought Brits had to have a license to own a gun."

She realized instantly what a stupid remark it had been and winced. Police here might not all go about armed, and handguns might be regulated more stringently than in the U.S., but it should hardly surprise her that illegal weapons could be had.

Agnes Harwood chose to ignore the inane comment. "Come with me," she ordered, "and be quick about it."

Lauren just stared at her, still trying to accept what she was seeing. Part of her simply could not credit that this was happening and kept insisting that the woman was harmless. "Now, Mrs. Harwood, you don't want to—"

"I'll shoot you where you stand if you don't do as I say."

All at once, Lauren believed her. The protuberant blue eyes that had regarded her with such indifference when they'd met a few days earlier were now lit with a too bright gleam.

Reluctantly, Lauren moved out of the relative safety of her room and into the wide, plushly carpeted corridor. At once she felt the cold metal of the gun press into her ribs as Agnes Harwood came up close behind her.

"Walk to the stairwell," she ordered.

Lauren heard the room door close and the click of the automatic lock and shivered. That small sound made her situation all too real. She was the prisoner of a madwoman.

Where was Adam when she needed him? He'd be back soon, wouldn't he? He'd been gone well over an hour. It was nearly noon.

Lauren had no choice but to obey as Agnes Harwood steered her toward the far end of the hall, but she slowed her pace as much as possible. There seemed to be no one else about in the quiet of late morning. Lauren found herself wondering if Mrs. Harwood had disposed of a real maid in order to get her disguise. She was relieved when they passed a room with an open door and she spotted another uniformed woman and a service cart inside.

The gun poked her again, harder this time. "Hurry," Mrs. Harwood whispered.

Instead, Lauren deliberately stumbled, catching

the edge of the open door. The real maid looked up, but they were past the room in a moment. Had she seen the gun? Did she understand the seriousness of the situation? That was probably too much to hope for, but Lauren had no intention of missing any chance to help herself out of this mess.

They reached the stairwell and Mrs. Harwood pushed Lauren upward. Could she stumble again, fall onto her captor so that she tumbled down the stairs? The older woman put an end to that scheme by taking the safety off the gun. The click sounded clearly in the enclosed space.

"No tricks. Just keep climbing."

They came out onto the roof of the high-rise hotel a few minutes later. It was another crisp, cool, early December day, and the view was spectacular, but Lauren was in no mood to appreciate either fact. She was searching desperately for some way to deflect Mrs. Harwood's aim, to make her fire the gun so that someone would hear and come to help. The trick was to not get shot herself in the process.

Talk to her, a small, frightened voice in her brain advised, striving for a rational solution. Did killers always want an opportunity to brag about their cleverness, or was that just one of those standard devices invented by novelists and scriptwriters? Lauren didn't imagine she had anything to lose by trying.

"Why are you going to shoot me?"

"I'm not going to shoot, unless you force me to." Mrs. Harwood sounded perfectly calm, her tone matter-of-fact. She might have been discussing plans for tea. "You're going to jump, you are. Right. Over to the edge with you, then. Let's get on with it."

Lauren held her ground, in spite of the intimidating sight in front of her. Adam had once said there was nothing crook or cop feared more than a nervous woman with a gun.

Think, she ordered her bemused brain. She'd had some self-defense training from Adam after the burglary. If Mrs. Harwood really was reluctant to shoot her, she might have a chance to use it.

"Why am I jumping?" Her voice shook a little on the question, but overall she was pleased with her effort to sound calm.

"Guilt. You killed my son, you did. Now you are filled with remorse. You are going to take your own life to make amends." She gestured again with the small weapon, motioning toward the low parapet that circled the edge of the hotel roof.

"I don't think my husband is going to believe that, Mrs. Harwood. He'll find out what really happened. You'll be tried and sent to jail." Did England have a death penalty? Lauren couldn't remember.

"No one will suspect me."

"You can't get away with murder."

Agnes Harwood started to laugh at that. Her bright eyes grew even more brilliant, and the iron gray curls that wreathed her weathered face bounced as she chortled.

"What's so damned funny?"

"You got away with murder," she chanted, waving the gun a bit wildly. "I got away with murder, too." Abruptly every trace of humor faded. "Thought I'd taken care of you once before, Lauren Kendall, but I was deceived."

"What are you talking about?"

"That's for me to know and you to wonder." Agnes

Harwood grinned obscenely at her intended victim.

"If you're going to kill me, you owe me an explanation." Lauren managed to say the words in a firm, no-nonsense voice, then spoiled the effect when she was unable to contain a horrified gasp. Mrs. Harwood had tightened her grip on the gun and aimed it straight at Lauren's heart. She held it with both hands, as if she'd had some training, and those hands seemed distressingly steady.

"I owe you nothing but a painful death. You took my son away from me."

"Mrs. Harwood, that wasn't me. I'm not the real Lauren Kendall." Lauren drew in a shaky breath. If only she could convince her adversary of the truth, she might still get out of this alive. "Listen to me, Mrs. Harwood. Lauren Kendall is already dead. There's no need to go through—"

"Dead? How?"

"She died in a fire. Years ago."

"Who are you, then?"

"My name is Jane Malte. I met Rob Seton after—"

"Seton!" Mrs. Harwood's second burst of laughter was even more uncontrolled than her earlier mirth. "I took care of him, I did."

Lauren blinked at her in confusion. Took care of him? She was almost afraid to ask what that meant. In the end she didn't have to. Mrs. Harwood was only too happy to volunteer the information.

"You weren't hard to find, you weren't. Not here in Leeds and not later. Took a while. You hid well, and I didn't know what you looked like then, not until I saw you one day at the window of that flat. You went back there. I saw that, too. Been following you, I had, until your interfering husband noticed."

"You never saw my face until Rob and I were living in that flat?" In spite of her present danger, she had to know if Mrs. Harwood had ever met the real Lauren. It didn't sound as if she had.

"Didn't I just say so?" Irritated by the question, the older woman glared at Lauren.

"And then you followed me to America?" Lauren still couldn't take it all in. It seemed too unlikely. "How—"

Again Mrs. Harwood cut her off. "Jon had a life insurance policy. That's where the money came from. I used every penny, I did, to make sure his death was avenged."

Lauren kept her eyes trained on the gun, hoping for an opportunity to grab for it, but in spite of her preoccupation with the past, Mrs. Harwood's aim never wavered.

"Took a while," she grumbled. "Nearly three years, but when the time came I was ready. I stayed and watched that night, too. Made sure he was dead."

The rambling words finally began to make a terrible kind of sense to Lauren. "Are you talking about the night Rob died?"

"What else, then?" The woman sounded impatient with her lack of comprehension. "How did you think he went over that embankment if it wasn't with a little nudge from another car?"

Lauren just stared at her, incapable of making a coherent response. Mrs. Harwood had become almost chatty now that she'd gotten started.

"He had to pay for what he did to my Jon. Now, if you'd stayed put, as you should have, it would have saved me a good deal of time and money."

"You . . . you looked for me after Rob died?"

The midday sun beat down on them, but Lauren had never felt so cold in her life. Even her worst nightmares couldn't compare to this. At least in them, at the end, she'd been drugged. Her dread of imminent death hadn't been nearly so intense.

"Time," Mrs. Harwood muttered, "so much time, and money, too, and then my own flesh and blood lied to me."

For a moment Lauren thought she meant her son had deceived her, but that made no sense. "Are you saying you followed me to Maine? How could that be? If you did you should have recognized me when Adam and I came to your house."

"I didn't know you as Lauren Ryder," Mrs. Harwood admitted, "and I thought that Lauren Kendall was dead. She should have been. Just proves that old saying that if you want a job done right, do it yourself."

"Mrs. Harwood, don't you understand? I didn't even know your son. I—"

"No more talking. Get over by the edge. Move."

Lauren took a step backward, and came up against the waist-high wall that served as the roof's only guard rail. One quick glance over the side reminded her how much she disliked heights. She closed her eyes against a wave of dizziness and concentrated on what she had to do. Mrs. Harwood did not want to shoot her. She wanted to have a chance at getting away with murder. That meant she might be provoked into coming closer.

I'm younger, Lauren assured herself. I'm stronger. I might even be crazier.

"I'm not going to jump, Mrs. Harwood," she said

firmly. "Lauren Kendall has already been punished for what she did to your son. She was executed for murder. I'm sure you'd have liked the way it was done."

Confusion momentarily blunted the older woman's purpose. She did not know what to make of the claim. "Already dead?"

"You thought so, didn't you? You just told me you thought Lauren Kendall was already dead. You were right."

"But you're here."

"I'm not Lauren Kendall. I'm Jane Malte."

The conviction in her voice seemed to give Mrs. Harwood pause. At the same moment Lauren glimpsed movement at the door to the stairwell. Someone was edging it open so slowly that she was certain he must know that she was here and in danger.

Adam.

She was sure he was the one on the other side of that door.

"Liar! Tramp! Don't try to confuse me. I'll see you get what you deserve, I will."

Mrs. Harwood leapt forward, so determined to force Lauren over the side that she seemed to forget for a moment that she had a gun. She came at her intended victim, both arms out in front of her, making it almost ridiculously easy for Lauren to catch hold of her wrist and twist until she dropped the weapon. It went off as it fell, but the bullet shot harmlessly up toward the sun.

Lauren felt a sense of great elation even as she tumbled to the surface of the roof with Mrs. Harwood on top of her. They landed with bruising force, but she scarcely felt the impact, for out of the corner of her eye she saw Adam burst through the stairwell door. He was closely followed by Jenny Barnes.

Then, without warning, everything abruptly went wrong. Mindless rage gave Agnes Harwood unexpected strength. She landed a series of punishing blows on Lauren's head and shoulders, then seized her arm in a viselike grip to haul her to her feet.

As she was forced inexorably closer to the parapet, Lauren struggled for purchase, losing a shoe in an effort to dig her heels into the roof's rough surface. Her bare foot dragged across it, abrading the skin and producing a burning pain that somehow seemed far worse than any of the aches and stings emanating from the other injuries Mrs. Harwood had inflicted.

Lauren's struggles to slow her captor's pace proved futile. She was pulled nearer and nearer to the edge until, with one Herculean effort, Mrs. Harwood slammed them both against the side of the parapet. A vicious kick knocked Lauren's feet out from under her and she was hauled ruthlessly up onto the top of the barrier.

Her sweatshirt rode up and Lauren could feel the blood welling on her bare midriff as her skin scraped against concrete. The top of the parapet was less than a foot wide. Before her terrified eyes, as she twisted and continued to fight for her life, there appeared a dizzying view of the distant street below.

Frantic, Lauren flailed at Agnes Harwood's hands, trying to break her merciless hold. Endless seconds passed as they grappled, poised on the brink of oblivion. Lauren contorted her aching body and bit the older woman's fingers but even that had no effect. Lauren could not break free.

With a desperate burst of energy, Agnes Harwood hurled herself over the edge. Lauren was lifted free of the roof. Her leg struck the parapet. Her arms, still caught in her opponent's grasp, were jerked backward, then down.

She was falling.

A scream caught in her throat just as strong hands grasped her around both ankles and hung on.

Lauren's rapid descent ended with bone-jarring suddenness. She felt as if she were being torn in two. A dead weight below dragged down on her arms until the muscles screamed. Above, as Adam's grip tightened, equal pressure ripped at the bones and tendons in her legs.

She didn't dare open her eyes. She was bent over backward, the upper half of her body dangling in space while the lower portion was flattened against the rooftop side of the hotel parapet. Her back, she decided in rising hysteria, was going to snap under the strain.

And then, as a piercing scream rent the air, one set of fingers at last released her. Lauren's body snapped upward, catapulted back to the safety of the rooftop and straight into Adam's waiting arms.

She kept her eyes squeezed tightly shut and clung to her husband's solid strength, but nothing could block out the sound of a body striking the ground.

Adam staggered backward with her, then gently held her in front of him so that he could inspect for damages. "Thank God you're alive. Where do you hurt, sweetheart? How badly are you injured?"

"I'll send for a doctor." Jenny Barnes's voice sounded very far away, very faint.

Lauren's breath came in great, sobbing gulps. She wanted to say that she ached all over, and that there was a burning pain in her foot, but before she could get a single word out the world began to turn to black around her.

Oh, God! she thought in sudden paralyzing horror. I'm going back!

Adam was worried about the woman in the chair by the bed.

Her pupils were as wide and dark, her expression as blank as when she'd first come to in his arms up there on the roof. Dazed, she'd let him carry her down to their room, but she'd refused to be put to bed. Reluctantly, she'd allowed the doctor Jenny had called to look at her injuries. None were severe, only bruises, bumps, and abrasions. After they were treated and Lauren had changed into a robe, she'd settled into that chair. She had scarcely moved since.

All the time the police had been in the room, she'd sat there, motionless and for the most part silent, speaking only when she was asked a direct question. She'd answered in a dull, lifeless voice and volunteered nothing.

Adam never wanted to live through anything like that scene on the roof again. From the time the maid had told him about the two women heading for the stairwell until he'd had Lauren safe again he'd aged ten years. It was ironic that he'd deliberately insisted they stay in the tallest hotel in the city. He'd had the idea that if he kept Lauren surrounded by the trappings of twentieth-century America she'd find it harder to keep identifying with Jane Malte.

They were alone at last, now that Jenny and her colleagues had gone. Late afternoon shadows were creeping into the room. The danger was past, but Adam felt tense and ill-at-ease. He could not quite shake the feeling that something was still very wrong.

He studied Lauren's face. He'd seen plenty of people in shock in the course of his career. Lauren's reactions were typical, but only up to a point.

"I thought I was going to lose you," he said aloud.

Lauren stirred listlessly under his intent scrutiny, but said nothing.

He wondered how much she'd really absorbed of the conversation around her during the last couple of hours. He and Jenny had developed a partial picture of Agnes Harwood's quest for revenge. That might be all they'd ever have, for she'd died of the injuries sustained in her fall.

He'd failed Lauren. Adam could not forgive himself for that. His mistakes had nearly cost her her life. Moving restlessly, he crossed the room to stand at the window and stare down at the street below. It was still cordoned off with police barricades.

If he hadn't quarreled with Lauren, she wouldn't have been alone in their hotel room. Agnes Harwood wouldn't have been able to get close enough to try to kill her.

If he'd made the connection sooner, Lauren would have had protection all along. He'd had it right in front of him the first day he was in Leeds. There had been an aunt, Sharon Wilks, listed in Jonathan Harwood's obituary. From Manchester, the newspaper had said. Whoever had written that account of the boy's death had assumed it was Manchester, England. Natural enough. That city wasn't far from Leeds. In this case, however, it was the wrong guess. Sharon Wilks lived in Manchester, New Hampshire. Adam felt now that he should have recognized her name at once. After all, it had only been five years ago that he'd arrested her son Greg for breaking into Lauren's house. Mrs. Wilks's first name had turned up in the investigation of Wilks's background, along with the fact that he had a long criminal record in the Manchester area.

A distant memory surfaced, something that hadn't made sense to Adam at the time. After Greg Wilks's conviction, he'd dismissed the anomaly as insignificant, but during the attack on Lauren, Adam had noticed that Wilks had said something odd. Five years later he couldn't remember the exact words. They were probably in the transcripts of the trial and he'd check when they got home, but in the meantime his memory was good enough to tell him that when Lauren had attempted to fight off her attacker, Wilks had muttered "she'll pay extra for that" or "she'll pay for the extra trouble." Words to that effect. The jury had assumed he meant Lauren. Now Adam suspected that Greg Wilks had been referring to his aunt, Agnes Harwood. He was almost certain she'd offered to pay him to kill Lauren and complete her revenge.

"A sister in New Hampshire must have been very convenient for her," Adam muttered, still staring down at the street. "Close to Boston. Close to Maine. I wouldn't be surprised if those two women in Darien were Agnes and Sharon."

He was startled when Lauren spoke. Apparently,

her thoughts had been paralleling his. "Was it Agnes Harwood I saw at that craft fair?"

"Looks like it."

He left the window and went to stand beside the chair. A little of the color had come back into her face, but she was still pale.

"She said her own flesh and blood lied to her, Adam. What did she mean?"

"Greg Wilks."

"The man who broke into my house?" Lauren snapped out of her stupor at that, staring at him with outright amazement.

"The same. He's her nephew." His lips twisted into a sardonic grimace. "We'll never be able to prove anything. Wilks would be a fool to admit he was hired to kill you."

"He meant to kill me?" She still sounded dazed, but her eyes were focused. Adam hunkered down in front of her and put his hands over hers.

"If he'd found you asleep that night, he probably could have made it look like an accident. A fatal fall down the stairs, maybe. Here's what I think happened. When she killed Rob, Agnes Harwood discovered that she didn't like doing the dirty work herself. Greg Wilks had already done time in New Hampshire for assault. Maybe he offered to help out. Maybe she asked. That doesn't matter. What's significant is that he apparently lied afterward, told his aunt he'd been successful in order to get the money she'd promised him for killing you. She'd already gone back to England. He must have figured that since she lived so far away, she'd never find out the truth. She probably wouldn't have, if we hadn't turned up on her doorstep."

Adam hated loose ends, but in this case he was forced to acknowledge that there was no way to tie them all off. He could only speculate. "Ironic, isn't it? He screwed up the job and because of that we met and fell in love and married."

"You arrived in the nick of time that night. Just as you did today." There were tears in Lauren's eyes as she squeezed his hands. "I couldn't have borne it if I'd gone back. Not after all we've been through."

He stared at her in confusion. "Gone back?"

"When I started to black out, up there on the roof, I thought—" She broke off as she caught sight of his bewildered expression. "Never mind. It doesn't matter. I'm still here." As if she couldn't quite believe it she repeated the words. "I'm still here."

"Lauren? What are you talking about?"

She kept her eyes on their joined hands. "It was silly. Impossible. Unlikely, anyway."

"What was?" He tugged free of her grip and lifted her chin with one finger, forcing her to meet his eyes.

Drawing in a deep breath, she blurted, "I thought I was going to come to back in the sixteenth century again!"

The idea disturbed Adam more deeply than he dared let on. He leaned closer to drop a kiss on her upturned nose and hug her cautiously, being careful not to cause more pain. Her back contained innumerable contusions. "I think it's time we left Leeds. I think we've found out everything we're going to here."

"I think you're right."

"It's pretty clear what happened."

"Is it?"

Lightly, afraid he might hurt her, Adam ran his

hands over her shoulders, then feathered a kiss on a fresh bruise on her cheek. "We can't change your past, but we can live with it. I suppose it was Jon Harwood's tragic death that caused the amnesia. You were morally responsible for it, and the guilt—"

"Adam," she interrupted, "what are you saying?"

"That we've been barking up the wrong tree looking for some mysterious amnesiac Rob Seton tricked into thinking she was Lauren Kendall. You are Lauren and always were. You just couldn't remember. It makes perfect sense once you think about the kind of person Fiona Innes is. She obviously made up the entire story about the impostor."

"But we have no proof I'm Lauren."

"Not so. We just didn't recognize what we were hearing. Agnes Harwood recognized you as Lauren, but given the circumstances, we—"

"Adam, no. You're wrong. Mrs. Harwood never saw me until after I lost my memory. I'm not Lauren Kendall."

"I know you aren't very happy about what we've learned. I'm not thrilled with any of that either, but when you think about it, what you did wasn't much worse than what a lot of other rebellious kids did during the seventies. You were trying to get your father's attention, his love. Then, over here, when a young man you were close to died, you couldn't deal with the fact that you'd been partly responsible for his death. You blanked it out, started over, became the person you truly were beneath that tough, rebellious exterior you showed the world. I'll bet Beaumont will agree with me."

"That's not exactly a point in your favor."

She rose stiffly, wincing as she shook free of the

protective circle of his arms. Belatedly, Adam realized that it wasn't just that she didn't like what he was saying. She honestly didn't believe his conclusions were the right ones.

"Lauren. Sweetheart. You have to be sensible about this. I'd like to have found proof I could take to court, but common sense tells me this is the answer we've been looking for. You are Lauren Kendall. Everything fits."

"What about my voice on that tape? Where did I get the accent?"

"Right here in Yorkshire, I expect. Honey, you lived at Miss Cogswell's for nearly two years. You must have had plenty of opportunities to hear the local dialect."

"So you're saying everything under hypnosis was just another fantasy, that all my dreams were fantasies?"

"It makes sense," he insisted. Why was she being so stubborn?

"What about my foot? You said yourself that a major injury must have left that scar."

"You did lose your memory. There could have been an accident you've forgotten about." Adam knew he was stretching, but it seemed imperative that he provide some explanation. "You were doing drugs in those days. If you tried freebasing cocaine there could easily have been a small explosion, not enough to cause a house fire, but enough to burn you severely as you tried to get out of the way." As he speculated, Adam decided the idea wasn't so far-fetched at all. "That could be why Rob treated the foot himself instead of taking you to a doctor."

His anger at the long-dead Rob resurfaced. Lauren

might have died from her injury. There was no excuse for such negligent behavior.

A heavy silence fell between them. In the room the shadows lengthened. Lauren took up Adam's earlier post by the window and looked down at the place where Agnes Harwood had died. He saw Lauren shudder as she realized it might have been her body that landed there, broken and lifeless.

"I won't keep the trust fund. I have no right to it, or to the house. I want to do exactly what we talked about doing if we found out I was impersonating Lauren."

He sighed. "I think it's fine if you go ahead with your plan to endow a shelter." She started to say more, but he cut in before she could get another word out. "We'll talk about it when we're home again. I promise. Another week or so isn't going to make much difference after seventeen years."

"I guess not." Her fingers toyed with the edge of the drapery. "You've never even considered that my theory might be right, have you?"

Adam's throat went dry. His chest felt unnaturally constricted. He kept hoping she'd abandon her crazy belief in some supernatural explanation. Just the thought that she could be so credulous created a tension between them that shouldn't be there, especially not now when the danger was past. They had succeeded in their mission to find answers. Why should he feel that he was letting her down just because he insisted on being rational?

"Honey, I've made a lot of compromises lately, accepted things I'd never have dreamed I'd be able to live with, but I won't lie to you and tell you that I can buy into this business about a ripple in time." He honestly didn't think he'd ever be capable of that kind of leap of faith. How could he believe a version of the facts that bordered on the ludicrous?

"You think I'm a fool," she said unhappily. When he didn't answer, unwilling to hurt her feelings, she turned her head and met his eyes. "Or maybe you think I'm losing my mind, after all. What if I am, Adam? What if it gets worse?"

"We'll . . . deal with it." Somehow, he had to close this ever-widening gap between them. He hadn't nearly lost her on that roof to give up on her now. "We're a team, Mrs. Ryder."

He wasn't sure she entirely believed him, and he couldn't blame her. She had to realize, as he had begun to, that in spite of their best efforts their marriage was on shaky ground. Not agreeing on what had really happened seventeen years ago might easily prove intolerable to them both.

"We've got a couple of days to kill before our flight leaves London for home." His palm glided over the softness of her hair, stroking, soothing, as he pressed her gently to him. "Let's try to salvage a vacation out of all this. Forget our troubles. Spend the time in London sightseeing. What do you say?"

"That sounds lovely, Mr. Ryder." The words were right, but her smile looked a trifle too bright.

Adam speared his fingers into his hair in frustration as she rested her head on his shoulder and snuggled closer.

Compromise. That seemed the only way out of this situation, and yet the possibility existed that their respective explanations of what had happened might be too far apart to ever be reconciled.

"Tell you what, sweetheart. I'll work on trying to

accept that your theory might be possible, if you'll work equally hard coming to terms with the fact that, until proven otherwise, you're stuck with living out Lauren Kendall's life."

Lauren's response did little to reassure him. She whispered, "I suppose I did inherit it, didn't I?"

Epilogue

It was not a mirror image.

The face in the painting was that of a much younger woman . . . a woman half her age . . . a girl, really.

Lauren Ryder's steps slowed until she came to a complete stop directly in front of the portrait.

The familiar eyes stared blankly back at her—large, not as widely spaced as she'd have liked, and in hue the exact color of the first forget-me-nots of spring. The other painted features, too, were her own. She had been painted in a watchful pose, regarding the antics of her betters with an expression that might have been disdain.

There was a certain sense of déjà vu about walking into a gallery and seeing *The Court of Henry VIII at Nonsuch* hanging on the wall. Lauren stared at the huge painting and fought against a rapidly growing sense of despair.

Something had gone from her relationship with Adam, in spite of all their efforts. She was just so terribly afraid, regardless of his protests and the ardent lovemaking they'd shared in the days since leaving Leeds for London, that in time he was going to turn from her, convinced that she was a hopeless case because she could not, would not give up her memories.

Jane Malte's girlhood was part of her now. She could remember just about everything, all the joy and all the pain, and the fact that though she hardly looked it, she was actually three years younger than Lauren Kendall had been. She would try not to refer to that, and she'd given up on the idea of calling herself Jane, but she had the awful feeling that she'd soon begin to resent that Adam was forcing her to live a lie.

Would he grow to hate her if she refused to betray a part of herself? Worse, would he regret his hasty decision to forgive her her sins?

In a way there wasn't much to choose between in their backgrounds. Jane Malte had killed a man in self-defense; Lauren Kendall had been responsible for Jon Harwood's accidental death. What if Adam someday decided that, despite his best efforts, he couldn't tolerate being married to either woman?

Out of the indistinct crowd murmurs came one familiar, much beloved voice, Adam's baritone. "So that's the painting that started it all."

He stared at it with considerable interest. It had been Adam's suggestion that they take a look at the portrait when he saw in the newspaper that it had been returned to its permanent home in a London museum. He'd never seen the actual painting, after all, only that small reproduction of it in a catalog. Reluctantly, Lauren had agreed.

She watched nervously and saw his fascination grow more and more intense. He seemed deeply affected by this first good look at Jane's likeness. Abruptly, against the rules, he did what she'd once tried to do. Adam Ryder reached out and touched the surface of the panel.

The guard's challenge came instantly, and three men in slate gray uniforms began to converge on them. Ignoring the distraction, Adam stood immobile, his finger still touching her painted face.

Lauren heard harsh words uttered in unfamiliar voices, but did not absorb any meaning. The guards seemed no more important than so many angrily buzzing flies. All her concentration was centered on Adam and the portrait.

For a fraction of a second it seemed to Lauren that Ned Teerlinck's face was superimposed upon her husband's features. Then she blinked, and the illusion vanished.

An aggravated voice addressed them, echoing the sentiments of his New York counterpart. Lauren was only vaguely aware of the muffled conversation that followed between Adam and a museum security team. When he took her arm and guided her out of the gallery, she went in silence. It was not until they were seated close together on a stone bench that faced a busy London street bathed in misty December sunlight that she spoke.

"There's one mystery left," she said quietly. "I still don't know for certain why Ned painted me . . . painted Jane Malte ten years after her death."

She glanced uncertainly at Adam. He'd always hated it when she referred to herself and Jane as the same person. She'd been trying to break herself of the habit but had found these last few days that it was becoming more difficult rather than less.

This time, however, her slip of the tongue didn't seem to bother him. He turned toward her and smiled. His expression left no doubt in her mind of his love for her. When he spoke it was with absolute assurance that he was telling her nothing less than the truth.

"It was painted by a man obsessed with you, a man in love with you in a way he'd never dreamed it was possible to love a woman, but that love was nothing compared to the love I have for you now."

"Adam? What are you saying?"

"That inside this museum is a portrait of my wife."

She hesitated, afraid to believe that at last, inexplicably, Adam was willing to accept that she had come to him out of the past. "You don't need . . . proof?"

"I know what happened now," he said with quiet confidence. "You were Jane Malte. Now you are called Lauren Ryder and this time around you are my wife. This time I have the power to keep you safe."

Lauren's gaze locked with Adam's. She saw her feelings for him reflected in his eyes, all the love, all the hope, all the trust of two people who were destined to be two halves of a whole.

She made her own leap of faith as she went into his arms. "It's time to go home," she whispered, holding him close and held tight in return. "It's time to get on with the rest of our lives."

Straight from the Heart by Pamela Wallace

Academy Award–Winning Author. Answering a personal ad on a dare, city girl Zoey Donovan meets a handsome Wyoming rancher. Widower Tyler Ross is the answer to any woman's fantasy, but he will have to let go of the past before he can savor love's sweet bounty.

Treasured Vows by Cathy Maxwell

When English banker Grant Morgan becomes the guardian of impoverished heiress Phadra Abbott, he quickly falls under the reckless beauty's spell. Phadra is determined to upset Grant's well-ordered life to find her spendthrift father—despite the passion Grant unleashes in her.

Texas Lonesome by Alice Duncan

In 1890s San Francisco, Emily von Plotz gives advice to the lovelorn in her weekly newspaper column. A reader who calls himself "Texas Lonesome" seems to be the man for her, but wealthy rancher Will Tate is more than willing to show her who the real expert is in matters of the heart.

Buy 4 or more and receive FREE postage & handling

MAIL TO: HarperCollins Publishers
P.O. Box 588 Dunmore, PA 18512–0588
OR CALL: **1-800-331-3761 (Visa/MasterCard)**

YES! Please send me the books I have checked:

- ❑ **YOU BELONG TO MY HEART** 108416-6 ......$5.99 U.S./$6.99 CAN.
- ❑ **AFTER THE STORM** 108205-8 ......$5.50 U.S./$6.50 CAN.
- ❑ **DEEP IN THE HEART** 108326-7 ......$4.99 U.S./$5.99 CAN.
- ❑ **HONEYSUCKLE DEVINE** 108406-9......$4.99 U.S./$5.99 CAN.
- ❑ **DANCING ON AIR** 108145-0......$5.99 U.S./$6.99 CAN.
- ❑ **STRAIGHT FROM THE HEART** 108289-9 ....$5.50 U.S./$6.50 CAN.
- ❑ **TREASURED VOWS** 108415-8......$4.99 U.S./$5.99 CAN.
- ❑ **TEXAS LONESOME** 108414-X ......$4.99 U.S./$5.99 CAN.

SUBTOTAL...... $________

POSTAGE & HANDLING...... $ 2.00

SALES TAX (Add applicable sales tax)...... $________

TOTAL ...... $________

Name________________

Address________________

City________________ State_____ Zip Code________

Order 4 or more titles and postage & handling is **FREE!** Orders of less than 4 books, please include $2.00 p/h. Remit in U.S. funds. Do not send cash. Allow up to 6 weeks for delivery. Prices subject to change. Valid only in U.S. and Canada.

M017

Visa & MasterCard holders—call 1-800-331-3761

Echoes and Illusions
by Kathy Lynn Emerson

Lauren Ryder has everything she wants, but then the dreams start—dreams so real she fears she's losing her mind. Something happened to Lauren in the not-so-distant past that she can't remember. As she desperately tries to piece together the missing years of her life, a shocking picture emerges. Who is Lauren Ryder, really?

The Night Orchid by Patricia Simpson

In Seattle Marissa Quinn encounters a doctor conducting ancient Druid time-travel rituals and meets Alek, a glorious pre-Roman warrior trapped in the modern world. Marissa and Alek discover that though two millennia separate their lives, nothing can sever the bond forged between their hearts.

Destiny Awaits by Suzanne Elizabeth

Tess Harper found herself in Kansas in the year 1885, face-to-face with the most captivating, stubborn man she'd ever met—and two precious little girls who needed a mother. Could this man, and this family, be her true destiny?

MAIL TO: **HarperCollins Publishers**
P.O. Box 588 Dunmore, PA 18512-0588
OR CALL: (800) 331-3761 (Visa/MC)

Yes! Please send me the books I have checked:

❑**PRAIRIE KNIGHT** 108282-1 .... $4.50 U.S./$5.50 CAN.
❑**ONCE UPON A PIRATE** 108366-6 .... $4.50 U.S./$5.50 CAN.
❑**IN MY DREAMS** 108134-5 .... $4.99 U.S./$5.99 CAN.
❑**DESTINY AWAITS** 108342-9 .... $4.99 U.S./$5.99 CAN.
❑**DESTINED TO LOVE** 108225-2 .... $4.99 U.S./$5.99 CAN.
❑**THE NIGHT ORCHID** 108064-0 .... $4.99 U.S./$5.99 CAN.
❑**ECHOES AND ILLUSIONS** 108022-5 .... $4.99 U.S./$5.99 CAN.

Order 4 or more titles and postage & handling is **FREE!** Orders of less than 4 books, please include $2.00 postage & handling. Remit in US funds. Do not send cash. Allow up to 6 weeks delivery. Prices subject to change. Valid only in US and Canada.

SUBTOTAL .... $__________
POSTAGE AND HANDLING .... $__________
SALES TAX (Add applicable sales tax) .... $__________
TOTAL .... $__________

Name______________________________
Address____________________________
City________________State__________Zip__________

M006